PRAISE FOR SE~~F~~

"Once again, the very funny Lou ~~...~~ ~~...~~ ~~...~~ ~~...~~ ~~...~~ ~~...~~ of murder, mayhem, and merriment."

—*Booklist* (starred review)

"Beautifully written and wickedly funny."
—Harley Jane Kozak, Agatha, Anthony, and Macavity Award–
winning author

"Lourey has a talent for creating hilarious characters in bizarre, laugh-out-loud situations, while at the same time capturing the honest and endearing subtleties of human life."
—The Strand

PRAISE FOR *AUGUST MOON*

"Hilarious, fast paced, and madcap."
—*Booklist* (starred review)

"Another amusing tale set in the town full of over-the-top zanies who've endeared themselves to the engaging Mira."
—*Kirkus Reviews*

"[A] hilarious, wonderfully funny cozy."
—*Crimespree Magazine*

"Lourey has a gift for creating terrific characters. Her sly and witty take on small-town USA is a sweet summer treat. Pull up a lawn chair, pour yourself a glass of lemonade, and enjoy."
—Denise Swanson, bestselling author

PRAISE FOR *KNEE HIGH BY THE FOURTH OF JULY*

Lefty Finalist for Best Humorous Mystery

"*Knee High by the Fourth of July* . . . kept me hooked from beginning to end. I enjoyed every page!"

—Sammi Carter, author of the Candy Shop Mysteries

"Sweet, nutty, evocative of the American heartland, and utterly addicting."

—The Strand

"[The] humor transcends both genders and makes for a delightful romp."

—*Fergus Falls Journal*

"Mira . . . is an amusing heroine in a town full of quirky characters."

—*Kirkus Reviews*

"Lourey's rollicking good cozy planted me in the heat of a Minnesota summer for a laugh-out-loud mystery ride."

—Leann Sweeney, bestselling author

PRAISE FOR *JUNE BUG*

"Jess Lourey is a talented, witty, and clever writer."
—Monica Ferris, author of the Needlecraft Mysteries

"Don't miss this one—it's a hoot!"
—William Kent Krueger, *New York Times* bestselling author

"With just the right amount of insouciance, tongue-in-cheek sexiness, and plain common sense, Jess Lourey offers up a funny, well-written, engaging story . . . Readers will thoroughly enjoy the well-paced ride."
—Carl Brookins, author of *The Case of the Greedy Lawyers*

PRAISE FOR *MAY DAY*

"Jess Lourey writes about a small-town assistant librarian, but this is no genteel traditional mystery. Mira James likes guys in a big way, likes booze, and isn't afraid of motorcycles. She flees a dead-end job and a dead-end boyfriend in Minneapolis and ends up in Battle Lake, a little town with plenty of dirty secrets. The first-person narrative in *May Day* is fresh, the characters quirky. Minnesota has many fine crime writers, and Jess Lourey has just entered their ranks!"
—Ellen Hart, award-winning author of the Jane Lawless and Sophie Greenway series

"This trade paperback packed a punch . . . I loved it from the get-go!"
—*Tulsa World*

"What a romp this is! I found myself laughing out loud."
—*Crimespree Magazine*

"Mira digs up a closetful of dirty secrets, including sex parties, cross-dressing, and blackmail, on her way to exposing the killer. Lourey's debut has a likable heroine and surfeit of sass."

—*Kirkus Reviews*

PRAISE FOR *THE TAKEN ONES*

Short-listed for the 2024 Edgar Award for Best Paperback Original

"Setting the standard for top-notch thrillers, *The Taken Ones* is smart, compelling, and filled with utterly real characters. Lourey brings her formidable storytelling talent to the game and, on top of that, wows us with a deft stylistic touch. This is a one-sitting read!"

—Jeffery Deaver, author of *The Bone Collector* and *The Watchmaker's Hand*

"*The Taken Ones* has Jess Lourey's trademark of suspense all the way. A damaged and brave heroine, an equally damaged evildoer, and missing girls from long ago all combine to keep the reader rushing through to the explosive ending."

—Charlaine Harris, *New York Times* bestselling author

"Lourey is at the top of her game with *The Taken Ones*. A master of building tension while maintaining a riveting pace, Lourey is a hell of a writer on all fronts, but her greatest talent may be her characters. Evangeline Reed, an agent with the Minnesota Bureau of Criminal Apprehension, is a woman with a devastating past and the haunting ability to know the darkest crimes happening around her. She is also exactly the kind of character I would happily follow through a dozen books or more. In awe of her bravery, I also identified with her pain and wanted desperately to protect her. Along with an incredible cast of support characters, *The Taken Ones* will break your heart wide open and stay with you long after you've turned the final page. This is a 2023 must read."

—Danielle Girard, *USA Today* and Amazon #1 bestselling author of
Up Close

PRAISE FOR *THE QUARRY GIRLS*

Winner of the 2023 Anthony Award for Best Paperback Original

Winner of the 2023 Minnesota Book Award for Genre Fiction

"Few authors can blend the genuine fear generated by a sordid tale of true crime with evocative, three-dimensional characters and mesmerizing prose like Jess Lourey. Her fictional stories feel rooted in a world we all know but also fear. *The Quarry Girls* is a story of secrets gone to seed, and Lourey gives readers her best novel yet—which is quite the accomplishment. Calling it: *The Quarry Girls* will be one of the best books of the year."

—Alex Segura, acclaimed author of *Secret Identity*, *Star Wars Poe Dameron: Free Fall*, and *Miami Midnight*

"Jess Lourey once more taps deep into her Midwest roots and childhood fears with *The Quarry Girls*, an absorbing, true crime–informed thriller narrated in the compelling voice of young drummer Heather Cash as she and her bandmates navigate the treacherous and confusing ground between girlhood and womanhood one simmering and deadly summer. Lourey conveys the edgy, hungry restlessness of teen girls with a touch of Megan Abbott while steadily intensifying the claustrophobic atmosphere of a small 1977 Minnesota town where darkness snakes below the surface."

—Loreth Anne White, *Washington Post* and Amazon Charts bestselling author of *The Patient's Secret*

"Jess Lourey is a master of the coming-of-age thriller, and *The Quarry Girls* may be her best yet—as dark, twisty, and full of secrets as the tunnels that lurk beneath Pantown's deceptively idyllic streets."

—Chris Holm, Anthony Award–winning author of *The Killing Kind*

PRAISE FOR *BLOODLINE*

Winner of the 2022 Anthony Award for Best Paperback Original

Winner of the 2022 ITW Thriller Award for Best Paperback Original

Short-listed for the 2021 Goodreads Choice Awards

"Fans of *Rosemary's Baby* will relish this."

—*Publishers Weekly*

"I should know better than to pick up a new Jess Lourey book thinking I'll just peek at the first few pages and then get back to the book I was reading. Six hours later, it's three in the morning and I'm racing through the last few chapters, unable to sleep until I know how it all ends. Set in an idyllic small town rooted in family history and horrific secrets, *Bloodline* is *Pleasantville* meets *Rosemary's Baby*. A deeply unsettling, darkly unnerving, and utterly compelling novel, this book chilled me to the core, and I loved every bit of it."

—Jennifer Hillier, author of *Little Secrets* and the award-winning *Jar of Hearts*

"Jess Lourey writes small-town Minnesota like Stephen King writes small-town Maine. *Bloodline* is a tremendous book with a heart and a hacksaw . . . and I loved every second of it."

—Rachel Howzell Hall, author of the critically acclaimed novels *And Now She's Gone* and *They All Fall Down*

PRAISE FOR *UNSPEAKABLE THINGS*

Winner of the 2021 Anthony Award for Best Paperback Original

Short-listed for the 2021 Edgar Awards and 2020 Goodreads Choice Awards

"The suspense never wavers in this page-turner."

—*Publishers Weekly*

"The atmospheric suspense novel is haunting because it's narrated from the point of view of a thirteen-year-old, an age that should be more innocent but often isn't. Even more chilling, it's based on real-life incidents. Lourey may be known for comic capers (*March of Crimes*), but this tense novel combines the best of a coming-of-age story with suspense and an unforgettable young narrator."

—*Library Journal* (starred review)

"Part suspense, part coming-of-age, Jess Lourey's *Unspeakable Things* is a story of creeping dread, about childhood when you know the monster under your bed is real. A novel that clings to you long after the last page."

—Lori Rader-Day, Edgar Award–nominated author of *Under a Dark Sky*

"A noose of a novel that tightens by inches. The squirming tension comes from every direction—including the ones that are supposed to be safe. I felt complicit as I read, as if at any moment I stopped I would be abandoning Cassie, alone, in the dark, straining to listen and fearing to hear."

—Marcus Sakey, bestselling author of *Brilliance*

"*Unspeakable Things* is an absolutely riveting novel about the poisonous secrets buried deep in towns and families. Jess Lourey has created a story that will chill you to the bone and a main character who will break your heart wide open."

—Lou Berney, Edgar Award–winning author of *November Road*

"Inspired by a true story, *Unspeakable Things* crackles with authenticity, humanity, and humor. The novel reminded me of *To Kill a Mockingbird* and *The Marsh King's Daughter*. Highly recommended."

—Mark Sullivan, bestselling author of *Beneath a Scarlet Sky*

"Jess Lourey does a masterful job building tension and dread, but her greatest asset in *Unspeakable Things* is Cassie—an arresting narrator you identify with, root for, and desperately want to protect. This is a book that will stick with you long after you've torn through it."

—Rob Hart, author of *The Warehouse*

"With *Unspeakable Things*, Jess Lourey has managed the near-impossible, crafting a mystery as harrowing as it is tender, as gut-wrenching as it is lyrical. There is real darkness here, a creeping, inescapable dread that more than once had me looking over my own shoulder. But at its heart beats the irrepressible—and irresistible—spirit of its . . . heroine, a young woman so bright and vital and brave she kept even the fiercest monsters at bay. This is a book that will stay with me for a long time."

—Elizabeth Little, *Los Angeles Times* bestselling author of *Dear Daughter* and *Pretty as a Picture*

PRAISE FOR *THE CATALAIN BOOK OF SECRETS*

"Life-affirming, thought-provoking, heartwarming, it's one of those books that—if you happen to read it exactly when you need to—will heal your wounds as you turn the pages."

—Catriona McPherson, Agatha, Anthony, Macavity, and Bruce Alexander Award–winning author

"Prolific mystery writer Lourey tells of a matriarchal clan of witches joining forces against age-old evil . . . The novel is tightly plotted, and Lourey shines when depicting relationships—romantic ones as well as tangled links between Catalains . . . Lourey emphasizes the ties that bind in spite of secrets and resentment."

—*Kirkus Reviews*

"Lourey expertly concocts a Gothic fusion of long-held secrets, melancholy, and resolve . . . Exquisitely written in naturally flowing, expressive language, the book delves into the special relationships between sisters, and mothers and daughters."

—*Publishers Weekly*

PRAISE FOR *SALEM'S CIPHER*

"A fast-paced, sometimes brutal thriller reminiscent of Dan Brown's *The Da Vinci Code*."

—*Booklist* (starred review)

"A hair-raising thrill ride."

—*Library Journal* (starred review)

"The fascinating historical information combined with a storyline ripped from the headlines will hook conspiracy theorists and action addicts alike."

—*Kirkus Reviews*

"Fans of *The Da Vinci Code* are going to love this book . . . One of my favorite reads of 2016."

—*Crimespree Magazine*

"This suspenseful tale has something for absolutely everyone to enjoy."

—*Suspense Magazine*

PRAISE FOR *MERCY'S CHASE*

"An immersive voice, an intriguing story, a wonderful character—highly recommended!"

—Lee Child, #1 *New York Times* bestselling author

"Both a sweeping adventure and race-against-time thriller, *Mercy's Chase* is fascinating, fierce, and brimming with heart—just like its heroine, Salem Wiley."

—Meg Gardiner, author of *Into the Black Nowhere*

"Action-packed, great writing taut with suspense, an appealing main character to root for—who could ask for anything more?"

—Buried Under Books

PRAISE FOR *REWRITE YOUR LIFE: DISCOVER YOUR TRUTH THROUGH THE HEALING POWER OF FICTION*

"Interweaving practical advice with stories and insights garnered in her own writing journey, Jessica Lourey offers a step-by-step guide for writers struggling to create fiction from their life experiences. But this book isn't just about writing. It's also about the power of stories to transform those who write them. I know of no other guide that delivers on its promise with such honesty, simplicity, and beauty."

—William Kent Krueger, *New York Times* bestselling author of the Cork O'Connor series and *Ordinary Grace*

SEPTEMBER
MOURN

OTHER TITLES BY JESS LOUREY

MURDER BY MONTH MYSTERIES

May Day

June Bug

Knee High by the Fourth of July

August Moon

September Mourn

October Fest

November Hunt

December Dread

January Thaw

February Fever

March of Crimes

April Fools

STEINBECK AND REED THRILLERS

The Taken Ones

The Reaping

THRILLERS

The Quarry Girls

Litani

Bloodline

Unspeakable Things

SALEM'S CIPHER THRILLERS

Salem's Cipher

Mercy's Chase

BOOK CLUB FICTION

The Catalain Book of Secrets

Seven Daughters

CHILDREN'S BOOKS

Leave My Book Alone! Starring Claudette, a Dragon with Control Issues

YOUNG ADULT

A Whisper of Poison

NONFICTION

Rewrite Your Life: Discover Your Truth Through the Healing Power of Fiction

SEPTEMBER MOURN

MOURN

JESS LOUREY

THOMAS & MERCER

Published by Thomas & Mercer, Seattle

www.apub.com

Amazon, the Amazon logo, and Thomas & Mercer are trademarks of Amazon.com, Inc., or its affiliates.

ISBN-13: 9781662519314 (paperback)
ISBN-13: 9781662519307 (digital)

Cover design and illustration by Sarah Horgan

Printed in the United States of America

SEPTEMBER
MOURN

Prologue

She cut a wide swath through the eleven other pretty young women. To a girl they had skin as\ white and creamy as lefse batter, blonde hair the color of sunlight on honey, and eyes as blue as a DQ raspberry slushie.

A brunette would have stood out like a turd on a salad bar in this bunch.

It didn't always work that way. Some years, a brown-haired girl could even win the Milkfed Mary, Queen of the Dairy title. But not this year. This year, the field was a flaxen army, with one Ashley Kirsten Pederson as its general.

"Lana, did you use my lip gloss?" Ashley demanded.

She couldn't believe she was being forced to spend another minute with these piglets, girls she definitely wouldn't hang with in her hometown. Probably they were all farm girls, maybe even in 4-H. Not her. She was just drop-dead gorgeous. Her parents happened to own a dairy farm, but that wasn't her fault. She planted her hands on her hips. "I asked, did you use it? Because your lips are super glossy and it sure looks like Cherry Sugar Kiss from here."

"No, Ashley, I did not take your lip gloss," Lana said, rolling her eyes. "I have my own."

Lana, for her part, was *not* a member of 4-H. She'd been involved in Head, Heart, Hands, and Health as a kid, back when she'd enjoyed riding horses and raising rabbits, but once she hit high school, she became busy with the demands of maintaining a 4.0 GPA, helping her mom run the farm, and keeping her new boyfriend, Bud, on second base.

Ashley gave her corn-silk hair one last fluff. "Fine."

She wasn't going to waste her time worrying about these Milk Duds. *She* was the queen this year. And thanks to her dazzling victory, Battle Lake was now in the enviable position of supplying more Milkfed Marys than any other town in the state of Minnesota.

Ashley'd made history.

A man wearing a pair of tiny headphones knocked before poking his face in the second-floor dormitory. "Ms. Pederson?"

Ashley swiveled and flashed her best smile. Her teeth were white enough to trigger migraines. He couldn't help but smile back.

"You'll want to grab your snow pants and coat," he said. "You're on in five."

Ashley took one last sip of diet cola, her main source of nutrition. She sucked the straw delicately, ice clinking in the glass, which was how she assumed movie stars drank their pop. Smiling at the glory that awaited her, she set her cola down and grabbed her quilted, pine-green Columbia parka and matching pants, both good to forty below, then floated down the cement steps that led to the massive Cattle Barn. She pranced through it and into the already-steamy, late-August morning.

The sun sparkled off her tiara and turned the sequins on her strapless cerulean gown into a million glittering sapphires. She waved and the cameras flashed, clicking and popping like firecrackers. She didn't lose stride as she crossed the pavement, her right arm in constant motion—elbow, elbow, wrist, wrist—and entered the front doors of the Dairy Building, which were held open for her.

She strode to the southwest corner of the edifice, passing the House of Cheese. It was a misnomer. There was no house, only a glassed-in display featuring the history of the cheese industry in Minnesota. On her left stood the Dairy Goodness Bar, which had been selling malts, yogurt, cheese, cones, sundaes, and icy-cold glasses of milk in three flavors since 1958. The line to the front counter already snaked outside the building, and those waiting for their calcium hit whispered excitedly as the newly crowned Milkfed Mary sailed past.

Overhead fans lifted Ashley's hair as she glided toward the refrigerated, glass-walled, octagonal booth. It was twelve feet high and nine feet across, rested on a four-foot base, and housed the most popular exhibit on the massive Minnesota State Fairgrounds.

The clamoring crowd shoved and hustled to catch a glimpse of the queen nearing her icy throne, parting like a high-sodium white sea so she could float through. Ashley felt like a rock star. Ever the professional, she paused for one final photo shoot in front of the glass-sided gazebo.

Organizers had recently spruced up the octagonal Milkfed Mary exhibit, and it carried the faint smell of new paint. The predominant color was white with red and blue trim. A single strand of scarlet twinkle lights crowned the top of the structure, and inside, behind viewing glass, twelve ninety-pound blocks of butter were arranged like a spreadable Stonehenge, eleven in a circle on the outside with one in the center: hers.

Ashley's grin inched up to her eyes, and in a move she'd practiced countless times in front of one of the full-length mirrors in her bedroom, she turned gracefully on her heel, showing just a hint of upper thigh through the slit of her gown, and slipped behind the blue curtain that separated the entrance of the exhibit from the excited crowd. The private area was really a small hall. To her left, four wooden stairs led to the exhibit's door. To her right were about a million plastic spoons. Dairy Goodness, whose kitchen was at the other end of the hall, had run out of storage space.

Ashley dropped her smile. "Are you ready for me?"

The sculptor nodded from her post guarding the exhibit's door. She was a fill-in this year and as nervous as a wicked thought in church. "You'll want to pull up those pants and zip your jacket before we go in. It's only thirty-eight degrees in the gazebo, and we've got a full day ahead of us."

Ashley adroitly tucked her gown between her thighs, illustrating the axiom that no one can wear a dress with snow pants like a Minnesota gal—they learned the skill in preschool and improved on technique from there. Once her lower half was swaddled, she zipped her jacket to her chin and tugged woolly mittens out of the pockets, yanking them tight. When she looked ready for a full-on blizzard, the sculptor marched up the four stairs, took a shaky breath, and pulled open the gazebo's only door. A rush of icy air met the wall of humid heat.

The crowd on the other side of the glass-walled booth went silent.

"Wish me luck!" Ashley called out in her sparkly voice, pausing for one more photo opportunity as a photographer ducked his head behind the curtain, against the rules, to catch sight of the queen entering her throne room.

Ashley Pederson was a natural, the Marilyn Monroe of Minnesota's dairy industry. That ability to turn it on and off for an audience was how she'd sailed through the judging, where she'd been required to bluff her way past torturous questions about the dairy industry and feign enthusiasm for pasteurized cheese.

How long can you keep milk after the expiration date?

Well, sir, it's best to drink it before it expires, but in a pinch, it's always better to drink old milk than fresh pop!

A nod of approval. *Excellent. And how important is calcium to the human body?*

Not very, unless you like having bones!

Ashley had the judges in stitches and the audience on the edge of their seats. When she was called forward with Lana and Delrita, the two runners-up, the weight of the crown on her head held no surprise, only a feeling of justice being done. And with it, the world became hers. Winning the title of Milkfed Mary, Queen of the Dairy promised local and even national media attention. She was scheduled to appear on *Good Morning America* next week, and there were whispers of her being invited on *Oprah*.

All she had to do was get through today.

When the last click faded, Ashley took her seat inside the booth, trying not to gag at the smell of greasy milk. She was lactose intolerant, and the blocks of Grade A unsalted butter surrounding her made her want to ralph. Instead, she sat prettily, not even twitching as the floor of the eight-sided booth began rotating slowly, allowing everyone a generous view of the magic happening inside, the only angle not visible the one behind the now-closed door to the booth.

And so opened the Minnesota State Fair, the country's second largest, with a tradition begun by the Midwest Dairy Organization back in 1965: on the first day of the fair, Milkfed Mary, Queen of the Dairy, chosen out of some eighty county dairy princesses and then twelve finalists, posed inside a glass-sided, rotating refrigerator as a larger-than-life likeness of her head was carved out of butter. For eleven more days after that, the runners-up were also immortalized in the special booth, but no butter carving was as grand as the first one of the fair, none as special as the queen's. That's what Ashley was telling herself as she shivered despite her parka and mittens. She felt a killer headache developing but refused to let it touch her smile.

She tried passing time by brainstorming what she'd do with her sculpture after the fair. Some past winners had donated their butter heads to their churches to be used in local festivals, either to make cookies and pies with or to twirl their corn on the cob on. Some women stored their heads in their chest freezer, between the venison sausage and the frostbitten hamburger, eager to preserve their glorious past.

Ashley envisioned something grander for hers. Maybe she would feature it as the centerpiece at her wedding next summer or donate it to Alexandria Technical College, where she was planning to study sales and marketing when fall semester began. The college president could build a refrigerated case and display the butter head in the main entryway, with a plaque making clear that Ashley, in fact, walked among them.

She rotated tranquilly, pats of butter falling to the floor from the sculptor's efforts. Even the rising tightness in her chest couldn't distract her from her happy place. She blinked rapidly and wondered why it was becoming so foggy in the booth.

The sculptor, for her part, worked busily and with a total focus. She'd begun the sculpting with a serrated bread knife to get the general shape and followed with a ribbon tool to refine angles. Her philosophy of butter carving was to not force the art but rather to let the face within emerge of its own accord. Fortunately, butter was a forgiving medium. Too much off the nose, and all she had to do was scoop some off the floor and slap it back into place. Bangs not high enough? Take a little from the rear of the head and paste it on the front.

The sculptor's work soon consumed her, and her nerves subsided as the many faces staring at her and Ashley as if they were zoo creatures faded. The world became a small, rotating, octagonal prison. The sculptor wouldn't allow music—it distracted her—and so the booth was as quiet as a tomb when the lights unexpectedly flickered out.

The outage lasted less than a minute. An eternity in an enormous black space filled with strangers. The audience panicked like spooked cattle, some screaming for their children or friends, others clambering toward glowing exit signs, still others holding their ground, sure someone would fix the problem soon.

When questioned later, the sculptor could recall only this from the one-minute blackout: violent retching and scrabbling from Ashley's side of the booth, the complete darkness, and a slash of brightness as someone opened the north doors.

Oh, and Ashley Kirsten Pederson, the fifty-fourth Milkfed Mary, Queen of the Dairy, proud owner of a promise ring from Dirk Holthaus, and soon-to-be college freshman, lying dead on the floor of the still-spinning octagon.

Chapter 1

As I snapped photos of Battle Lake's newest butter queen rotating in that over-the-top refrigerated booth, blissfully unaware that the lights were about to snap out and change my life forever, I had the leisure to wonder at the circuitous route by which I found myself back at the Minnesota State Fair for the second time in my life. After graduating from Paynesville High School, I'd moved to the Twin Cities to spend the next ten-plus years haphazardly pursuing an English degree, escaping the accumulated demons of my small-town past, and generally drinking too much.

A wake-up call and possibly the cat-clawed hand of fate had steered me to Battle Lake this past spring. The relocation came with a double-wide trailer and a dog. The house and pooch-sitting were only supposed to have lasted through the summer, a fact I'd rejoiced in once the dead bodies started blowing through town like ghoulish tumbleweeds.

Murdered dead bodies, to be exact, and they'd all been connected to me.

My beginning in Battle Lake had actually been auspicious. I'd strolled into an assistant librarian position that had coincidentally opened up a week after I'd moved to town. It didn't pay great but was full-time, and life became financially comfortable after I supplemented that income with a part-time reporting gig for the *Battle Lake Recall*.

Emotionally comfortable, less so, especially after I stumbled upon a corpse my first solo day at the library, found another in a seventy-year-old safe a month later, yet another—this one missing part of his scalp and all of his pulse—at an isolated cabin in July, and a final one in a gully just a few weeks ago with a bloody hole through her teenage spine.

If you're counting, that's four bodies in as many months.

You know those people who always win stuff? Radio call-in shows, door prizes, pull tabs, scratch-offs—they can't help but get lucky? Well, I'm the yin to their yang, the shadow to their light. Their luck brings them money, concert tickets, and fruit baskets, and mine brings me cadavers. I figured my karma must be off. Maybe my chi got dinged a little somewhere along the line or my planets were misaligned. Whatever it was, I'd recently vowed that there was no way I was going to get involved in another murder investigation as long as I lived.

I was only a librarian and part-time reporter, after all.

My initial instinct, once the bodies had started lining up, had been to ditch Battle Lake. That same bail reflex had kept me out of serious relationships and in the bottle for the last decade, following in the footsteps of my father, one Mark James, prolific drinker and real-life crash test dummy. He'd killed himself and another person in a head-on collision my junior year of high school. After that, I was a pariah in Paynesville and only too happy to leave the second I graduated.

A series of events had convinced me to stay in Battle Lake despite the bodies piling up with freaky regularity, however, and as much as it scraped and chafed, that's what I was going to do. It was a new idea, this sticking-it-out approach. It looked good on paper.

At least that's what I was thinking until the lights flatlined in the Dairy Building at the exact moment I noticed something odd about Ashley through my camera's viewfinder. I pressed the shutter button just as the room went inky black, not sure what I'd seen, and began to swallow my tongue in the sudden darkness. I couldn't keep the yelp from escaping.

I was mortally terrified of being trapped in dark spaces, specifically haunted houses, but a Dairy Building would do in a pinch.

I had good reason.

Right before my sophomore year of high school, Jenny Cot had invited me to the State Fair with her family. My dad was still alive, and by that point in my life, his drinking had affected most of my friendships. Because I couldn't have people over, they eventually stopped including me in their lives outside of school. Jenny's invitation was an unexpected treat, an opportunity for a fifteen-year-old to leave her dysfunctional family and travel to glamorous Saint Paul. No one would drink and then expect me to get in the car with them behind the wheel, the adults wouldn't fight on the trip down and back, and people would actually care where I was going and when I was going to return. It was a slice of TV-ready perfection that I was at pains not to screw up.

In fact, I didn't sleep the night before, twisting in my sheets as I imagined all the ways the trip to the Cities could be thwarted: Jenny could change her mind and choose to bring a closer friend. Even if she still wanted to bring me with, I might say something stupid in the driveway and her parents would realize they'd rather not have me around. Or my dad would stumble out of the house drunk and shame us both, and the Cots would leave without me.

The list was endless, spinning and growing and striking down hope wherever it touched. When Jenny and her family actually arrived to pick me up the next morning, I was bone-tired and edgy. I gritted my teeth when my dad went out to meet them, still sure he was going to mess it up somehow.

But he didn't.

And I got to go.

The car ride to the State Fair was exactly as I'd imagined it. Her parents even held hands and joked with each other. We played "I Spy" for most of the trip. The sun shone warm and clear. It was the ideal fair day, Jenny's dad, Craig, kept reminding us with a smile in the rearview mirror. Jenny and her older brother told him to lay off after about the sixth time, and I pretended to laugh at him along with the others, but I couldn't stop watching him. *That's how a dad is supposed to act,* I told myself.

At the fairgrounds, I found myself pleasantly overwhelmed by the crowds and the smell of fried foods and the buzz of a thousand conversations happening at once. I'd never been far from Paynesville except when our volleyball team, for which I was a perennial benchwarmer, played away games. The loud and colorful State Fair was both scary and thrilling. I bound the joy at discovering the largeness of the world to Mr. and Mrs. Cot.

I would have done anything for them that day.

They even bought us food—a corn dog for me and cheese curds, fries, and pizza for their kids. My stomach still rumbled after I ate the corn dog, but I saw how much the food cost and so turned them down when offered more.

I'm good, I said. *I had a big breakfast. Thank you, though.*

We walked the Mighty Midway together, and then Craig and his wife offered each of us ten dollars to do our own thing. Jenny's brother grabbed the money and ran. I was reluctant to leave the Cots, but Jenny was excited to explore without her parents and tugged relentlessly at my arm.

We agreed we'd all meet up at the Space Tower in two hours.

I let Jenny lead us, and she did—straight to the Haunted House. I'd never been inside one before and felt apprehension like a wet lick up my spine as we stood outside the Victorian mansion. It was surrounded by a black wrought iron fence that was as welcoming as bones jutting from a graveyard. The windows of the two-story building were curtained with rotting lace, and a permanent cloud seemed to hang over the building. Faint screams emanated from inside. The overall impression was of a ravenous monster biding its time until someone was stupid enough to walk into its belly.

Couldn't we go on the River Raft Ride, I asked, *or check out the wild drum music we heard strolling past the International Bazaar?*

But Jenny was dead set on the Haunted House, and I was her guest. I took a breath and reevaluated the situation. Sure, the house was maliciously terrifying, but other than that one gray cloud directly over it, the day was warm and sunny, and laughing groups of people waited in line for their chance to enter. I could do this. I slapped on a brave smile and got in line. When it came our turn to enter, we handed five precious dollars each to the teenager working the door.

"Don't worry," he said, raising his eyebrows at us. "No one gets out alive."

Ignoring him, we went in as a pair, creeping along the dark hallway. The lighting was a mixture of shadows and electric candle flickers. We clung to each other, picking our way through. The carpet felt soggy underfoot, and the air had a metallic smell, like spilled blood. Ahead, a low moan made Jenny jump and then giggle. Surprisingly, her fear made me less scared.

This is just a pretend house, I told myself. *Relax and enjoy it.*

We soldiered on, pushing past sticky cobwebs and feathers set near the floor to brush against our naked ankles. Mirrors lined the halls, reflecting faces in excruciating pain, their eyeballs hanging out, grisly mouths gaping. The wallpaper seemed to melt and bend as searching fingers pushed through it, stopping just short of groping us.

Our steps grew slower until Jenny was nearly riding me piggyback, pushing me to go first. I did. The very next second, I was greeted by Jason Voorhees, bloody axe in one hand and knife in the other.

I screamed, my stomach and heart switching places, and grabbed for Jenny's hand. She buried her head in my back and we dashed past, catching our breath.

"What was it?" she squealed.

"Jason from the *Friday the 13th* movies." I laughed, adrenaline pounding through my veins. "Let's see what's up ahead."

"I don't want to go any farther," she begged.

Looking back, I should have caught the tone in her voice. She wasn't joking anymore, but I was too pumped up on fear to catch her switch in mood. "They don't let you turn back," I said.

So I led her along, happy to no longer be paralyzed by fear. We found ourselves in a dimly lit room the size of a large walk-in closet.

Red liquid poured down the walls, and in the outline of a door, a dismembered skeleton dropped goopy intestines from one bony hand to another like a macabre Slinky. I was pulling Jenny toward the next grody doorway when a creak behind us announced danger. Before either of us could turn, the *Texas Chain Saw Massacre* guy grabbed Jenny around the neck with one hand and revved his chain saw with the other.

The stranger's closeness made my knees weak until I noticed the Voss label emblazoned on his machinery, marking it for the child's toy it was. I laughed shakily and reached for Jenny's hand to haul her away from the monster and out of the room.

I clasped it just as she fell to the ground in a dead faint.

Her head hit the floor with a ripe thud, and in the dimness of the room, it looked like her real blood was joining the fake gore. I tried to drag her away from the man with the chain saw, who didn't seem to notice that Jenny had passed out. He laughed in our direction and twisted to greet the gaggle of kids approaching from behind.

In a reaction I still can't explain to this day, I carried Jenny out of that small room instead of calling for help. It was a primitive animal instinct, wanting to protect her and hide her from the monster, but part of me also wanted to run from people discovering what'd happened.

Her parents would be so disappointed in me for allowing her to get hurt.

They'd told us to take care of each other.

It was the Bride of Frankenstein who stopped me at the next station. I was dragging Jenny by her arms, her head lolling toward the floor. The Bride appraised the situation quickly and flicked on the lights in the hall, revealing a worn and dingy space as impermanent as a stage. She grabbed a phone from behind a panel and called for help, and Jenny was whisked outside and into an ambulance within minutes. It took me longer to find her parents, and then her brother, and the four of us hurried to the hospital.

Jenny received ten stitches on her scalp, and I took her and her parents' quiet demeanor during the long ride home as anger at me.

They never invited me out again.

Afterward, in a ridiculously exaggerated response to any mention of haunted houses, my feet started to sweat and my intestines went soft and rumbly. It was an overblown reflex, I knew, but one I carried with me through the rest of high school. Even now, almost fourteen years to the day after the event, that fear was as powerful as a sleeping giant inside me, as awoken by the lights snapping out in the Dairy Building.

I should never have come here. The initial State Fair assignment had seemed pretty cherry, offered to me by Ron Sims, publisher, editor, marketer, layout director, and chief reporter at the *Battle Lake Recall*. Even though I was a part-time reporter, he acted all-the-time bossy.

Go to Saint Paul and cover our very own Milkfed Mary getting her head carved out of butter, he'd said. *Write about all the Battle Lake farmers showcasing their work. See what the 4-H kids are up to. We're having a special State Fair issue, and it'll be chock full of your articles.*

He'd sweetened the pot by offering me his camper trailer, which I could park on a State Fair lot paid for by the Battle Lake Chamber of Commerce. Without a good reason to turn down an all-expenses-paid week in the Cities, I had asked Mrs. Berns, my assistant librarian, to run that show; coaxed my friend Jed to stay with my cat, Tiger Pop, and Sunny's dog, Luna, at the double-wide; and driven the camper to the northeast end of the fair.

I'd arrived early enough to snag a spot underneath the water tower, near the bathrooms and showers. I'd set up camp yesterday afternoon, feeling like it wasn't a bad deal. That was, until the Dairy Building went black, compressing my highest-pitched fears into one convenient package.

True, this place was bigger than the Haunted House and none of the folks crowded around were going to yank out chain saws or tickle me with Freddy Krueger blades, but the sensation was just as I remembered it. Blackness. Strangers pushing and yelling. Little sparks of panic flashing like fireflies, igniting tidal waves of terror. The smell of the fair didn't help—mini doughnuts, animals, dust.

Jess Lourey

I was just about to howl when a brilliant sliver of light sliced through the absolute black. Someone had cracked a door. We all sighed. We were in a building, civilized humans. Moments later, every light in the building switched back on, washing the interior in a safe yellow glow.

At first, none of us made eye contact. I think we were all embarrassed. No one likes to discover they're two minutes of darkness away from devolving into a cave person. Soon, people chuckled uneasily and began to crack bad jokes: *How many cows does it take to change a light bulb, anyways?*

All I knew was that I wanted to skedaddle. I kept my head down and made for the one lighted exit in my line of sight, taking me right past the butter-carving exhibit. The booth's floor was at shoulder level, and at first glance it appeared empty except for some blocks of butter that had been knocked over. Milkfed Mary and the sculptor must have panicked when the lights went out and started flailing for a door.

They were no more cowards than the rest of us.

Suddenly, a woman a few feet away from me screamed. I figured it was a delayed reaction, or maybe somebody'd discovered their purse had been stolen when the lights were out. Either way, I wanted to keep moving, but the crowd surged, trapping me against the booth. That's when a second shriek, this one a long, continuous wail, escaped from behind the nearby blue curtain to my left.

My throat grew tight. It sounded like someone was hurt back there. I was reaching to yank open the curtain when the butter-carving booth finished a rotation and I realized what had made both people scream: on the booth floor, a cherry-red hand stuck out between two felled blocks of butter.

Chapter 2

Had Milkfed Mary been crushed by falling butter in an ironically dairy-themed re-creation of the *Wizard of Oz*?

The booth turned inexorably, bringing first her blonde hair into view and then her eyes, open and sightless. The woman next to me was also staring into the booth. She gurgled.

"Do you have a phone?" I asked her, my eyes hot.

She nodded at her purse but made no move to open it. The crimson and completely dead Milkfed Mary, Queen of the Dairy, had her transfixed. I dug into the woman's purse and dialed 911 for the second time in my life.

"What's your emergency?"

Sweet Jesus, I hadn't thought this through. My best bet was to make it swift and vague. "I'm at the State Fair. In the Dairy Building. Milkfed Mary was getting her head carved out of butter, and something terrible happened to her."

"Can you be more specific, ma'am?"

"I think she's dead. Send someone quick." I hung up, dropped the phone back in the woman's purse, and made for the blue curtain, from which a scream still emanated, though it'd grown fainter.

Real quick, let's get one thing straight: I wasn't going back there to be a hero. I'm no Wonder Woman. What I am is a lifelong prisoner of guilt, sometimes on work release but never far from my cell. How that shakes out is that, in a crisis, I usually know what the appropriate action is, which leaves me one of two choices:

- act immediately, or
- prepare to get squashed beneath so many what-ifs and so paralyzed by fear of karma catching up with me that I will spend the next lifetime *wishing* I'd acted, turning the missed moment over and over in my head like bloody rosary beads.

Thank you again, Jenny Cot and Leatherface.

So I yanked that curtain back, scared as a kicked dog, fully expecting to discover loads of people squished like Milkfed Mary, a floor full of bright-red Flat Stanleys with only one person inflated enough to still be shrieking. Imagine my relief to see only the butter-head artist sobbing and being comforted by a red-suited woman with a cell phone in her hand and a strange expression on her face. Behind them, hundreds of boxes of spoons lined the wall, which ended in a door.

Blergh. The sculptor already being comforted left me with the short-straw job: I needed to step into the gruesome booth and make sure nothing could be done for Milkfed Mary.

Though I'd recently vowed to avoid corpses at all costs, I had to be 100 percent sure she was beyond suffering. *Curse words.* I swallowed my fear and forced myself up the steps that only the sculptor and a reigning queen and her court should ever travel.

I opened the door.

A wash of icy air scented with the oily yellow smell of one thousand pounds of butter chilled my skin.

Goose bumps popped up across my flesh.

Inside, the floor turned, slowly and relentlessly, exhibiting its ghastly cargo. Milkfed Mary, Ashley Pederson of Battle Lake, Minnesota, lay sprawled on the floor, red as an apple and still as a rock.

Only minutes earlier, I'd watched her in her full youthful glory, hamming it up for the cameras and basking in the attention she'd earned. But now, her lifeless body curved around the white carving station in the center of the booth. Two butter slabs pinned her right arm, and another trapped her left leg. Only one hand wore a mitten. I was leaning forward to check her pulse when I was pushed roughly from behind.

It was the red-suited woman who'd been comforting the sculptor. She was all business, grimacing at me from beneath her perfect helmet of hair. "The State Fair EMTs are almost here. They need to get at her."

I moved out of the way but not before looking through the glass of the booth at the hundreds of people staring up at me. I had a flash of Ashley's last moments, on display like a crown jewel.

Or a two-headed goat.

It gave me a shiver that stuck with me as I hustled out of the booth, away from the curtain, and down the long hall of spoons. I suddenly wanted nothing more than to take a bath in Purell. But even in my benumbed state, I wondered what'd turned Ashley's skin that color. Was it some sort of dairy virus, or a latent but deadly Oompa-Loompa gene triggered by a constant thirty-eight-degree temperature and slow circular movement?

More importantly, had I just exposed myself to something contagious?

I lunged outside into the blistering heat and breathed deeply. A parked ambulance flashed its lights to my right, and behind it, two police cruisers pulled up. Of course the State Fair would have its own health and security personnel on the grounds.

I strode past the amphitheater and River Raft Ride to Clough Street, took a right, and ducked into the first bathrooms I spotted. Inside, I literally and figuratively washed my hands of the whole ordeal. It wasn't my fault she was from Battle Lake, right? I didn't know her personally. The ambulance would haul her body away, and the police would find out what'd happened to her, not me.

I'd cover the story, of course. I'd report on any information the police released, but that was as far as it would go, because while Ashley's death was terribly sad, it had nothing to do with me.

Once I'd scrubbed the top layer of skin from my hands and face, I headed north to my trailer, keeping my head down and my hands to myself. The place was so crowded that I couldn't walk a straight line for more than four feet. The smell of roasting meat competed with the sweetness of fresh Tom Thumb Donuts and cinnamon-baked nuts.

Overhead, the Sky Ride carried people from one end of the fair to the other. They laughed and dangled their feet while sipping cool drinks and pointing out the sights, oblivious to the horror at the Dairy Building. How long until word of the queen's death spread? Would it clear out the crowds? Increase them?

I shoved those thoughts away and navigated toward the campgrounds. My trailer was a neat little twenty-two-foot vintage Airstream that Ron had remodeled inside to look like an early-1970s opium den, complete with white shag carpeting and beaded curtains. He'd even applied those little flower-shaped stickers to the shower floor, which I believe were invented to keep stoned people from slipping down the drain.

That was all fine because I had a bedroom in the rear, a kitchen with an electric stove, a dining room table, and a pile of books I'd been meaning to read. And right now, I wanted nothing more than to be alone to regroup and pretend I hadn't just seen my fifth corpse since May. Ron would be calling me and ordering me to cover the story soon enough.

I unlocked the door, hitched it behind me, and dropped onto the nearest chair.

"Mira? Surprise!"

Chapter 3

I leaped to my feet. "Mrs. Berns?"

"Well, it ain't Cher. Who pooped in your pants?"

"What?" I sniffed the air.

"You look like you just found out your cat died. It didn't, by the way. I checked your place before I left, and Jed's doing a fine job. A couple redecorating touches to up the vibe, but those were necessary after last night's party." She pursed her lips and made a show of looking around. "Speaking of vibes, what the hell was Ron Sims smoking when he decorated this place?"

In deciding to quit drinking last month, I'd experienced more challenges than the average Joe. Mrs. Berns was my favorite one. I took a deep breath, more like a gasping for air really, and started at the beginning. "Why are you here?"

"I was listening to 103.3 out of Fergus. You know the station?"

I nodded. Or had a nervous tic. It looked the same.

"They were 'getting the Led out' when all of a sudden, they announced a contest. The first person to answer three questions correctly about Neil Diamond wins two tickets to his State Fair concert and backstage passes to meet him afterward."

"Neil Diamond's at the State Fair?"

Mrs. Berns tsked. "You might be cute, Mira James, but smart don't always park in your garage. *Of course* Neil Diamond is at the State Fair. Didn't you see all those old ladies with DiamondHead T-shirts walking around?" She indicated her own bedazzled top. It featured a life-size, three-dimensional rendering of Neil Diamond's head and shoulders. His face floated above an open-collared shirt, and a healthy patch of black hair that was either glued or sewn on sprouted from the vee of his collar, which was located on the part of the shirt that covered Mrs. Berns's lower tummy.

"That's fake chest hair, right?"

"If by 'fake,' you mean it isn't really Neil Diamond's, you are correct. Now stop interrupting." She cleared her throat. "I was baking bread in the nursing home kitchen when the contest was announced. By the time I got my hands clean, three people had called in and lost. They answered the first two questions, but the third stumped 'em. I knew all the answers, of course, but I couldn't get through." She threw her hands in the air, reenacting her exasperation.

"I was redialing, redialing, but there were so many idiots clogging up the line that I couldn't make contact. Finally, a ring! The announcer picked up, and he asked me question number one. 'What was the first song Neil Diamond wrote?' he asked. 'Hear Them Bells,' I told him, and you can bet I was right. Then he says, 'What type of scholarship did Neil Diamond go to NYU on?'"

"Charisma?" I asked.

"Nope. Fencing."

I pointed at the blade she had strapped to her waist. "That explains the sword."

"It's an épée. Neil will appreciate the symbolism. Anyhow, those were the easy questions. Number three was a killer."

Did I mention Mrs. Berns is eighty-nine if she's a day? We should all be so lucky to age this gracefully. Here she was, her lipstick bright and shiny, her apricot-tinged hair crisp with curls. In fact, a curler or two may have still clung to her scalp, which just added to her general je ne sais quoi. I loved the woman even though she drove me up a wall. Or maybe because of it.

"And what was the third question?"

"'Which Neil Diamond song contains the words "danced," "night," "brand-new day," "lovers playing," and "romantic play"?' And understand that the man has a gobzillion songs."

"I don't know," I said. "Which song?"

Mrs. Berns crossed her arms triumphantly. "'September Morn.' And voilà!" She pulled two laminated tickets out of the purse slung over her forearm. "You and me are going to meet the man! Monday night!"

"Whuh?" I was on sensory overload. "But it's only Thursday. And I'm not a DiamondHead."

"All it takes is one show, sister."

That wasn't the point I was arguing. "Why are you here now if the show's not until Monday?"

"What else do I have to do? I'm retired."

My chest tightened with worry. "Um, actually, you're my assistant librarian. I left you in charge for the next ten days."

She waved her hands. "Pah. A monkey could do that job. I left Curtis Poling at the wheel."

Curtis Poling, the Battle Lake Senior Sunset resident who periodically fished off the roof into the grass below. His eccentricity made him a town legend, but he was sharp as a knife and completely responsible. He'd do for the moment. "OK. How'd you get out of the nursing home?"

"Paid a woman to pretend she was my daughter and sign me out for a family vacation."

"And you paid that same woman to drive you here?"

"No, I hitchhiked."

My jaw dropped. "That's dangerous!"

"You're a fine one to talk, Ms. Finds Dead Bodies. And it's not as bad as it sounds. The first woman drove me as far as Alexandria, where I wandered around pretending I had dementia until a nice older couple stopped for me. I told them I was from Saint Paul and didn't know where I was. They drove me to the Lyngblomsten Nursing Home right over here on Como, where a friend of mine stays. She was in on the plan and welcomed me like her roommate." Mrs. Berns grinned. "If not for the kindness of strangers."

I dropped into the nearest seat.

"You don't need to look like such a sourpuss. I'm here and I'm fine. What's wrong with you, anyhow? When you first walked in here, you looked like you saw a . . ." A shadow passed across Mrs. Berns's face as she stared at me, her eyes growing wider. "Oh no. Tell me you didn't."

I tried swallowing but didn't have enough spit. I knew where this conversation was going. "Didn't what?"

She scowled. "Find another dead body."

Yep. I sat up straighter. "Technically, I didn't *find* it."

She shook her head. "Someone OD on hotdish-on-a-stick right at your feet?"

"Worse."

"You see one of those Sky Ride bubbles crashing to the ground and crushing young lovers below, popping them like slugs?" She nodded knowingly. "I always suspected that was going to happen. You wouldn't catch me on one of those death traps."

"Worse."

She leaned toward me, her eyes bright. "Out with it, then."

I drew a ragged breath. "Ashley Pederson, the newest Milkfed Mary, Queen of the Dairy? She died about an hour ago while she was getting her head carved out of butter. I was there, but so were a thousand other people," I added defensively.

"Woof." She pushed her sword toward her front and fell onto the bench across from me. "I'm surprised they let you outta your car. You're the Grim Reaper in person. So how'd that little demon die?"

"'Little demon'?"

"Yep." She floofed her hair. "Her parents are nice folks, but they spoiled that girl rotten. She was as mean as the day is long. That's what happens when you never say no to a pretty girl."

I'd never met Ashley in person—I'd planned to interview her immediately after the butter carving—but had on occasion run into her parents when stopping by the *Recall* office. They were pleasant people whose life, by all accounts, rotated entirely around their only child.

"They're going to be devastated."

"That's an understatement. So how'd she kick the bucket?"

I held myself. "I don't know. It started out everything was fine. Ashley was waving at the crowd, smiling. She stepped into the carving booth, and the sculptor followed her. Everyone was snapping pictures, me included." I indicated the camera still dangling at my neck.

"They're in there for not more than five minutes, the sculptor carving and Ashley posing, when the lights in the whole building snap out. Actually," I continued, realizing something that had eluded me, "*all* the power went out. I know because the ice cream machines stopped whirring, too."

I saw the tableau emblazoned on the back of my lids. "When the lights came back on, Ashley was dead in the booth. And her skin was the brightest red I've ever seen."

Mrs. Berns nodded as if she'd expected this. "Probably the goat milk cartel offed her. They're always conniving for their slice of the dairy market. You said this happened just this morning?"

"Yeah."

"Well, let's see 'em."

"What?"

She pointed at the camera still around my neck. "The pictures. You said you were snapping them right before she died. You probably captured her last breath."

My intestines spasmed. The camera suddenly felt heavy, like a yoke. I took it off and handed it to her, remembering the feeling that I'd had watching Ashley through my viewfinder just before the lights went out. "You know, I noticed something odd about Ashley as the building lost power."

"Probably her guardian angel flying the coop," Mrs. Berns said as she turned on the camera.

"No, that's not it. Go to the last picture." I stood and leaned over Mrs. Berns's shoulder as she scrolled through the photos. The thumbnails displayed the image of a young blonde in perfect health, a crown glittering on her thick hair.

I stabbed my finger at the camera when she reached the end. "That one."

Mrs. Berns selected the photo and made it as big as the screen would allow. "It's a picture of the back of her head."

I squinted. "I know."

"What could possibly be odd about the back of someone's head?"

I blew out a puff of air, frustrated. "I'm not sure. I didn't quite have it when I took the shot. It was more of a sensation than a formed thought. Maybe if I upload the photo to my computer and enlarge it?"

"Maybe, but it'll have to wait." She handed the camera back to me. "We need to go."

"Where?"

"To the scene of the crime, girl! You've gotta cover it for the paper. People'll be dying to know what happened." She laughed dryly at her word choice. "So turn that frown upside down, and let's hit it."

I violently shook my head. "No."

"You can't just sit here and mope." She stood. "If there's as many people around as you said, no one can pin this one on you. She probably just choked on some flying butter, and you'll feel better once you find out it was some freak accident."

It would be nice to know she wasn't murdered, which I was ashamed to say had been my first thought. "You know I swore no more murder investigations the same time I gave up drinking," I said, already starting to cave.

She held out her hand. "We're not investigating. You'll be doing the job you were sent to the fair to do: write articles about Battle Lake."

"I don't know . . ."

"I saw some deep-fried Nut Goodies on a stick on my way over here," she coaxed.

I stood up straight. "You didn't."

"I did. Let's go. I'll buy you one."

I sighed. I hated being cheap, but not enough to do anything about it. "Fine. But you're going to tell me all about this redecorating Jed's done at my house. And we're not doing any investigating."

"I'm sure we won't need to."

And with those optimistic words, I took her hand, and we stepped out of the Airstream and put our feet onto the most dangerous path the two of us would ever walk.

We wouldn't come out of it together.

Chapter 4

The deep-fried Nut Goodie line wasn't long.

Unless you're an addict.

"What's the holdup?" I stood on my tiptoes. "How long do they take to make? How do you think they fry it without it melting?"

"Would you relax?" Mrs. Berns said. "For five dollars a pop, let's assume they're using space technology."

When we finally reached the front, Mrs. Berns traded the clerk an Abe Lincoln for what looked like a windblown funnel cake on a stick. "Where's the Nut Goodie?" I asked.

The man behind the counter smiled. "We freeze it, bread it, fry it, and sprinkle powdered sugar over the top. Trust me—it's in there."

Not convinced, I turned away and sniffed at it. It smelled like a doughnut.

Mrs. Berns pinched my arm. "Shit or get off the pot."

"Fine." I bit in, expecting molten lava to sear my tongue. Instead, my mouth was filled with warm, chocolaty, nutty maple goodness. I moaned. "I might need some time alone with this."

She smiled smugly. "You're welcome."

"No, seriously. Try this." As she ducked her head in for a taste, I pulled the fried Nut Goodie back. "On second thought, you should get your own."

She shook her head in disgust and took off toward the Dairy Building. I followed, whispering endearments to the fried candy bar as I nibbled at it.

Nut Goodies had been a part of my life for more than a decade, ever since I'd bought my first green-and-red-wrapped one on a whim at a gas station. Out of the wrapper, the candy is round, brown, bumpy, and looks about as appetizing as a hairball. One bite, though, and you'll be hooked. You first encounter decadent chocolate, which is quickly countered by a satisfying peanut crunch, and finally, complete immersion in a blissful wave of maple-candy center. I'd eaten them quick, like a naughty habit, and slow out of the freezer, but never deep-fried before. The holy trinity was complete.

My private ecstasy was cut short by the horde of rubberneckers and camera crews lining Underwood Street and curving around Judson Avenue. The chocolate that'd just brought me so much joy abruptly grew leaden in my stomach as the reality I'd been trying to avoid ever since the Dairy Building went black hit home.

A young woman had just died.

The death was new, but already the front of the building was lined with teddy bears, pom-poms in Battle Lake's signature red and blue, and flower bouquets. I swallowed the starchy taste in my mouth, chucked my licked-clean Nut Goodie stick, clipped on my press badge, and tugged out my pad and pen. Mrs. Berns, who was nowhere in sight, had been right: I had a duty as the only Battle Lake reporter at the fair to cover Ashley's death.

Near me, two young, golden-haired women were laying daisies near the door to the Dairy Building, which was cordoned off with police tape. Next to them, a KSTP interviewer was speaking to her cameraman.

"OK. Ready," she said. After a countdown and a signal, the light on the camera snapped on, and her face became somberly animated. "Hello! I'm Angela Klein, reporting live from the Minnesota State Fair. Today, in a tragic turn of events, Ashley Pederson, Battle Lake native and recently crowned fifty-fourth Milkfed Mary, Queen of the Dairy, died.

"In a time-honored State Fair tradition, Ms. Pederson was inaugurating the fair by posing as her head was carved from butter. She and the sculptor, Glenda Haines, were sitting in the rotating, refrigerated booth supplied by the Midwest Dairy Organization when the lights temporarily went out in the building. When power returned, Ms. Pederson was discovered dead in the booth. At this time, police have not ruled out foul play."

A weight, heavy as a gravestone, pushed down on my shoulders. The announcement brought back the image of Ashley's slack face and brightly colored skin. I sighed. As much as I wanted her death to be from natural causes, it was time to face facts. Someone was to blame. Eighteen-year-old beauty queens with their lives in front of them didn't just keel over and start glowing like cherry lollipops.

The interviewer turned toward a thick-necked teenager. "Here with us is Dirk Holthaus, Ms. Pederson's boyfriend. How'd you find out about her death, Dirk?"

He blinked and adjusted his letter jacket, which must have been an XXXL. The medals sewn on the front jangled, and I squinted, trying to figure out what sports he was in. "I was in the building when it happened. I saw the ambulance take her away." He ducked his eyes. "Her mom was there, too."

The interviewer nodded sympathetically. "What can you tell us about the circumstances surrounding her passing? Did she have a heart condition, or was she in some way predisposed to premature death?"

He seemed to struggle, whether with the questions or his recent loss, I didn't know. I also didn't recognize his name or face, which meant he wasn't from Battle Lake. It was odd for an Otter Tail County girl to date an outsider, though summers brought vacationing families from the Cities to the region, so maybe that's how the two of them had met. I jotted down his name and placed a question mark next to it.

Dirk responded, "I don't know anything."

The edge in his voice made me wonder how long they'd been dating. He didn't seem broken up at all. Rather, he acted peeved, like he'd been interrupted in the middle of a *Diddy Kong Racing* session. I wrote his behavior off as shock. Grief hits in all sorts of ways.

I watched as the news crews finished interviewing bystanders. I couldn't help but notice that the two blondes in the background had been retrieving and then placing the same daisies near the entrance of the building since the cameras had started rolling. If my guess was right, they were Milkfed Mary runners-up who might give me some quotes I could use. I wasn't coldhearted enough to interview Dirk, even though he didn't seem like he'd mind, hanging around the door of the Dairy Building as he was.

When the crowd dissipated to regular fair size, I strode up to the daisy-droppers, both of whom had apparently come from the same Pretty Blonde Girl™ mold. "Hi. I'm Mira James. From Battle Lake. Mind if I ask you a few questions?"

Their expressions tightened at the mention of Battle Lake. "Sure," they said in unison.

I nodded at the flowers. "I can't help but notice that you've been moving the same bouquets around for a while. What's up?"

They exchanged glances, and the shorter of the two spoke in a high-pitched, almost childlike voice. "You said you're from Battle Lake?"

"Yeah," I held up my notebook. "I'm a reporter for the paper there."

They looked at each other again before the shorter one ventured another question. "Did you know Ashley?"

"I'd never met her. I knew her reputation."

This interested both of them, judging by the light it ignited in their faces. I continued, improvising based on what Mrs. Berns had told me. "I got the impression that she didn't have a lot of friends at school. I took it she was one of the mean girls."

The taller girl spoke. "That sounds like her." She offered her hand. "I'm Delrita, and this is Brittany, by the way. Our chaperone told us to come down and act busy around the flowers. I think they want to make things look good."

Interesting. "What things?"

Brittany interjected in her slide-whistle voice. "*Every*thing. The Milkfed Mary pageant is a big deal. A queen has never died before, not at the State Fair. I guess they don't want the whole industry to get a bad name. We were told to stay as long as there're cameras around."

I studied the stress lines under their eyes. "That's pretty cold."

Brittany shrugged. "It's the beauty pageant world. It's a lot about appearances. Hey, you've got something on your face. Right here."

She pointed at the corner of her mouth, but once I started licking around mine, I realized she was being kind. If my tongue was any judge, I had a perfect rim of Nut Goodie circling my lips with a little powdered sugar dusted in for good measure.

"Thanks," I mumbled, pulling a tissue out of my purse. Eager to change the subject, I asked them what they knew of Ashley.

Delrita spoke up. "We're only supposed to focus on the good stuff, you know? It's part of the Milkfed Mary creed."

I stuffed the now-brown tissue back into my bag. "OK, what *good* stuff did you know about Ashley?"

They both squinched their foreheads as if trying to remember the procedure for splitting an atom.

"She was pretty," Brittany finally offered. Delrita nodded, eager that they'd landed on something.

"Anything else?" I prodded.

Delrita glanced around. No one was paying us any attention. She sighed deeply. "Look. We didn't like her much. She thought she was better than everyone else. She made fun of dairy farms and people who worked on them. And she stole things."

This perked me up. "Like what?"

The girls glanced quickly at each other, and then Brittany found her shoes very interesting.

"Ask Lana," Delrita said.

"Lana?"

"That's all I can say. Really." She shook her head so vigorously that hair fell over her eyes. "We're supposed to be putting on a united front."

I could feel them closing off. "One more quick question. Do you think she died of natural causes?"

Delrita hugged her elbows. "I've lived on a farm my whole life. I've seen animals born, and I've seen them die, but I've never seen anything drop that fast and turn red as a stoplight. Me and some of the other girls think she was poisoned."

There it was, my worst fear given voice.

Someone had murdered Battle Lake's Milkfed Mary, Queen of the Dairy.

"Well, thank you for your time. I appreciate you talking to me." When they nodded and returned to their flower-moving business, I took off into the crowd, a sugar-and-stress headache knocking at the back of my skull.

Mrs. Berns materialized alongside me. "What'd you find out?"

"Not much. You?"

"Not much."

A glint in her eye suggested otherwise, but my headache kept me from pursuing it. "You got any ibuprofen?"

Mrs. Berns dug in her purse and came out with two red-and-white tablets. As I made spit, I prayed they were over the counter. "Where are you headed now?"

"I want to play some Midway games. Last year, I won a big Scooby-Doo at the pool tables. Care to join me?"

"No thanks. I need to find someone named Lana, and I think I know just where to look."

Chapter 5

The Midwest Dairy Organization housed Milkfed Mary and her runners-up in the top floor of the Cattle Barn during their State Fair appearances. At least that's what the people at the information booth told me.

The barn was a huge brown brick structure that looked like an industrial concert hall with a stretched-out A-line roof for a hat. Over the door hung the blue, white, and green words CATTLE BARN, painted two feet high above an ornate and somber bull's head carved from what appeared to be granite.

As I craned my neck to peer up the bull's nostrils, I decided that being forced to sleep in the Cattle Barn was a raw deal. Cows tramped in and out, and the air was heavy with the aroma of sweet straw and gritty manure for ten feet on each side of the building.

Once I stepped inside and climbed the steep, curving cement stairs to the second floor, however, I was greeted by a surprisingly neat dormitory, one enormous room containing twelve beds side by side, six on the left wall and six on the right, a few vanities sprinkled around, portable closets to hold gowns, and a bathroom complete with shower, toilet, and sink. Sunlight streamed in from grand windows constructed of sturdy glass blocks along the far wall, book-size squares of light piled one on top of another until they were twenty feet tall. At this level, the odor was more stale bedding than cow butt, and the facilities were no worse than my digs in the trailer.

Two closed doors led off the far side of the gigantic main room, one marked CHAPERONE and the other marked OFFICE. Since the place was currently uninhabited, I strode across the expanse to try both doors. They were locked. I considered snooping in the dresser drawers, but since most girls no longer embroidered their names on their underwear, I didn't think it'd do any good, as I was up here solely to verify the name of one of the contestants.

The Lana who'd been mentioned must have been a Milkfed Mary, after all. How else would Delrita, Brittany, and Ashley, all from different sides of Minnesota, know her? But there were easier ways to find out than riffling through underwear drawers. I'd just come to satisfy idle curiosity, really, to keep busy so I didn't have room in my head for the image of Ashley's dead eyes. I was on my way down the curved stairs when I heard footsteps coming up from below.

My heart started hammering. A woman had been murdered this morning, and here I was snooping around her dormitory. It wouldn't look good, which was exactly why I shouldn't have gotten involved. I couldn't escape without passing whoever was coming toward me, and there were precious few places to hide upstairs unless I wanted to cower behind a rack of off-the-shoulder taffeta gowns. I settled for slipping back up the stairs so I could walk back down more nonchalantly. After all, who doesn't get lost in the Cattle Barn?

My foot was on the first step, descending for the second time, when I heard the sniffling. Whoever was coming up was weeping. *Shoot.* I wasn't good at dealing with criers. Actually, I wasn't a fan of any emotion. If I had my way, all honest interaction would involve hand puppets.

I tried making myself invisible, but as soon as the woman ascending rounded the corner, I knew that would be impossible.

I found myself face-to-face with Carlotta Pederson, mother to the recently deceased fifty-fourth Milkfed Mary, Queen of the Dairy.

She looked like she'd been smacked by a train.

Chapter 6

"Mira? Is that you? Ron said you'd be at the fair. He said I should look for you. I just talked to him, to tell him about . . ." Her voice cracked. Tears rolled down her face, settling in lines that hadn't been there the last time I'd seen her.

"I suppose you heard," she finally squeezed out.

I opened my mouth to reply but closed it when I spotted the two police officers bringing up the rear. They were followed by the woman in the red power suit whom I'd seen trying to calm the sculptor earlier this morning. I moved to stand closer to Mrs. Pederson, hoping Red Suit wouldn't recognize me.

While Carlotta and I hardly knew each other, I felt an immediate need to protect her. Regardless of what others thought of Ashley, Carlotta had just suffered an unimaginable loss. Her swollen face was a painful reminder that no one adores you like your mom, and no amount of love was insurance against loss.

"We're here so I can point out Ashley's things. You'll stay with me, won't you, honey?" She glided past me as she spoke, her voice seeming to come from far away. I must have been her only remotely familiar face.

"Of course." I followed her into the dormitory, the other three on our heels. There was no point in asking Carlotta how she was doing. She was moving as if her spine had been crushed and she was only staying upright out of habit.

She rambled to the nearest vanity and reached for a hairbrush with an ornate silver handle. She held it toward the sunlight streaming in from the windows, and the rays played off the blonde strands captured in the bristles. "I gave Ashley this brush for her first Communion. I used to comb her hair with it before she went to bed. A hundred strokes on each section." Her voice remained eerily detached.

"I'm so sorry," I croaked, feeling her pain despite my best efforts.

I knew that level of agony, that bottomless falling, the elevator plummeting to an end that never came. I'd spent part of my childhood and all my teen years wishing my dad out of my life, and then when he disappeared in a screeching crash of metal, I felt as lonely as a box. I wanted to somehow comfort Carlotta, but I was afraid to touch her. She trembled with sadness. It crawled on her skin like bugs, parted her hair, leaked out her ears.

Guilt drove me, though, and I stepped forward and tentatively patted her shoulder. She turned, fell into my arms, and sobbed, her disconnection cracking beneath the most basic human touch. "She's dead! My beautiful baby. How could this happen? Why her? Why can't anyone tell me what happened?"

The uniformed officers shifted uncomfortably. They both appeared fresh-scrubbed, maybe four years younger than my twenty-nine. One of them hadn't been shaving long.

"I'm so sorry, Mrs. Pederson," I said. "Do you have someone at the fair with you? You shouldn't be alone at a time like this."

She clung to me. "My husband is on his way. You'll help me, won't you, Mira? You'll help me find out what happened to my baby. Won't you?" She pulled back and locked eyes with me. Her expression was etched with a wild fierceness, leaving me only one answer.

"Of course I will."

That wasn't good enough for her. "Promise me. Promise me you'll find out what happened to my little girl."

Those were the words people spoke when unimaginable pain befell them. They were unmoored words, a kettle hot to bursting letting off necessary steam. Most listeners would write them off to extreme grief. I, the prisoner of guilt, tattooed them on my heart.

"I promise."

And with those two words, my personal vow to avoid all future murder investigations shattered like a bad-luck mirror.

Chapter 7

Carlotta held eye contact for another moment, nodded resolutely, and then released me to cradle the hairbrush as if it were an infant. "My sweet baby. My poor, poor baby."

With the help of the police officers and the staid but keen-eyed red suit woman I guessed was the Milkfed Mary chaperone, Mrs. Pederson made her way around the dorm, pointing out her daughter's duffel bag and gowns. Their location and contents were photographed, as was the entire room, from every angle. Mrs. Pederson wasn't allowed to remove any of Ashley's belongings. Rather, the police officers collected them with their gloved hands and carried them out, even gently peeling her daughter's brush from Carlotta's hands before leading the way down the stairs.

The three of us followed, me with a hand on the shaky Mrs. Pederson. The chaperone trailed at a distance. She had an icy demeanor, but inside she must have felt terrible. Talk about a profoundly bad job of looking after someone. I couldn't imagine it was her fault, but that was probably empty solace.

The police officers waited for us at the bottom of the stairs. "Mrs. Pederson, we need to go to the station now."

"I'll go with," I said. In for a penny, in for a pound.

"I'm sorry," the nearest officer said. "You can't ride in the police car."

My stomach dropped. Riding separately would mean unhooking Ron's pickup truck from the Airstream, and I had no idea how to do that. I could figure it out, though, even if it meant reasoning with a crowbar. "Can you give me directions?"

Mrs. Pederson shook her head. "It's OK, Mira. Steven is meeting me there. You've met my husband? He'll take care of me."

Sadness squeezed my ribs. "Is there anything I can do?"

She gripped my arm. The fervor that had struck her earlier had dissipated. "Pray for me, Mira. Pray for me and my girl's soul."

The police led her away, supporting her as they walked. The chaperone followed for a few feet before turning back to me. There was a pleasant non-expression on her face, but it constricted into something darker. "You were the girl who tried to get into the booth after Ashley died."

"Not me." I met and held her gaze.

She studied me for five uncomfortable seconds, apparently coming to the conclusion that I wasn't one to abandon my lies easily. She changed tactics. "What were you doing in the dormitory just now?"

Defensive was my normal posture, but my brain was so thoroughly rooted in sympathy that it took me a moment to jump tracks. "I was looking for Mrs. Pederson."

You lie enough, your fibbing muscle becomes as toned as a weight lifter's bicep.

The chaperone mulled this one. From a distance, one might describe her as attractive in a motherly way, but up close, she had a Nurse Ratched vibe. A lot of that was due to her hair and clothes, which were stiff and perfect, but she also wielded iron behind her eyes. She unsettled me a little.

"How'd you know Mrs. Pederson would be here?" she finally said.

"I didn't. I was hoping." Before she came up with a counter question, I threw one back at her. That's Subterfuge and Camouflage 101. "What's your name?"

"Janice Opatz," she said icily. "I'm the Milkfed Mary chaperone."

Exactly as I'd surmised. I raised my eyebrows just enough to indicate it'd occurred to me how lousy she was at her job, then continued my offensive charge. "That's your room off the dormitory above?"

"Yes."

"And your office is the one next to it?"

"No, that's . . ." Some instinct drew her up short. If her age was any indicator, she was a veteran chaperone, which meant she owned a juiced-up shit-sniffer. I was surprised I'd gotten this far. "I didn't catch *your* name."

Now that I'd promised the impossible to Mrs. Pederson, I figured I had better do my best to keep all avenues open. "Mira James." I held out my hand. "I'm from Battle Lake."

Janice shook it, offering me a Switzerland smile. "I'm sure I'll see you around."

I mirrored her expression. "I'm sure."

She resumed following Mrs. Pederson and the police, and I headed to the Midway to search out Mrs. Berns. My head was full, and I needed someone to help me sort everything out. I was so deep in my muddied thoughts that I barreled right into a very tall young man with a sign on a stick.

"Oh! I'm sorry," I said.

He regained his balance, allowing me to read his placard, which said, FREE THE COWS! I glanced over my shoulder into the barn I'd recently exited. The heifers inside appeared more comfortable than most humans at the fair—they had fans blowing on them; they got brushed, fed, and watered regularly; and they could poop right where they stood and someone else cleaned it up. I knew a lot of men and more than a few women in Battle Lake for whom, if you threw in a working television, that would be paradise.

Twenty or so other protesters milled nearby, their signs also denouncing some aspect of the dairy industry. It made me exhausted just to read them, so I strode off without any further interaction.

I cruised to the Midway and sought out the games area, which was lined with stalls—balloon darts, frog fishing, basketball, Skee-Ball, ring toss, break-a-plate or Whac-A-Mole, rubber duck grab—probably fifty kiosks in all ringing the sides with more in the middle. I noted as I walked that either my black mood had affected my senses or I'd stumbled into the seedier side of the fair.

Likely both.

The game booth workers cajoled me to buy three darts for five bucks or try my luck with a basketball. The crowds were thin here, and so the barkers were aggressive, insulting me when I walked by without acknowledging them, catcalling and hooting.

"Hey, baby, you wanna pump my gun? Every girl's a winner at this booth!"

"Where you going? Spend some time with a lonely carnie! I promise I won't bite, sweetheart."

The farther in I walked, the higher my hackles rose. I'd tripped into the dark side, a mangy place populated with cheap polyester dolls, warped prize mirrors, and T-shirts adorned with pictures of large-breasted women and sexist slogans. It felt like everyone around me had developed flashing eyes and sharp incisors, and when I dared a glance up, I met the gaze of the short-range-shooting booth operator, who was suggestively eating a Hot Pocket.

Someone tapped my shoulder. "Where's the fire?"

"Mrs. Berns!" My relief was immense. The sleaziness of the moment melted. A family walked past, their little girl smiling at her massive puff of cotton candy, and the wolves retreated into the shadows.

"Who else? Check these out!" She was cradling two stuffed pit bulls, each the size of a wide-screen TV. "I would have won *three*, but he kicked me out. Said there was a limit, but I didn't see a sign."

My heartbeat slowed to normal. "Maybe he meant a limit to good taste?"

She acted like she didn't hear me. "Can you carry one of these? A strong wind picks up, and I'll have to choose between me and them."

I hoisted one on my shoulder and grabbed the other with my free hand. "We should probably get these and you into a taxi. It's been a long day. Where're you staying?"

Mrs. Berns grinned. "Can I buy you dinner? Deep-fried pickle? Chocolate-dipped bacon? Teriyaki ostrich skewers?"

My shoulders tightened as I realized where this was headed, and all the trauma of the day came home to roost. "Oh no."

"Oh yes." She started walking toward my camp. "There's plenty of room in that pimpmobile Ron passes for a trailer. No sense in me wasting my money on a hotel room. Besides, I already unpacked."

I picked up my pace to catch up with her, no small feat while balancing two huge pooches. "I go to bed early."

She snorted. "You think there's anyone in Battle Lake doesn't know that? You've gotta be drier than lint by now, all those nights with just you, the TV, and your animals." She made herself cackle. "Don't worry. I won't put a dent in your lifestyle. Now let's go store these dogs. I don't want people to think I'm a show-off."

I considered telling her that with the épée still strapped to her waist, people thinking she was a show-off might be the least of her worries, but why point out a ding in a person's windshield when they were happy to have the car running?

And truth be told, I was more than a little relieved Mrs. Berns would be staying with me. I didn't want to be alone tonight. I trudged behind her, the bizarreness of the day fully catching up to me and wiping me out, and it wasn't even suppertime. By the time we reached the campgrounds, I was dragging. I felt like I'd walked to the State Fair from Otter Tail County.

Barefoot.

"You left the door open," Mrs. Berns said.

I shook my head, not even bothering to look. "No I didn't."

"Well, then it opened itself, because it's swinging in the wind."

I glanced up. She was right.

I shuddered as my body scraped the bottom of the adrenaline barrel. After finding Mrs. Berns in the trailer earlier today, I'd been extra careful to lock the door on my way out. No way had it sprung open on its own.

Someone had broken in, and there was a possibility they were still inside. I set down the pit bulls and was reaching to pull Mrs. Berns away from the Airstream when I was sideswiped by my third shock of the day.

Chapter 8

Kennie Rogers, Battle Lake mayor and perpetual thorn in my side, stood on the top step wearing some sort of Christina Aguilera weave on top of her platinum hair. Mrs. Berns reflexively seized a pit bull and hurled it at her.

There was more power in those stewing-chicken arms than I would have guessed, because she knocked Kennie Rogers's hair-adjacent monstrosity right off.

"What in the hell'd you do that for?" Kennie demanded.

Mrs. Berns shrugged. "You had an animal on your head."

Kennie stepped down so she could retrieve the three-foot strands of Barbie-blonde hair woven with startling oranges and pinks. While her hairpiece was relatively modern, I couldn't help but notice that her clothes were screaming to be released from the 1980s. Her tight rainbow shirt, ankle-pinned Guess jeans, and acid-green jelly shoes looked like exactly what I'd worn in my high school senior photo, and I was ten years younger than Kennie. She plopped the weave back on lopsided. "In an effort at day-tawn-tay, I'm going to pretend I didn't hear that."

Détente? Kennie Rogers was to diplomacy what termites were to wood. Though to be fair, she and I'd reached an uncomfortable truce recently, after the Battle Lake chief of police had dumped her for God. I felt sorry for her, which wasn't the same as liking her but was better than wanting to drown her.

"What're you doing here?" I asked.

She drew herself up tall. "As mayor of Battle Lake, it is my right to see how city funds are being spent." She pointed at the ground. "The trailer's spot was paid for by the chamber of commerce, you know."

It was still a marvel to me how Kennie got away with her thick southern accent. She was Battle Lake born and raised, except for a short stint in beauty school, which hadn't stuck. "Fine. But how'd you get in the trailer?"

She smiled archly. "Key from Ron. I'll be helping myself to the bed in back, thank you."

I rubbed my ear. I must have misheard. Kennie, stay *here*?

"Oh no," Mrs. Berns piped in. "You're not crashing with us. And even if you are, that's my bed."

Not only had I heard correctly, but apparently they both intended to stay with me. That was it. I was full up for the day. I turned and walked away. My plan was to find a nice barn, pretend I was a cow, and live it up for the rest of my life. Worst-case scenario, I'd get committed and sent someplace where at least the people *knew* they were off their rockers.

"Where're you going?" both women called out in unison.

I kept my stride.

Kennie continued, her voice cajoling, "That mean you don't want to know when Johnny'll be here?"

I stopped.

My blood ran hot and cold, creating little explosions where the temperatures collided. Johnny Leeson was the Adonis of Battle Lake. The mere mention of his name brought delicious quivers. He had thick and wavy dirty-blond hair, eyes blue enough to scare off clouds, a sensuous mouth, and arms that could pick you up and throw you over his shoulder, if he weren't such a nice guy.

He and I had a history, and like most histories, it was riddled with conflicts and misunderstandings. Johnny was sexy, kind, and smart, and too good for me. That last one was the root of most of our problems. That, and my Dork Wattage shot off the charts when he appeared. It was his hands that really made me lose my way. They were sunbrowned, big and capable, his fingers lean and perfectly proportioned. I couldn't look at them without imagining them tangled in my hair, or moving down my naked back, or pulling me in fiercely for a passionate kiss that set us both on raging, all-consuming fire.

Of course, none of that had yet to happen outside of my fertile imagination.

"Might wanna put your leg down," Mrs. Berns called out. "I think you just sprayed that gentleman."

I blushed and nodded at the cowboy striding by. Then I turned and marched past the ladies, up the steps, and into the trailer. "We're going to sit around the table and figure out who's staying where, like civilized folks. Come on."

I hadn't migrated to Battle Lake expecting to change my lousy luck with the opposite sex. In fact, I hadn't even moved there expecting to find a guy who used correct verb tenses, so when Johnny sailed into my life all open and sweet and smart, I had no idea what to do with him. Keeping him at arm's length had worked OK so far, but I could feel my reserve crumbling. "He's coming to the State Fair?"

"Saturday," Kennie confirmed, taking one of the seats inside the trailer. "His band's playing. They just booked it, filling in for a cancellation. He made me promise not to tell you, but as your friend, I couldn't do that. He shows up to surprise you, and there you are all tree-frog ugly with your hair uncombed and wearing no makeup. *Ugh*."

"I never wear makeup, Kennie."

She pursed her lips and nodded, her expression saying, *And see where it got you?* "Where did you leave off with Johnny, anyhow?" she asked. "Have you two even gotten to first base?"

"Doubt it," Mrs. Berns said, taking the bench by the door. "Mira'd have better luck falling up than she does falling in love."

They both giggled. I didn't like this sudden switch to them teaming up against me.

I scowled. "Johnny and I've decided to back it up a little. To be friends, and see where that goes."

"You can't back up from nowhere, girl," Kennie said.

"Yeah," Mrs. Berns agreed, leaning forward to high-five Kennie. "I think you have to be somewhere to back up from it, honey."

Sad but true.

My past was sprinkled with men who had drinking problems, thought that making sure you were awake first constituted foreplay, and/or were so afraid of commitment that they didn't even own permanent markers.

I changed the subject to distract from the sudden thrumming in my rib cage. Nothing like imagining your crush on a big stage, shaking his hair and singing for strangers, to make a gal hot. It's primal. It's mysterious. It explains how Roy Orbison and Bob Dylan ever managed to get laid.

"So you're up to see the sights?" I asked Kennie, figuring I'd ease into asking where *else* she could stay.

She made a scoffing sound. "Oh no, baby. Sightseeing isn't a tax write-off. I'm up here to *work*." Kennie said this loud, as if the IRS may have planted a hidden microphone behind Ron's lava lamp. "Battle Lake has a booth here, for one day only. It's going up a week from this Saturday, on 'I Love the Fair!' day. All the proceeds will go to the municipal liquor store. I wanna get in some of that vodka with gold flecks in it, but Bobbie said we can't order stuff that might not sell unless she's got more cash in the pot."

I furrowed my brow. I'd never fully understood the concept of city-owned liquor stores, though the financial investment made sense the more time I spent in Battle Lake, where Old Milwaukee was one of the four food groups. That aside, a Battle Lake fundraiser at the State Fair actually sounded like a great idea, which made me suspicious. Kennie was known for her brainstorms, but not one of them had been good. In fact, most of them weren't even legal. "How're you going to raise the money? Specifically, what kind of booth is this going to be?"

She smiled like a satisfied cat. "That's a big ol' surprise."

Uh-huh. Thought so. "And you need to be here *a week* early to set up?"

"Yes." She raised her voice. "I must work while I am here at the Minnesota State Fair." She drew it down to a whisper. "But between you, me, and the wall, I'm going to also reacquaint myself with one Mr. Neil Diamond."

Any camaraderie Mrs. Berns had shared with Kennie at my expense vanished. "What do you mean, 'reacquaint'?"

Kennie fluttered fake, glitter-sprayed lashes. "A girl's gotta have her secrets. But if you insist. I have a little history with Neil. We shared a special night many years ago. I think he'll be pleased to see me again."

"Were there five thousand other people there, sharing this special night?" Mrs. Berns asked, her eyes narrowing. "And did you have to pay to get into this special night, and was there stadium seating?"

"Now, now," Kennie said, leaning back and crossing her legs. "No need to be jealous."

Mrs. Berns scowled, then grabbed me by the arm and led me to the back of the trailer and into the only room with a door. She'd already laid her clothes across the bed and had my suitcase packed near the door. "She can stay here, but if you tell her I have backstage passes, I'll pee on you while you're sleeping."

My eyes widened. "Was that called for? Couldn't you just ask me to please not tell? Also, I didn't even know *you* were staying here."

Mrs. Berns ignored the last part. "If Kennie finds out I have backstage access to Neil, she'll steal those passes from me as sure as you and I are standing here." She tugged my ear. "I know how weak you are. You cave at the drop of a hat. Now, you keep my secret, and I'll throw in a little something extra for you on Neil night. Deal?"

I yelped and rubbed at the side of my head. "You don't need to bribe me. How about I just don't tell her?"

Mrs. Berns studied me doubtfully, but she left my ear alone. "When you're sleeping. Remember," she hissed, before striding back into the

RV's main room. "We agreed, Kennie," she announced. "I'm the old lady, I get the back bedroom. I need my sleep, plus I snore like a buzz saw. The two of you can take the fold-out beds in this main room."

Well, I guessed that was decided.

Kennie glanced from me to Mrs. Berns, not trusting us. She understood squatter's rights, though, and replaced her look of doubt with a broad smile. "Fine. Isn't this going to be fun? Just like a slumber party."

And those words were the last I heard before I entered the third circle of hell.

Chapter 9

It should come as no surprise that Mrs. Berns and Kennie Rogers were appalling roommates.

For starters, I learned that first night that Mrs. Berns was not exaggerating about her propensity for snoring. It was like trying to fall asleep in the middle of a rip-roaring lumber camp. And the sunrise brought no relief. Oh no. Turned out Kennie had some sort of disorder that required her to hum when she wasn't talking. I'd never been around her when she was quiet for any length of time, so I hadn't noticed before. The next morning, though, when I tried to piece together the little I knew about Ashley's death into an article, there she was: *Hmmmmmm hmmm hummmm.*

It was toneless, tuneless, and a prescription for making a quiet gal climb the walls.

I thought Kennie was giving me a reprieve when she left the trailer the next morning to find breakfast, but in an apparent effort to make our "slumber party" a multisensory experience, she vomited in an empty cookie bucket on her way back. Apparently, a breakfast of corn dogs and deep-fried Twinkies followed by a ride on the Scrambler had been her undoing.

Mrs. Berns wasn't silly enough to go on any rides, but she did love morning cheese curds, which gave her farts that sliced through metal. Those, combined with the unexpected September heat, transformed the Airstream into a Dutch sulfur oven.

I was sitting at the trailer's kitchen table, wondering if there was room for me in the cow stables, when the ringing cell phone in my pocket made me jump. Ron Sims had forced the cell on me, and as his was the first call I'd received on it, I was startled by the ringtone, a jarringly tinny rendition of Barry White's "I'm Qualified to Satisfy You." Had he given me his wife's phone? His insurance agent's? I snapped it open to end the song. "Hello?"

"What do you know about Ashley?" Ron had never been a loquacious man, but his speech was more clipped than usual.

I dragged in a deep breath. "It's terrible, isn't it? I don't know much, probably less than you. I ran into Carlotta, though, right after Ashley was . . . right after Ashley was found. That poor woman looked terrible."

Silence at the other end. A cough. "I need an article before tomorrow. It'd be ideal if you could find out what happened to Ashley by then."

I pulled the phone away from my head in disbelief, stared at it, and then shoved it back to my ear. "What? How am I supposed to find out how she died by *tomorrow?*"

"Press conference. In an hour, at the Dairy Building. They're announcing the cause of death. Get me the story."

Click.

I was left with a lot of bluster and nowhere to aim it. A raucous rumbling from the back room pulled me out of my funk. Mrs. Berns was waking from her nap, and I didn't want to be sitting here when the smell caught up with the sound. I snatched my notebook and pen, shoved them in my big embroidered purse along with my press pass, threw my camera around my neck, and took off toward the Dairy Building.

The day was bright, the sun at its zenith. It was one of those dog days of summer that was so hot, you wished your skin had a zipper. I pulled out my oversize sunglasses and plowed through the crowd, snagging bits of conversation about the rides, or the baby animal exhibit, or whether Pig Lickers or gyros were a better option for lunch.

The frenetic mood of the fair changed when I neared the Dairy Building. The crowds were still packed as tight as grapes, but they were quieter, whether out of deference to Ashley's recent passing or because they thought that's what the camera crews circling the building expected, I couldn't be certain. I slid toward the entrance, stopped short by the mountain of flowers and stuffed animals that had grown since yesterday. The entire front of the building was flanked with memorial offerings.

Apparently, Ashley had become the sweet princess in death that she'd never been in life.

I stepped around a hyperbolic television reporter intoning into his microphone something about "a fallen queen taking her last breath" and pulled out my press badge for one of the police officers at the front door. He glanced at it and nodded me in.

It was creepy being back in the building where Ashley had died. I counted fifty-plus people inside, which seemed like a lot unless you were in a cavernous pole barn with a cement floor. Yesterday, the place had been wall-to-wall bodies, thrilled to be part of history as Milkfed Mary commenced the State Fair. Today, most of the people resembled vultures instead of fairgoers, leaning forward to catch a whiff of the luridness surrounding Ashley's death, something that would sell papers and coerce people to keep watching through commercials.

I stroked the laminated press pass hung on a lanyard around my neck, considering the pseudo credibility it conveyed. Then I tugged at my navy-blue sundress, trying to free a wedgie as I studied the guys on each side of me. They both wore button-down shirts and ties, tape recorders in hand.

I turned my attention to the rear of the building, where a make-shift stage had been set in front of the glass-sided butter-carving booth. Minnesota flags had been placed on each side of a podium, the orga-nizers almost successful in their effort to obscure the gruesome booth, which was crisscrossed with police tape. Reporters snapped photos of the refrigerated gazebo, angling for a clear shot, but I didn't have the stomach for it.

A lone woman stood next to the podium. She was short with badly permed dishwater-blonde hair. She wore a cheap suit, the pants of which were a little too short, exposing the tops of her wilted dress socks. Her appearance brought to mind a mad scientist, someone too distracted to worry about how she appeared. Even from here, though, I could see the wrinkles around her mouth and eyes that indicated she smiled frequently, under better circumstances.

She fidgeted under the snapping of cameras before stepping behind the podium at some unseen signal. She adjusted the microphone and leaned into it. "Hello." Her voice scratched its way out of her throat. She coughed and started again. "My name is Kate Lewis, and I'm the current president of the Minnesota State Fair Corporation. Thank you for joining us here today."

We were about to find out what'd happened to Ashley.

Chapter 10

Cameras rolled. Reporters stood at the ready, pen or tape recorder in hand. I mimicked their behavior, snapping off four or five shots of Kate before pulling out my pencil and notepad.

"As you know, yesterday, Ashley Pederson of Battle Lake passed away while . . ."

There was a hiss behind the president, and I craned my neck to see Janice Opatz emerge from behind one of the Minnesota flags to shoot knife eyes into Kate's back. She looked as well put together as she had at our last meeting, though her outfit today was an appropriately somber gray.

Ms. Lewis rerouted her speech. "Ashley Pederson passed away at the State Fair. We won't have full toxicology reports for another four weeks, but initial results indicate that she died of malicious poisoning."

The room buzzed like a hive.

Ashley *had* been poisoned.

I shook my head, thinking immediately of Mrs. Pederson. I hadn't spotted her in the building when I'd entered, but surely she knew by now that her daughter had been murdered. My heart cracked a little for her.

I waited for Ms. Lewis to continue, but she scurried off the stage, herded by Janice, who followed closely. I watched them go. That was a smooth move on Ms. Opatz's part, distancing her role as chaperone from the crime. There'd been no mention of Ashley's Milkfed Mary status or the dairy industry in the entire—brief—announcement. It seemed a little cold. *Bet on me not omitting that info from my article.*

A man in uniform replaced Kate Lewis at the podium. "Hello. I'm William Kramer, Saint Paul chief of police. I would like to concur with Ms. Lewis's statement that we believe Ms. Pederson was poisoned and to assure the public that we're doing everything in our power to solve this case. I'd also like to offer my sincerest condolences to Ms. Pederson's family and friends."

Hands shot up in the audience. Chief Kramer pointed to someone near the front.

"This is a homicide investigation?"

"Yes. Next?"

Another hand. "What poison was used, and any likely suspects?"

"We won't know for certain until the tox screen returns, and until then, we're considering all avenues open."

"How did she get the poison?"

The chief grimaced. "If we knew that, the case would be closed. We do have reason to believe that she ingested it shortly before entering the booth."

"Are the other girls in danger?" This question from a woman in the back.

"We are operating under the assumption that this was an isolated incident, but we're taking the necessary precautions to ensure the safety of all the Milkfed Mary contestants."

Reporters vied for the chief's attention. "When will this building reopen?"

"That depends on the investigation. We're shooting for Monday."

The man next to me raised his hand and spoke before he was called on, his voice echoing in the building's vast corners. "How does this murder affect the embezzlement investigation that the State Fair Corporation is undergoing?"

The reporters pecked and clucked like excited chickens at this new thread, but the chief didn't twitch. "They're two completely separate investigations. One has no bearing on the other. Thank you for your time." He raised his hand, a clear signal that the press conference was over, and ignored the hollered questions that followed him off the stage.

I scribbled notes on my pad—*check on Mrs. Pederson and see what she knows about poison, find background on Janice Opatz, Chief Kramer: "we're considering all avenues open," embezzlement?*—before turning to the reporter next to me, the one who'd asked the embezzlement question.

He was also writing in a notebook, and his grim expression reflected how I felt. I held out my hand. "Excuse me. My name is Mira. I'm a reporter from Battle Lake."

He kept writing. "Where?" His tone wasn't unfriendly.

"Small town, a couple hours northwest of the Cities. Too far away for me to have heard about the embezzling that you just asked about. Can you tell me what you were referring to?"

He stopped to study me, taking my measure. "Battle Lake. That's where the murdered girl was from."

"Ashley. Yep."

"You knew her?"

I shrugged. "I saw her around town. She was younger than me. What have you heard about her?"

"Sounds like your average eighteen-year-old beauty queen—self-centered, shallow. That's about all anyone knows." His eyes narrowed. "You could probably scoop all of us with your connections."

I tried out an easy laugh. Pretty sure it sounded like a goose honk. "I'm not much of a scooper. So what's this about embezzling?"

He ran his fingers through his hair and spoke reluctantly. "Not much to tell. The attorney general is investigating the Minnesota State Fair Corporation, and the rumors are that someone's been skimming money. There's no public funds involved because the State Fair's been a private business since the 1940s. But still, it'd look bad for Minnesota if a certain woman dragged the good name of the fair through the mud with her."

"Kate Lewis, you mean?"

He smirked. "She's the president, isn't she? This murder is probably the best thing that could've happened to her. Takes the limelight off of her while bringing attention to the fair."

"But it's bad attention."

He chuckled, but there was no humor in it. "There's no such thing as bad attention when you're trying to make money. Have you seen how many people are out there?" He shoved his thumb toward the front door, where folks were jostling for a glimpse into the disbanding press conference. "The fair's shattering attendance records. Hold on."

He reached for a chirping cell phone in his jacket and glanced at its screen while I noted that his ringtone wasn't a hot-monkey-love song. "Say, gotta go." He dropped his notebook into his pocket and pulled out a card. "Here's my number. Call if you hear anything about Ms. Pederson's death, OK? We could trade info." Then he turned away into the phone call.

I looked down at the business card. Chaz Linder, *St. Paul Pioneer Press*. I shoved the card into my purse, along with my notebook and pencil, and stole toward the refrigerated booth that'd been the scene of Ashley's last moments. Police were stationed around the stage, busy arguing with a camera crew who wanted a close-up. I took advantage of their distraction and slipped to the far edge of the stage and around the back, using the flags that hid the booth to conceal my movements.

From this side, with my back to Dairy Goodness and the stage to my right, I could access the booth unseen, as long as nobody peeked around the stage. I planted my fingers on the glass. It was cool to the touch but not refrigerator cold.

I perched on my tiptoes to get a clear view of the interior. It'd been scoured clean, not a trace of butter or murder to be seen. The rotating floor was still. I cast a quick glance over my shoulder. The ruckus with the camera crew had gained volume, which meant no one was paying attention to me. Curving close to the booth, I ducked around to the side with the entrance and peeked through the blue curtain.

The door to the booth was padlocked, and a shadow walking toward me from Dairy Goodness forced me to drop the curtain. *Nothing to see back here, folks.* I was about to scurry out the way I'd come when a meaty hand clamped down on my shoulder, turning my mouth as dry as dirt.

"You're in big trouble, miss."

Chapter 11

Why did police chiefs always have meaty hands? I'd be more inclined to cooperate with them if their mitts were normally proportioned.

"I'm sorry, Chief Kramer. I thought my partner went back here."

Saint Paul's chief of police checked my press pass, which clearly identified me as a reporter for the *Battle Lake Recall*, and then raised his eyebrows to indicate I had one chance to revise my story for plausibility.

"Not my *partner*, exactly," I said, scrambling. "Chaz Linder, with the *Pioneer Press*? He's the one who asked you the embezzlement question."

"I know." This close, he smelled like Old Spice. The gray of his beetling eyebrows intensified his brown eyes, eyes that'd seen lots of liars in their time.

"I wanted to ask him about the embezzlement because today was the first I'd heard of it, and I thought I saw him come back here. Is there anything you can tell me about that case?"

To be a good liar, you have to have an innate sense of when you've gone too far. As the chief cocked his head, I realized I'd passed that point when I first opened my mouth. I waited to see what the consequences would be.

He sighed, brushing aside my question about embezzling and getting to the heart of the matter. "I'm sorry for the loss your town must be feeling, but you're not going to help by getting in our way. The police department knows what it's doing. Let us find out who killed

Ms. Pederson, and I promise we'll contact your paper when we know anything for sure. Deal?"

He could have made life difficult for me, but instead was letting me off the hook. Strangely, his kindness made my eyes go blurry with unshed tears. It must have been the stress of the last twenty-four hours. I pretended to brush hair from my face. "Sure. Thanks. Can I go?"

He nodded and pointed toward the front door. I tromped outside, past the memorial of flowers and stuffed toys, past at least three television crews sharing the news of the tragic "Princess Poisoning" (based on the little I knew of her, Ashley would *not* have been happy with the demotion, but alliteration was its own force), and across the street to the Cattle Barn to check out the dormitories. I owed Ron a story, and I still didn't have much. I was hoping to flesh it out by interviewing Lana.

The cows inside the barn looked as happy as ever. Maybe "unconcerned" was a better word. Or "regal." Was I getting obsessed with cows now? I usually saved that type of laser focus for Chief Wenonga, the hot, twenty-three-foot fiberglass statue I'd left behind in Battle Lake. That man, well, that *fake giant* with a six-pack as tall and wide as a refrigerator, was a hottie. He'd kept me mental company since I'd arrived in Battle Lake. Strong and silent, just like I liked 'em. Probably, someone needed to stage an intervention for me.

But back to the cows.

They lowed and ate and pooped, and I walked past them on my way to the dormitory to see if the remaining princesses were around. When I spotted the police officers at the base of the dorm stairs, however, my plan and I did an about-face. One run-in with an officer a day was my quota.

I didn't have many options left. I wasn't ready to return to the stinky steam bath of the trailer, so I decided to stroll the fair to organize my thoughts. My favorite place so far was the International Bazaar, a huge tented area laid out like a world market. Food booths rimmed the outside, and in the center, tiny shops were arranged in rows, separated by narrow aisles with musicians sprinkled here and there. I could hear easy

Jamaican reggae played live near the hot sauce booth and walk ten feet to sample spicy olives from Greece while listening to dizzying Egyptian drumbeats emanating from the booth one over with the mummy out front.

The air was redolent with curries, vinegars, and the smell of sweet rice, and people bargained and hollered for my dollars and rearranged their shiny silks and cheap Austrian crystal jewelry to catch my attention. It was anonymous chaos, and I loved it.

By nature, I was a catch-and-release shopper. I liked to buy stuff on impulse, confident that it'd fill a hole in my life. Within twenty-four hours, however, I'd realize I'd wasted my money, and so I would return whatever bauble had grabbed my attention. It was a bad habit, one I was going to break as soon as I bought the diamond-shaped prism throwing sunny rainbows across the walkway.

Twenty dollars later, a rainbow in my pocket and a vegetarian gyro in my hand, I ambled through the wall of fair smells and sounds back to the Silver Suppository, as I'd affectionately nicknamed the Airstream. Happily, Mrs. Berns and Kennie were both gone. I lugged my laptop out on the front steps to write the article. At least there'd be a breeze.

Carlotta's face was in my mind the entire time I wrote.

Battle Lake Loses Ambassador

Ashley Kirsten Pederson, 18, a recent Battle Lake High School graduate, died on the opening day of the Minnesota State Fair. Pederson was beginning her duties as Milkfed Mary, Queen of the Dairy when the tragedy occurred. Police believe she was poisoned, and that she unknowingly ingested the poison shortly before entering the butter-carving booth. They don't yet have a suspect.

Kate Lewis, president of the Minnesota State Fair

60

Corporation, broke the news at a press conference the day following Ashley's death. According to Saint Paul police chief William Kramer, they're "considering all avenues open." The chief said that he believes Pederson's murder was an isolated incident and that none of the other contestants are in danger. He sent his condolences to the Pederson family and to the town of Battle Lake.

Pederson was enrolled at Alexandria Technical College, where she planned to attend the sales and marketing program in the fall. She is survived by both parents, Carlotta and Steven Pederson, as well as her paternal grandparents, Ivy and Steggard Pederson. Funeral arrangements are pending.

I searched for the very slow State Fair wireless network and sent the article snail-crawling through cyberspace to Ron's desk.

As it flew, I thought, *That's not enough.*

I need to help Carlotta.

Chapter 12

The sun the next day promised another scorcher. I got up and out early to find—no surprise—that the Dairy Building was still cordoned off. The security detail out front had all the warmth of palace guards in London, standing stiffly with an angry set to their jaws.

It wasn't entirely their fault.

The crowd of well-wishers and memorial stockers had grown impossibly larger, and a wall of teddy bears threatened to collapse on the guards. Three young women were lighting a white candle, which they placed next to a handwritten sign that read, WE LOST YOU TOO SOON. LET THE ANGELS GUIDE YOU. The candle was outshone a million times by the sun, already volcanic even though it wasn't yet 9:00 a.m.

I turned toward the Cattle Barn, considering the oddness of humans. No way had all these people met Ashley, and if they had, by all accounts, they wouldn't have liked her. But she represented something to them, maybe lost youth or a rip in the bonds of community, that they wanted to repair with flowers and tears. Whatever it was, I was grateful for its appearance, at least for the surviving Pedersons' sake.

Inside the Cattle Barn, my heart gave a little skip as I saw the door to the dormitory was unguarded. I hurried toward it just as Janice Opatz came down, followed by a compact, well-dressed man who looked closer in age to me than to her. I tried to disappear, but too late.

Janice caught sight of me.

"Mira." She covered the ten feet between us as her companion stayed back to speak with the police officer who'd followed them down.

"Hi, Janice. Are the girls up there?"

She glanced behind her absentmindedly. The movement of her hair released her signature scent, a combination of disinfectant soap and Aqua Net. "No. They're no longer staying on the grounds. They'll return soon, we hope. What can I do for you?"

"Um, nothing." The fib came quickly. "I'm here to cover some Battle Lake dairy farmers for the paper."

"I see. Where are their stalls?" She stared at me archly, but I wasn't biting.

"Over there," I said, indicating the entire barn. "Can I ask you something?" When she didn't respond, I continued, scratching an itch that I'd had since I'd first laid eyes on her. "Did you used to be a Milkfed Mary?"

Her hands went immediately to her hair, which she fluffed despite its resistance to movement. It was a perfect shell of black. "First runner-up, 1977."

I smiled encouragingly. "How long have you been a chaperone?"

"Three years after I wo—" She caught herself. "Three years after I ran. I've been the chaperone since then."

I made a mental note to research the 1977 pageant. Janice had just about said she'd won, which was not the same as being first runner-up. "And as chaperone, you were present the whole time Ashley was in the booth?"

"Of course."

"You didn't see anything unusual?"

"I already answered that question for the police. Surely you were there, too?"

"Yes," I said, distracted by an agitated scuffle between a cow and her milker. "Right up front, taking pictures. I snapped something peculiar about the back of Ashley's head, but I keep forgetting to enlarge the photo so I can figure out what it was. Say, I don't suppose you know where I could find the sculptor, do you? Glenda Haines?"

"I don't suppose I do." Janice again glanced over her shoulder. I followed her gaze. Her companion and the police officer had finished their conversation and were staring impatiently at us. "If you'll excuse me."

I watched her and the guy leave, considered asking the police officer, now stationed at the base of the stairs, where I could find the sculptor, and thought better of it. I needed to remain under the radar.

Instead, I spent the better part of the day walking the grounds, my head spinning as I tried to figure out who'd want to kill a young queen. I supposed one of the girls she'd beaten out for the title might have offed her because of jealousy, but that seemed like a long shot. Statistically, her boyfriend or her family were more likely to kill her. No way had Carlotta been involved. A person couldn't fake being that broken. I didn't know her husband, Steven, well, but she'd said he hadn't even been at the fair when Ashley died. Dirk bore more looking into, however.

My brain was fried from thinking of all the angles and the sun was well past noon when I found myself in front of the Leinie Lodge Bandshell Stage, where Johnny and his band would be performing tonight. The Thumbs' music was an original mix of folk and rock with a bluesy edge. Johnny'd started the group with three high school buddies. While his friends had settled permanently in Battle Lake, Johnny had been the wild card, intending to return to Madison to begin his graduate program in horticulture this fall. When a convergence of events had kept him in the area, though, he'd decided to focus time on the band.

If they'd been invited to play the State Fair, it must have been paying off.

The stage was empty, but people were sitting around on the grounds, picnicking and generally taking a rest from the fair. A group of three young blondes wearing tank tops snagged my attention. Two of them looked like Delrita and Brittany, the flower-placing team I had met outside the Dairy Building the day of Ashley's death.

I didn't recognize the third.

I strolled over, at first keeping to the perimeter so as not to draw attention to myself. When I was within fifty feet, I verified that they were the two runners-up. Brittany wore her hair in a jaunty ponytail, and Delrita had hers fully feathered in a retro-Farrah flip. They both seemed shiny and full of life, as did their companion. I would have loved to have been able to listen in to what they were talking about, but there was no way to slip in close enough without them noticing. I settled for the direct route and clomped on over.

"Hi, remember me?"

Brittany shaded her face against the sun and looked up. "Sure, you're that girl from Battle Lake," she squeaked in her high-pitched voice. "From the newspaper. Mira, right?"

"Right. Mind if I join you?"

"Not if you buy us a beer."

I scrutinized Delrita to see if she was joking. Her blue eyes were dead serious.

"How old are you guys?" I asked.

"I'm twenty-two," Delrita said. "Brittany is twenty one. Megan here is twenty-one, too."

Those were three lies, back-to-back. I had an ethical dilemma for two whole seconds before I acknowledged that they were adults by the looks of it; if they didn't get it from me, they'd get it from someone else; and they'd give me more dirt if I played nice. As long as they weren't driving, I was cool with that. "Be right back. What kind do you want?"

"Lite," they all sang in unison.

I returned with three frothy plastic cups. The beer smelled bitter and wonderful on this steamy day, and I was glad to hand off the temptation. "You a Milkfed Mary, too, Megan?"

"Yup. I came in last." She said it matter-of-factly. I liked her for that.

"I ran into Janice," I said, putting out feelers. "She mentioned you guys aren't staying at the dorms right now. Where're you at?"

Delrita wiped off her beer mustache. "The fair officials put us up at a Days Inn down the road. They promised we're moving back to the dorms Monday and getting back on track with our regular duties on Tuesday, though."

I leaned forward, genuinely curious. "What are those duties exactly?"

Brittany shuddered. "The big one is sitting in that sick booth with a bunch of butter. Like, how gross is that going to be? Janice says the show must go on, though."

"And they're using the same refrigerated booth Ashley died in?" I couldn't believe that the authorities would allow that.

"Yeah."

Delrita chimed in. "Lana Sorensen's first. She was the runner-up, but now she's the queen. She gets her butter head carved Tuesday after some bogus mourning ceremony where the crown is officially passed over to her."

Megan elbowed her. "I told you not to say it like that. Besides, you're next. Right after Lana."

The Lana from whom Ashley had stolen something, according to what they'd told me when we'd first met. She *was* a Milkfed Mary. "I'm amazed they won't let you skip the butter-carving part of the pageant. It seems a little gruesome."

"You don't *know* gruesome," Delrita said, her tongue loosening from the beer. "If you had to see the type of stuff we put up with— taping our boobs, slathering hemorrhoid cream under our eyes so they don't look puffy, starving ourselves to fit into those stupid gowns." She chugged her beer for effect. "It's like we're little kids being babysat. Today is the first time any of us have been on our own since Ashley died, and we had to sneak out to do it."

Megan added her two cents. "Yeah, Janice keeps a tight watch. I'm a light sleeper, and sometimes I wake up and she's just standing next to one of our beds."

The other two girls shivered. They'd heard this story before.

"Doing what?" I asked.

"I dunno," Megan said, shrugging. "I sat up once to ask her, and she shushed me back to sleep. I think she's checking in on us. She takes her job real seriously."

I already knew that. "Why do you put up with this pageant?"

Brittany spoke, her voice so high I was surprised it didn't bring dogs running. "Different reasons. Some of us have been on the pageant circuit our whole lives and we're used to it. Some do it for the money. The Milkfed Mary winner gets a full ride to college *and* $10,000. That can come in pretty handy." She paused for a minute. "I think Ashley did it for the fame."

"I guess she got that," Delrita said darkly.

Chapter 13

Ashley had indeed. She'd be forever famous for her death rather than her life. It was tragic. I glanced toward the sun dropping closer to the horizon. "You ladies have curfew?"

"Not if they don't know we're gone." Megan chuckled. "We snuck out. We're supposed to be on lockdown."

I took note of their casual clothes. "What're the three of you doing tonight?"

"You're looking at it," Delrita said. "There's a rockin' band here in a few hours. We're scoping out the cherry spots. You wouldn't believe how hot the lead singer is. Did you see the posters? His name is Johnny something."

"Leeson," I said, suddenly having second thoughts about how cool it would be to see my crush playing for a big audience. The whole world would soon be in love with him.

"That's right," she said, pitching her voice low. "'Mrs. Delrita Leeson.' How does that sound?"

They giggled, and I fought a flame of jealousy.

Johnny'd always been the pied piper when it came to the ladies. They loved that effortless smile, his easygoing personality, that wavy hair, and those strong hands. He'd never paid much attention to the attention, but I didn't know what business of mine it was anyhow. I'd made a clear point of telling him we were just friends. Gawd, it was bad enough when adults played games with *each other*, and here I was doing it with myself.

I stood. It was time to go. "Have fun. Maybe I'll see you all later." They waved happily at me, all taut and blonde and smiling, as I tromped away, figuring I could kill time until the show by doing research for my Battle Lake Bites food column. Ron had offered me the gig when I started at the *Recall* last spring. I'd changed its name but otherwise kept the mission: find food representative of Battle Lake specifically, and Minnesota in general.

I'd surveyed most of the food booths since I'd arrived but only eaten at the tame ones—Salem Lutheran Church for breakfast, Chinese food or tofu-on-a-stick for lunch, gyros or a bucket of salty, fresh-cut french fries for supper. If I was going to find food that screamed "Battle Lake," however, it needed to be a little bit quirky, a tad unexpected, and flirting with inedible. I strolled past the deep-fried Twinkies and the pudgy pies, the latter appearing to be cherry pie filling deep-fried in a white-bread pocket. I stopped at the Low-Carb German Meat Rolls and waited my turn in line.

"Excuse me," I asked when I reached the front, "but what's a German meat roll?"

The harried woman behind the till barely spared me a glance. "Sliced beef rolled around diced pickles, sautéed onions, and spicy mustard."

My mouth watered a tang, but it'd been years since I'd eaten red meat. Swallowing something that was smart enough to find its way home creeped me out. "Thanks." I moved on to the adjacent booth as twenty people jostled to take my spot.

The next stall featured blood sausage. On a hunch, I walked around to the back, where I saw empty boxes that had once contained beef blood, heavy cream, and lard. My stomach twisted, but I decided that if I walked away from everything I wouldn't eat, Battle Lake Bites would never have become the popular column it was. A woman appeared out the rear door and tossed an empty pig intestines box onto the pile.

"Hi! Sorry to bother you. My name is Mira James."

She shook my hand. "Karen Hipple. What can I do for you?"

"Can I ask how you make your blood sausage? I write a column for the *Battle Lake Recall*, and I'd like to possibly feature your recipe in our State Fair issue. I'd give you credit."

She smiled. "Sorry. It's a secret."

"Not even a hint?"

She indicated the boxes. "Not beyond what you see here."

"Thanks anyways."

On my way back to the thoroughfare, I almost bumped into a fair-goer cradling a cardboard plate full of the blood sausages. They looked like coiled slugs. Gagging, I made my way to the Scotch-eggs-on-a-stick booth and waited my turn in line. "Excuse me, how do you make your eggs?"

"They're pork sausage over hard-boiled eggs, fried and put on a stick."

Of course they are. "What do you put in the pork sausage?"

"Are you allergic?"

"No, I'm writing a recipe column."

"Sorry. Trade secrets."

Ach. This was going to be harder than I'd thought. I dragged my feet to the Schraufnagel's Famous Loaded Brats booth, not feeling hopeful, and again waited in line. "Hi. Yeah. I'm writing a recipe column. I need your recipe. I'll give you credit. You in?"

The kid behind the counter appeared confused. "They're just brats."

"What kind?"

"Pork. The cheapest."

Lips and buttholes. I pulled out my notepad and wrote that down. "And what do you do with the brats?"

"You can come around back and I'll show you, if you like. The owners are off until the suppertime rush."

I raised my eyebrows. I'd been invited behind the wizard's curtain. "Thanks!"

I let myself in the back door and was rewarded with the acrid smell of sauerkraut and mustard blending with the primordially delicious aroma of cooking bacon. If that smell could be canned and put into a hair dryer, there'd be a lot more well-coiffed folks walking around.

The booth, which was really a trailer outfitted to be a kitchen, was crammed tight. I squeezed between boxes and deep fryers to interview the kid, who didn't look more than seventeen. I read his name tag. "This your summer job, Greg?"

"Yeah. My aunt and uncle own the business. They make me work every State Fair. I'm missing a canoe trip with my buddies this week. Last summer it was baseball camp."

Ooh. Bitter nephew. Perfect source for secret family recipes. I prodded him. "So, first you take a cheap pork brat."

"Yup. From Costco. Generic sausages."

"Then what do you do with it?"

"It's gotta be raw." He grabbed a sample sausage from a plastic bin. It was limp, gray, and would get a XXX rating if it starred in its own movie. He slapped it on the white laminate countertop. "You slice it the long way, like so. Then push the insides as far into the skin as you can."

The pallid meat made a gooshy sound as he shoved it around with his fingers. I smiled wanly at the line of people outside clambering up for their very own tube steak. They poked their heads up toward the window like chickens trying to see into the corn bin, but the trailer was set four feet off the ground, and they couldn't view much past the front counter.

"OK, then load the channel you just made with sauerkraut. The more the better. It kills the sausage's aftertaste. Once it's full, you pinch it closed and wrap the whole brat, stuffing and all, with raw bacon. You gotta use toothpicks to keep the bacon in place at the ends. If we have time, we grill the whole works on low heat. If we're busy, we deep-fry it." He dropped it into a fryer basket, and the grease sizzled and spat angrily.

The smell of frying bacon intensified.

"How do you know when it's done?"

"It floats, like so." The enhanced wiener popped to the surface, the toothpicks and ends of the bacon black and crispy. He grabbed it expertly with a pair of tongs and inserted a stick into the bottom. Juices ran down the wood. He handed the whole package to the grateful woman at the front of the line. I watched her slide him a five as she bit into the volcanic bratwurst. She opened her mouth to let heat escape and then bit down again, the bacon crunching between her teeth.

I returned my attention to Greg. "Do you want me to use your name in the article?"

"Please. It might piss off my uncle enough to fire me."

"Deal. Thanks for your time."

He didn't respond, already too busy frying up brats to sate the hungry crowd outside his window. These sausages were preloaded, so he just pulled them out of the fridge and dropped them in the hot grease.

Outside, I noticed the smell of frying oil clung to me even after I put distance between myself and the Schraufnagel booth. I decided to distract myself with a deep-fried Nut Goodie.

"Any chance I can get back there and see how you make the magic?" I asked when I reached the counter.

The woman laughed as she traded me heaven on a stick for a fiver. "No chance."

"Thanks anyways."

I walked and munched, making my way back to the Airstream. I hadn't showered that morning, so my plan was to rinse off and prep myself for the Thumbs' State Fair debut tonight.

Johnny and I were just friends, but that didn't mean I wasn't going to look hot.

Chapter 14

In an unusual turn of good luck, Mrs. Berns and Kennie were nowhere in sight when I returned to the trailer, though their presence lingered in several unpleasant ways. I grabbed a pair of cutoff jean shorts, a white T-shirt, a hairbrush, shampoo, a toothbrush, and a towel, and headed to the public showers. The water pressure was good, though the floor had the slime of perpetual wetness. I made it quick, got myself toweled and dressed, and headed back to the trailer smelling like cucumbers and sandalwood.

I brushed my hair and loosely braided it so it'd dry wavy. After slapping on a single coat of mascara and some lip gloss, I settled in to organize my notes and type the Battle Lake Bites column, which I thought turned out quite nicely.

State Fair Food Edition: Fry, Baby, Fry

For those of you who couldn't attend the Minnesota State Fair this year, the *Recall* is bringing the fair to you. Today's issue reveals the secret family recipe for Schraufnagel's Famous Loaded Brats, a State Fair standard, shared with us by Greg Schraufnagel. The recipe is simple but delicious. One bite, and you'll be hooked.

Schraufnagel's Famous Loaded Brats

6 servings

Ingredients:

1. ¼ cup olive oil
2. 6-pack uncooked bratwurst
3. 6 slices bacon
4. 1 16 oz. can sauerkraut
5. Toothpicks

Slice open the bratwurst the long way. Push aside the innards. Stuff each wiener with sauerkraut and squeeze shut. Wrap the whole brat in bacon, starting at the top and working your way down. Pierce the bacon with a toothpick at each end so it stays tight. Using olive oil, cook over medium heat on stovetop, covered. When both bacon and wiener have lost their grayish hue, place them on a grill for 5 minutes or until crispy. The broiler setting on your oven will do the same. When cooked to your desired crispness, place in a bun and serve. Or, if you want to do it State Fair–style, insert a Popsicle stick and enjoy!

I emailed Ron the recipe before settling in to read for two peaceful hours. That's what I told myself anyhow, but in the back of my mind, I was hoping Johnny would track me down at the Airstream. To that end, I practiced various provocative poses until I got bored with being a silly girl and just fell into the story.

A half an hour before Johnny's band was supposed to go on, I unbraided my hair, ran my fingers through it, and stepped into the still-warm night. The sun was settled on the horizon, throwing out lavender and tangerine shadows. The air smelled like caramel apples and clean straw, and all around the campground, people talked and laughed. Because the campground was really just a parking lot, camp-fires weren't an option, but some people had brought their own barbe-cue grills and were clinking beers in a toast and passing the ketchup. It felt very communal and summery. I strode to the concert site with a spring in my step.

When I arrived at the bandshell, I looked around to make sure I didn't see anyone I knew before buying a mineral water. Being incog-nito felt good after so many months in the fishbowl of Battle Lake. I stretched a little mentally, relaxing into the evening.

I was paying for my water when I felt the tap on my shoulder. My esophagus twitched. I turned.

Kennie stood behind me, hands on hips. "I told Mrs. Berns that you'd come dressed like a refugee. Would a little makeup kill you?" Her face wasn't helping her argument, as it appeared to be drowning in green eye shadow, blue mascara, peach-colored blush, and coral lipstick.

Mrs. Berns popped up alongside her. "You look fine. You look like you." She scratched her arm and studied all the people. "It sure is fun to fart in a crowd, by the way. No one knows where it came from." She effortlessly illustrated her point, and sure enough, the people around us began wiggling their noses and glaring suspiciously at one another.

I sighed. "What're you two doing here?"

"Moral support." Mrs. Berns smiled. "Now let's get up close, where we can see that boy shake his moneymaker."

I let them lead me through the crowd, disappointed I'd lost my ano-nymity but figuring it was better to go quietly. They elbowed through the audience until we were positioned front and center, where we were surrounded by pretty young things. I glanced around for Brittany, Delrita, and Megan, but couldn't spot them. A sound check drew my attention back to the stage, where Johnny was entering with his bandmates.

My breath caught in my throat and my secret parts did a happy dance.

He looked glorious, his worn Levi's hanging low on his narrow hips. His faded Led Zeppelin T-shirt did more to define than cover his broad shoulders, accentuating the tanned lines of his arms and the muscles in his chest. He pushed his hair out of his eyes and studied the crowd as if searching for someone.

I ducked reflexively.

Mrs. Berns whistled. "She's over here, Johnny! She got as close as she could."

Johnny glanced over, a little smile tugging at the corner of his mouth. His gaze locked with mine, and I melted in all the right places. I waved weakly, and he gestured back before finishing his sound check.

Soon, the band was in full swing. The music rocked the night and got the audience moving. Johnny's quiet confidence translated well onstage. He prowled from end to end like a lion, tossing his hair and singing about love and loss. His voice was deep and full, with a rumbling, sexy rasp.

Every fiber in my brain was trying to pull me away from that stage, reminding me that I was the gal who had trouble expressing serious emotion, that my relationships always ended badly, that Johnny was too good for me, that I wasn't meant for a happily ever after. My heart was succumbing, though, and my body was being oppositionally defiant.

Dang. Johnny looked *good* onstage.

I gave in and let my body run the show, at least for a little while, raising my arms and shaking my rear alongside Mrs. Berns and Kennie, reveling in the moment. A screaming ovation brought the Thumbs out for one, then two, and finally three encores. Midnight hit before the show was over.

The last ringing note left me feeling warm and happy with just a tinge of loneliness as the musicians strode offstage. I was hoarse from singing along, and Mrs. Berns and Kennie looked as spent as I felt. "Should we head back to the trailer?" I asked.

They nodded.

We were on our way when Flapjack, one of Johnny's friends and an occasional roadie for the Thumbs, jogged out from backstage. "Hey, ladies. You wanna come back? You know, have a Battle Lake get-together?"

In the first subtle act in their combined lives, Mrs. Berns and Kennie turned him down and pushed me forward. "We won't wait up," Kennie said.

I followed Flapjack, feeling suddenly shy, and hung on the perimeter of the backstage area while the band members packed up. When Johnny spotted me, he jogged over, ignoring the gaggle of female admirers waiting for his autograph. "You made it! What'd you think of the show?"

Sweat had curled his hair around the nape of his neck and pressed his shirt to his firm body. My mouth was suddenly dry, so I licked my lips. "It was great. You are rock hard."

He blinked oddly as I realized what I'd just said. I concentrated on melting into oblivion.

"I mean, *you* rock hard. Really good. Good show." *Kill me now.*

He nodded, the peculiar expression still on his face. "Do you want to go for a walk?" He shoved his hands in his front pockets. "We had to unload and set up as soon as we got here, and I haven't had a chance to see the fair. It's probably mostly closed down, but we could check?" He raised his voice hopefully.

Why he would want to hang out with the queen of the dorks escaped me, as it always had, but we were friends, and friends walked around together after midnight, didn't they?

"Sure." I smiled tentatively. "I know my way around pretty well by now."

We took off, our shoulders almost touching as I brought him up to speed on Ashley's death, seeing Mrs. Pederson, and rooming with Mrs. Berns and Kennie. Talking to Johnny had always been easy, once I got past the nerves his sexy grin and sunbrowned hands gave me. He was sympathetic at all the right spots and laughed when I mentioned my roomies' bad habits. As we cruised the fair, I kept surreptitiously pinching my thigh to remind myself that Johnny and I were focusing on building a friendship, but it was hard to deny that the air between us felt electric. I just wanted to pull his firm body against mine, get on my tiptoes, and plant a kiss right on those full lips. When I looked around to break the spell, I realized we were near the campground.

"Um, this is where I'm staying." I stopped, glancing into his bottomless blue eyes. "It's getting late, you know? I should probably go in."

He was studying my mouth as I spoke. "Sure."

The intensity made me shiver. I turned my head to the side so I could focus. "Where're you all staying tonight?"

"The band and I are at a hotel in one of the suburbs close to the fair. I have to leave early tomorrow to get back to the day job." He stepped in closer. If I let myself, I could rest my hand on his chest without leaning forward.

"How long are you staying at the fair?" he asked, his voice close, intimate.

"Another week or so." Could he hear my heart beating? Could everyone? "Ron wants me to cover all the Battle Lake stuff going on. And like I said, I promised Mrs. Pederson I'd see what I could find out about Ashley."

"I can come back next weekend." His voice had dropped. "You could show me the fair in the daytime."

"That'd be great," I said, drawn to his mouth as he leaned forward. My pulse hammered. I couldn't believe it was finally happening. The Adonis rock star was going to kiss me.

One of his hands pushed my dark hair from my face and the other slid to my lower back, pulling me gently forward. Blood pounded in my toes, my fingertips, between my legs. My knees buckled slightly at the smell of him this close, clean sweat and fresh-cut grass.

This was really happening. We were going to have our first kiss. "Mira," he whispered, his voice nearly a growl. His mouth was inches from mine, and I imagined the softness of his lips. I let him pull my hips to his, shivered at the hardness of him when our bodies met. I saw him close his eyes and bridge the final distance, and . . . I pulled away. I couldn't do it. This wasn't meant for me. It was a mistake.

"Good night," I said as I darted toward the trailer. "I'm sorry."

I didn't look back.

Chapter 15

I sneaked out early the next morning to avoid Mrs. Berns's and Kennie's questions about my night with Johnny. If I wasn't going to answer them for myself, I certainly wasn't going to answer them for those two. I headed toward the Agriculture Horticulture Building south of the campground for a scheduled interview with a Battle Lakean.

A person could walk from one end of the State Fair to another in less than half an hour, quicker if the place was just waking up, like now. The farmers and 4-H kids were out and about, but otherwise, people slept on in their trailers and tents.

The air was cooler than it had been the last couple days and smelled fresh, with a crisp hint of the fall to come. The temperature was supposed to hit the lower eighties by noon, though, which would cook that leafy smell from the air soon enough. I zipped up my cotton jacket and swung into the Salem Lutheran Church Dining Hall for tea and pancakes on my way. The sound of clinking plates under an aroma of fresh-brewed coffee was welcoming, and I entered the screened-in area glad for company but not wanting to talk to anyone.

While I ate, I eavesdropped on farmers in a friendly game of one-upmanship, trying to out-story each other. An old guy in a red plaid shirt had been coming to the State Fair for longer than anyone here—more than forty years—so he swept that round, but his friend in the jean jacket had grown the largest pumpkin in fair history three summers ago. He'd snagged a grand prize ribbon and bragging rights for eternity. There was much laughing and hearty slapping on the back, and the dark coffee kept flowing.

By the time I left, it was 9:00 a.m., and I was feeling almost normal. I wanted to fall in love with Johnny, but it just wasn't in my cards. Better to avoid it altogether than suffer the inevitable pain. I had more important things to focus on anyhow, most notably helping Mrs. Pederson find out what had happened to her daughter and doing my job for the *Battle Lake Recall*, which today involved covering the launch party of Henry Sunder, a Battle Lake legend whose third book was being released today in the Ag-Hort Building, as the regulars called it.

It was a bit of an odd location, as all his books were about hunting and trapping, but Henry was a peculiar man. He resided in the woods south of town, living off the grid. He'd been known around town as a hermit until about five years ago, when he discovered the internet and iUniverse while visiting the library. Since then, he'd written several books espousing his life philosophies, including the need to live off the land and generally keep your nose clean. He'd arranged for iUniverse to publish his tomes on demand, and sold them to people all over the world by advertising on a modest website, www.earthwarriorbooks.com.

About three years ago, he'd also met a woman online, a fan of his books, and they'd gotten married. She'd produced fraternal twins from the union: a boy named Hunter and a girl named Gatherer.

They called her Gathy.

Henry was a nice enough guy if you overlooked a few peculiarities. Specifically, he brushed his teeth with twigs and charcoal because he believed toothpaste was a scam, he sewed all his own clothes by hand and so always looked like he was headed to a casting call for a Neanderthal movie, and although he washed and brushed his hair, he'd never cut it in his adult life. It hung halfway down his back, ending as a buttocks curtain. Years ago the hairs must have given up any idea of working as a unit, leaving the ends to split every which way.

The book he was releasing today was called *Entrails, Ears, and Bones, Oh My! How to Use the Whole Animal*. He must have had a friend in high places at the State Fair, because when I entered the Ag-Hort Building, I found him dead center in the round floor plan, right next to the information booth. He was surrounded by his books and wore a peaceful smile.

"Hey, Henry. How's business?" I asked as I strolled up.

He stood to greet me. "Mira! Thanks for coming. I just arrived myself."

"Well then, welcome to the fair. I've been here since Thursday." My chest tightened. "It's been a wild ride."

His face sobered. "Terrible thing about that Pederson girl. They know what happened?"

"Poisoning, they think."

His chin pulled back. "How'd she get her hands on poison?"

I shrugged, laying my hands out. "Someone probably slipped it to her, but no one knows how. They can't even be sure what kind of poison it was until the toxicology reports are complete, and that could take weeks."

His face loosened. "My heart aches for Carlotta and Steven. If anything ever happened to Hunter and Gathy . . ." He shook his head. "Lisa's home with the kids, by the way. They're helping me put together a care package for the Pedersons. A community's got to come together when tragedy strikes."

I tipped my head, wondering what would be in a Sunder care package. A soft purse made from the skin of a bear's nose? Water bottles crafted from dried pig bladders? It didn't matter. It was the thought that counted, and Henry was a good person. I interviewed him for more than an hour, sneaking in questions between his conversations with customers. I wrote the answers on paper with a pencil, even though I had the *Recall* laptop slung over my shoulder.

At the end of our Q and A, I slapped my notebook shut. "Thanks, Henry. That'll make for a good article." People were starting to crowd into the building, forming a line in front of his table. "Want me to bring you some food around lunchtime?"

He grinned and held up a clear bag filled with red-flecked dried meat. "Brown-bagging it."

"OK. See you around."

He waved before commencing to sign copies of his books for a gaggle of admirers wearing animal-skin vests and headbands. Some people might say he had a cult following, with the emphasis on "cult," but everyone gets to choose their own spot in the world.

I found a wooden bench in a quiet spot in the round building. I yanked out the computer and fired it up, preparing to organize and email the article on Henry. Feeling lazy, I almost hoped that the wireless wouldn't link. No such luck.

In a classic work-avoidance move, I checked my email before typing. I saw one message from Jed, my house sitter, two from the Battle Lake library, and one from—my heart started pounding—"JohnnyLeeson@ yahoo.com."

We'd never emailed before. Was this advance warning of a restraining order? A request to please forget I knew him? My fingers were suddenly trembly, and I decided to read the emails in the order I'd received them. Johnny hadn't emailed me until five o'clock this morning, so he'd be last.

I clicked on Jed's message, and like him, it was short, sweet, and vaguely troubling:

> Mir, the house is fine. Tiger Pop sure likes the catnip, doesn't she? I can see why.
>
> Luna says hi. Don't ask Mrs. Berns about the bathroom wall.
>
> Love, His Jedness

The first library message was written by Curtis Poling, whom I was surprised to see knew how to email. He must be at least ninety and came across as an old-fashioned guy, but I should have known better than to judge a book by its cover, especially when it came to Battle Lake's elderly.

> You call this work? I sit at a desk and talk to people about books all day. You might want to worry about me taking your job for good, except it's cutting into my fishing time. There's a box of books came in the mail for you. We'll leave them until you get back.
>
> Curtis Poling

When I opened the second library email, I saw it was also from Curtis, written a day after the first:

> Everything's still good. Those of us from the Senior Sunset who're mobile are taking turns. We've extended the hours, and some of the ladies took it upon themselves to dust every book and wash every leaf on every plant. You could read by the reflection of clean surfaces here, I swear.
>
> You remember Loretta Applet from the Sunset? Turns out she used to be a grant writer. Said she's coming out of retirement to see what money she can scrounge up for the library. I had to kick her off this computer to email you. Oh, and I'm donating my collection of fly-fishing books. First editions, good as new.
>
> We're having the time of our lives. Don't hurry back.
>
> Curtis Poling

The Japanese had it right: respect the elderly, for they are amazing. Feeling better since finding out my home, animals, and primary job were in order, I took a deep breath and double-clicked on Johnny's email, immediately had second thoughts, and clamped my eyes shut before I could read the short message.

I'm normally a rip-the-Band-Aid-off-quick sort of gal, but I guess I didn't want to find out Johnny had once and for all realized what a loser I was. Sigh. *Enough. Get it over with.*

I opened one eye, then the other:

> I'm sorry about last night. I shouldn't have rushed things like that. It was good to see you.
>
> Johnny

The hammering in my ears receded. I glanced around to make sure I wasn't being filmed for some prank show, but saw only families eating apples, sniffing flowers, and giving Henry a wide berth. A little smile tugged at my mouth.

Johnny was sticking with me.

I didn't want to think too hard on what that meant, so I closed the email and began typing my coverage of Henry's book release:

Local Author Takes His Wares to the State Fair

Battle Lake native Henry Sunder launched his latest nonfiction book at the Minnesota State Fair. The book, *Entrails, Ears, and Bones, Oh My! How to Use the Whole Animal,* is the third installment in the Don't Get Left Behind series. The first two, *Tracking for Dummies* and *Putting Meat By: How to Make One Day's Hunt Last through the Winter,* sold so well that Sunder was invited to the State Fair to celebrate the publication of the third.

Sunder is a Minnesota treasure who loves and respects the land he's grown up on. He can track a deer for miles over dry ground, catch fish with his hands, and make camp in a snowstorm. He's a throwback to the pioneer days, when people didn't own what they didn't need. When asked why he prefers his frontier lifestyle, Sunder said, "Because anything else ain't truly living."

His launch party was well attended. Sunder plans to use the money he makes off his most recent book to buy replacement parts for his windmill and a new crossbow for his wife. He said he also promised his children, Hunter and Gathy, a new set of picture books.

He's currently at work writing his fourth nonfiction book, tentatively titled *Puff It, Stuff It, or Make a Muff of It: 101 Uses for Prairie Grass*.

I proofed my work. Looked good to me. I wasn't normally a fan of hunters, having found them to be a monosyllabic, selfish bunch in general, but I couldn't help but admire a person who lived in rhythm with his world. I punched the "Send" button and, while I was online, began to search for information on Milkfed Mary, 1977, the year Janice had said she'd won the first runner-up title.

The Midwest Dairy Organization kept a pretty snazzy website with a separate page for each of the Milkfed Mary pageants. Unfortunately, the pages consisted of a brief press release and were entirely focused on the queen. Her runners-up didn't get so much as a mention. Shelby Spoczkowski had been 1977's winner, and the only two things I could definitively say about her after viewing the article were that she didn't like facial hair—despite a headful of curly, dark tresses, she was completely eyebrow-free—and mozzarella cheese was her favorite dairy product.

I was just about to email myself a copy of the 1977 Milkfed Mary press release for later perusal when the cell phone Ron had forced on me jangled in my purse. A passing mother held her children tighter at the sound of Barry White's croon, and I made a mental note to change the sex-drenched ringtone.

"Hello?"

"James. Ron Sims. You interviewed Henry." It was a statement of fact, not a question.

"Were you sitting by your computer waiting for the article to land on your lap?"

"Yes," he said matter-of-factly. "I received the recipe article yesterday and realized you were sending me one a day to make it look like you were actually working."

I smiled. He'd found me out. "You're a putz."

He didn't respond. "What else did you uncover on Ashley Pederson?"

"I don't have anything new," I said, sighing. "The other contestants are staying at a hotel, so I have to wait until they return to the fair tomorrow to interview them. I want to track down the sculptor and ask her what she remembers. And last but not least, the butter carvings will resume on Tuesday. Let's hope the police were right and Ashley's death was random and isolated, or this fair is going to turn into a hall of horrors."

Ron was quiet for a couple beats. "I think Carlotta knows what kind of poison was used. Call and ask her."

"What?" I sputtered. "Why can't *you* ask her?"

He didn't respond. "Also, people here are talking about an older man Ashley was seeing. Find out about that."

"Wait. What older man?"

"Right now, it's just rumors. Get me the story."

Click.

The evil word echoed in my head. Rumors—the brutal side of small-town life.

The thing was, there was a kernel of truth in every piece of gossip, which was why it was so dangerous.

Chapter 16

With Ron's directives still ringing in my head, I got up with the sun on Monday and headed to the Dairy Building, escaping the humming gas snore that was Mrs. Berns and Kennie for the fourth morning in a row.

The first thing I noticed when I neared the building was that the security guards and the sprawling, makeshift memorial of stuffed animals, flowers, candles, and signs were gone. On the one hand, the cleared sidewalk allowed fairgoers to resume walking past this area without being reminded of death, but on the other, it broke my heart how quickly the evidence of Ashley's murder could be wiped from the fair.

That knowledge spurred my already-strong desire to find her killer. Someone's death shouldn't get swept under the rug so the fair could go on.

I peeked inside to see fair workers scuttling around like mad hatters late for tea. The place wasn't officially open for business, but it looked like it would be in time for the passing-of-the-crown ceremony tomorrow. All police officers and yellow-and-black police tape had been removed from the exhibit. That boded well for the return of the princesses to the dormitory, and sure enough, when I walked over to the Cattle Barn, I saw no uniformed officer guarding the dorm entrance. Instead, a teenage boy attended the bottom of the steps, his face afire with pimples and hope beneath his cowboy hat.

He held up his hand as I neared, palms facing me. "You can't go up there. I'm a Milkfed Mary bodyguard, and it is my sworn duty to keep anyone from entering."

I tried to peek over his shoulder. "So the princesses have returned? They're back upstairs?"

"Just one." His eyes were silly with love. "She's the only one I guard."

I wondered which of the newly returned milk-fed sirens had convinced this poor Future Farmer of America to watch the stairs for her, and why. Best to trick him. "I know. She asked me to stop by."

"Really?" His expression was puzzled. Clearly his instructions hadn't covered this scenario. "She didn't mention that."

"She told me to tell you on my way."

He glanced up the stairs, then back at me, uncertainty connecting the dots of his acne like a constellation. "Maybe I should go up with you."

I pursed my lips. "You *know* she wouldn't want that. She needs this time up there uninterrupted, or she wouldn't have asked you to guard the entrance. Right?"

He scratched his head beneath his cowboy hat. "I suppose."

"Absolutely right." I patted his shoulder. "I'll tell her what a great job you're doing. This shouldn't take more than a couple minutes." I gave him a brisk nod and started up, trying to walk as quietly as a cat. I didn't make it far before a thought occurred to me, and I tiptoed back down. "It goes without saying that you can't let anyone *else* up. She was very clear about that. If someone tries to get past you, holler."

I'd been in the wrong place at the wrong time enough to know that it's not a good idea to be overly present in the area where a murder investigation is taking place. If the police—or worse, Janice Opatz—returned, I wanted a chance to spin a good excuse before they caught me.

"Understood." He tipped his hat resolutely and turned back to face the crowd of cows, steadfast in his clarified duties.

I crept back up the stairs, watching for the creak I'd heard the first time I'd climbed them. It had been where the steps curved sharply to the right, but by sticking to the outside, I avoided it.

The door at the top was ajar, and inside, I heard huffing.

And puffing.

Rather than blow the door down, I cracked it slightly more. I spotted movement on a bed at the far wall but couldn't make out who was on it with my one eye staring through a crack.

Behind me, I heard my cowboy friend say urgently, "You can't go up there!"

"I most certainly can. I'm the girls' chaperone. Now get your hands off of me."

Uh-oh. It was Janice. My heart quickened. Should I rush forward and satisfy my curiosity or retreat and talk my way out of this?

Well, that was an easy one—curiosity was a vice I took great pains to gratify. I stepped into the dorm and marched swiftly toward the bed.

Two bodies writhed on top.

My mouth dropped open when I saw who they were.

Chapter 17

"Delrita?" I hissed. "What're you doing screwing around with Ashley's boyfriend?"

The petite blonde pulled her face off Dirk Holthaus, the moose in a letter jacket that KSTP had interviewed in front of the Dairy Building the day of Ashley's murder. Delrita's hair was disheveled and her shirt unbuttoned, revealing a pink, lacy, snap-front bra.

"She had something in her eye," Dirk stammered, jumping off the bed. "I think I got it." He fumbled with the zipper on his pants.

"With your *tongue?*"

"Yeah." He tugged the zipper closed. "I had to get in real close."

"Forget it," I said, disgusted, turning to Delrita. "Janice Opatz is on her way up, so unless you want to answer to her, you'll find a place to hide me and Dirk but quick."

Delrita's mind was surprisingly agile when she was cornered. She pointed behind her. "The office. Janice isn't allowed in there. I have a key." She pulled it from her pocket, jumped to the far side of the long room, unlocked the door, shoved us in, and locked it behind us just as Janice's voice came from the top of the stairs.

"Delrita? What're you doing here?" The chaperone's voice was icy. "The parade begins in ten minutes. All the princesses need to be there."

"I had cramps," she said so smoothly that I was tempted to ask her for lying lessons. "I had to come back for some aspirin."

Janice's clacking footsteps echoed across the hardwood floor. "You *do* look flushed. Are you sure it's just cramps?"

"I'm fine. You don't have to be all up in my business."

"Maybe the problem is that I wasn't paying enough attention to your business," Janice said ominously.

Delrita didn't respond, but I could hear the stare down through the thick wood of the old-fashioned door. Delrita must have won, because shortly, the older woman harrumphed. "Parade," she said, her voice growing more distant. "Ten minutes. There's news crews everywhere waiting to see the Milkfed Marys welcomed back to the fair."

Sixty seconds later, Delrita opened our door. It was just in time, as Dirk was breathing down my neck. He struck me as one of those guys who'd mount anything that stood still for long enough, so I'd wiggled as much as I could while still keeping my ear to the door.

I stared across the dormitory, worried Janice might sneak back. There was no movement. Only the lines of ball gowns and scattered makeup, jewelry, and hair spray, evidence of pageant princesses prepping for a parade, and the two rows of beds lining the walls, straight out of the dwarves' attic in *Snow White*.

"What was that last comment about?" I asked a smug Delrita. She looked proud she'd gotten rid of Janice so quickly.

"What?"

"Janice saying maybe she wasn't keeping a close enough watch on you."

"Who knows with her." Delrita shrugged, avoiding my eyes. "She's crazy as a two-headed loon. Dirk, you should probably go."

"See you later?" he asked pitifully.

"I'll call you." She watched him walk out and then went to make her bed.

I couldn't believe her nonchalance. "So, how long have you been fooling around with Ashley's boyfriend?" I sputtered.

She fluffed her pillow and kept her back to me. "You mean *Lana's* boyfriend?"

"I mean Dirk, that big oaf who was getting dirt out of your eye with his mouth."

"Yeah." She turned to face me. "He was Lana's boyfriend before Ashley stole him."

I tried to puzzle out the logistics of that. Milkfed Marys came from all over the state, and I didn't think they'd have that much time to socialize with one another outside of the pageant, forget meeting and stealing each other's boyfriends. "Where's Lana from?"

"Carlos."

Ah. A wide spot on the map forty-five minutes southeast of Battle Lake. It *was* possible that Lana and Ashley had crossed paths outside of the pageant. "How'd Ashley meet Dirk?"

"I dunno." She twirled a lock of blonde hair. "One of those preliminary Milkfed Mary events last spring, I suppose. All I know is when I first met Lana, she was set on marrying Dirk, and then he started sleeping with Ashley."

That had to hurt. "Did Lana know?"

"She'd have to be an idiot not to. We all did." She rolled her eyes, then walked to a vanity and sat down to freshen her makeup, her back rigid.

"And who knew *you* were sleeping with him?"

"That's new," she said lightly. "We've just been messing around this past week. It's still a secret."

I wouldn't count on it. "So when you told me a few days ago to ask Lana about what Ashley steals, you meant Dirk."

"Yup."

I didn't see any reason to point out that Delrita herself was in that same boyfriend-pinching camp. I'd already intuited that she operated on a different set of principles than the average person. "But I heard that Ashley was seeing an older guy. Dirk's about her same age."

Delrita's shoulders clenched. "Where'd you hear that?"

Her reaction interested me. "You know. Small-town gossip. Remember that I'm from Battle Lake."

"Mmm."

She was definitely acting cagey. "So, do you *know* what older guy she was seeing?"

"Not really." She applied a coat of sparkling pink lip gloss. "Some of the girls thought she was snogging some dude who worked for the company sponsoring the pageant, but I doubt it. She doesn't seem like the type who could pull in the older guys. She wasn't a real deep pool, if you know what I mean."

And a lot of older guys weren't great swimmers, at least when it came to pretty young blondes, but that was something Delrita would learn on her own soon enough. "Do you know his name? The guy some of the girls thought she was seeing?"

Her reflection in the mirror analyzed me as she placed a silver, rhinestoned circlet on her head. Its protruding combs disappeared into her flowing blonde hair, anchoring the tiny crown. "Not really. It was Swedish sounding, I think."

Whatever she was hiding, she clearly wasn't gonna give it up easily. I changed the subject. "Where's Lana now?"

"Probably at the parade, which is where I better be. Can you help me into this dress?" She stood from the vanity, unbuttoned her shirt, unsnapped her bra, and dropped her pants with not a hint of self-consciousness. Clad in only a pink thong, she pointed at a rose-gold sequined gown, likely as hot as a convection oven on a day like today.

"How long do you have to wear this?" I asked, averting my gaze and stepping away from her to pull the heavy dress off the dowel.

"The parades last a half an hour, and then we can wear what we want."

"Do you think Lana'll be free after the parade?" I held out the gown. "I want to talk to her about Ashley."

Delrita's blue eyes flashed. For the first time, I noticed she didn't have eyebrows, or they were so light as to be invisible. "Don't tell her about Dirk."

"I don't care about Dirk." This was mostly true. He'd fallen down the suspect list in light of recent events. He didn't care enough about Ashley to be faithful to her, so it was unlikely he cared enough to kill her. "I want to know how she thinks Ashley got poisoned."

"Probably all that stupid diet cola she chugged. Said it made her feel like a movie star to use a straw to drink it. That's where I'd put poison if I wanted her to drink it. Anyways, Lana's in meetings with Janice for the rest of the day to get ready for the handoff of the crown tomorrow." She stepped into the gown, and I zipped the back.

She kept talking. "That's your best bet for talking to Lana—after the passing-of-the-crown ceremony. She needs to stick around and be sociable. Janice said."

All tucked into her gown, with her tiny tiara and blue eye shadow, Delrita was as pretty as a doll. She slipped into her strappy heels and smiled sweetly at me before heading down the stairs.

For the life of me, I couldn't decide if she was friend or enemy.

Chapter 18

The sun was ending its arc, sending shadows across the streets, when I finally returned to the trailer after another day spent wandering the corners of the fair, weighted by the puzzle of Ashley's death.

"Where have you been?" Mrs. Berns stood outside the trailer, bony arms crossed in front of her and her eyes accusing. She was wearing the same outfit she'd arrived at the fair in—Neil Diamond shirt with 3D chest hair, elastic-waisted shorts, tennies, sword at her waist. I'd managed to mostly avoid both Mrs. Berns and Kennie since Saturday, and it seemed as though I hadn't missed a thing.

"Talking to a Milkfed Mary," I said, counting each item on my fingers, "eating some fried rice over at the International Bazaar, checking out the baby animal exhibit, cruising on the River Raft Ride, taking . . ."

"It was one of those metaphorical questions," Mrs. Berns said. "You're not supposed to answer it. You're supposed to apologize for not getting here sooner. I almost left without you!"

"For where?"

She grabbed my hand and yanked me into the trailer. On the inside wall over the door, she'd hung a banner proclaiming it NEIL DIAMOND ROCKS MY WORLD NIGHT. She pointed at it. "Didn't you see the sign on the way out this morning?"

"It was early when I left," I mumbled. Truth be told, I'd forgotten about the concert entirely. "You sure you don't want to take Kennie?

I need to do some follow-up work on my Ashley article." I decided against filling her in on Delrita's escapades.

"No, *I do not want to take Kennie,* and I forgive you for asking only because you're like the village idiot when it comes to Neil Diamond. You have no idea what you've been missing, girl. Once you get a taste, you'll eternally hunger for more."

"Then maybe I shouldn't go," I said, hopefully. "I don't want to set myself up for an addiction that I can't feed."

"Shush, and come along."

I reluctantly followed her out and to the Grandstand, trailing a few steps and acting like I didn't know her when the security guards at the entrance to the outdoor stadium confiscated her épée. She attempted to persuade them that it was a cane, but nobody was buying. When she pretended to cry, the head guard promised her she could pick it up after the show.

Inside the amphitheater, I was floored by the massive crowd, thousands of people of all ages coming together for the open-air Neil Diamond concert. The crowd was predominantly female and aged fifty or older, and all around the amphitheater, eyes glittered with fanaticism, reflecting the stage lights.

I heard ladies excitedly chattering about following Neil Diamond around the country, and I noticed more than a few fans with tears streaming down their faces, staring at the stage as if waiting for the second coming of Christ. As we made our way through the general admission area and down toward the stage, we passed an impromptu poetry recital, women overcome by their love for Neil and driven to compose sonnets in his honor.

"Neil, Neil," one woman in a short-sleeved concert T-shirt was intoning, "you make me feel special when you sing a tune, and I know, this girl's gonna be a woman soon." She looked to have been a woman for at least six decades, but I had to admit there was a certain girlish glow in her face as she waxed poetic. I didn't get to hear the entire verse of the woman she passed the torch to, but it started out, "To America, you bade us come, and I'm saying *yes*, to a night of fun."

"Mrs. Berns," I whispered, feeling conspicuous. "Name me a Neil Diamond song."

She pressed her lips into a firm line and looked away. "The shame. Now come on. We're right up front."

She pinned an "All Access" badge to my sundress and fanned out her elbows to launch us through the crowd. I was amazed as we passed level after level, descending lower and closer to the front, until we ended up in the plaza area, center stage, standing room only. These were the best concert seats I'd ever scored, and I couldn't hum a single song by the star of the show. *Jeez Louise*. Around me, people chattered like magpies on speed. Their anticipation was contagious.

That's when it came to me. "Sweet Caroline!" I yelled, grabbing Mrs. Berns's shoulder.

"I'm not angry," she said. "I'm disappointed. Now shut up. I think he's coming out."

Sure enough, there was some commotion stage left. The crowd dialed it down to an intense hum, doing their best impression of a gigantic electric generator. Overhead, the moon had punched in, and the night was absolutely gorgeous, warm with a light breeze. I smelled hot dogs and popcorn and the spicy cologne of the man next to me. Although I was warm, goose bumps speckled my arms as I got caught up in the charge of sharing an experience with fifteen thousand other people.

In a short while, the band trickled out, followed by a sexy older guy wearing a tight black button-down shirt with a head of beautiful, thick, and graying hair. "That him?" I asked.

My gaze walked him up and down as I tugged at Mrs. Berns to get her attention. "Is that Neil Diamond?" When she still didn't answer, I looked over in time to see her bent double and wrestling something out of her shorts. "For god's sake, what're you doing?"

One good yank, and she was holding a pair of authentic granny panties—white, elastic-hemmed, and approximately the size of a bedsheet. She whooped triumphantly and chucked them toward the sexy older guy. They fell short, landing on the shoulder of a security guard with his back to the stage. He grimaced and batted them away.

"Don't worry," she told me. "I got plenty more where that came from. I sewed them into the lining of my clothes this morning. Even have a couple bras up here." She patted her lumpy shorts.

Good lord. "Glad to hear you came prepared." A change of subject seemed in order. I nodded toward the stage. "You know, you weren't lying about him. He's one silver fox."

"Wait until he opens his mouth."

As if on cue, he picked up a microphone. "Hello." His voice was impossibly deep and mellow. It made me shiver a little in my down below. "I'm thrilled to be back in Minnesota, one of my favorite states in the world. How're you all doing?"

Screams filled the outdoor arena, wild, lingerie-laced, sexual-fantasy screams. He chuckled. "I'm doing good, too. How about I sing for you? This is one of my favorites. I call it 'September Morn.'"

His voice rolled through the Grandstand and soared to the stars and back. He wasn't flashy—no costume changes or dance moves—but he put on a great show. Ten songs in, I asked Mrs. Berns if I could throw a pair of her underwear onstage.

"Sure," she agreed amiably, if a little smugly. She was reaching down to pluck me a pair when I spotted something very bad out of the corner of my eye.

"Mrs. Berns."

"I'm trying. Hold on. This one's sewed up good."

"Mrs. Berns."

"I think it's one of the super-reinforced undies," she grunted. "It feels like it's made out of burlap."

"Mrs. Berns," I said urgently. "Is that Kennie?"

She glanced up just in time to see Battle Lake's mayor, in full groupie regalia, rushing the stage, wiping out security guards like bowling pins. She was a little Norwegian and a lot buxom to be wearing the black bustier over a spandex skirt. She resembled a human tube of toothpaste that someone had squeezed in the middle and then dressed in fishnet stockings and five-inch heels, topping it with thick makeup and an updo.

"I love you, Neil!" she screamed. "It's me, Kennie Rogers! Remember me? It's me, Neil!"

Neil strolled to the opposite end of the stage, belting out "Solitary Man" without breaking stride. I tried to elbow through to Kennie, who was about twenty feet to my right, but there was no moving in this tight crowd. I don't know what I'd have done if I caught her. Probably tossed a pair of Mrs. Berns's underwear over her head to calm her down.

She made it all the way to the thin wall separating the crowd from the stage. Behind that barricade stood a line of security guards. The one nearest Kennie whispered something to her, and she smiled ecstatically. When he hoisted her on his shoulders, she pumped her bespangled arms in the air and cheered.

The guards began to pass her down the line on their shoulders, like she was the only sandbag that could stop the flood. They were moving her closer and closer to Neil, and my jaw dropped as a thought struck me: Maybe Kennie *actually* did know him. Maybe for once she hadn't been stretching the truth, and she was now going to join this rock god onstage in front of thousands. Next to me, Mrs. Berns watched, her open-mouthed expression mirroring my own.

When Kennie was directly beneath the superstar, on her back and resting on the broad shoulders of four security guards, she reached up as if to welcome Neil into her arms.

Time stood still.

A stage camera turned to her, projecting her face fifty feet high on both of the immense concert screens. Her smile curved beatifically as she reached for the music man, but alas, it wasn't to be. The guards didn't stop. They kept passing her down the line, farther and farther from her idol, until she was out of sight, and, presumably, out of the Grandstand.

Neil's face replaced hers on the concert screens, and the moment was gone.

"Well, that's one way to get kicked out of a concert," Mrs. Berns said with something like admiration. "I prefer toking on the wacky tobacky myself, but no way am I going to risk it—the show isn't even half-over."

"You smoke pot?" I asked, wondering what plan Kennie was currently hatching to sneak back into the Grandstand. She wasn't a woman who gave up easily.

"Helps my glaucoma. There's a great many advantages to getting old, but we don't like to tell you pups too much. Gotta have a few surprises when you grow up."

I smiled, putting Kennie's mini-drama behind me to enjoy the rest of the concert. For the record, though, I knew I'd be thrilled to grow up into a Mrs. Berns.

We swayed to the music, danced to the numbers that rocked, and generally partied like it was 1999. The concert was off the charts, and when it was time to head backstage, I was surprised to find myself excited.

"What should I say to him?" I said.

"Lemme do the talking." Mrs. Berns fluffed her hair. "*Always* let me do the talking."

As we were ushered past the security, our badges were checked again, and we were ushered into a large room replete with bottles of icy champagne and trays of fruit, cheeses, prosciutto, and other meats I couldn't pronounce. Mrs. Berns took a Tupperware container from her purse and began filling it.

"No use having this all go to waste," she said to no one in particular.

I sniffed at the food but was too nervous to eat. The room was filled with other people who wore badges similar to ours, presumably also radio contest winners. Many of them held posters and T-shirts in their shaking hands, or autograph books, and most were clothed in their best—dresses, heels, ties. The few people my age or younger were not quite as spiffy, but they looked as awestruck and out of place as I felt.

We all shuffled around, trying to appear as though we'd spent most of our lives backstage. *No biggie. I'm with the band.* The only person I recognized besides Mrs. Berns was the woman from the press conference—Kate Lewis, president of the State Fair Corporation. She appeared as rumpled and mad-scientisty as she had then and, if anything, paler and more distracted. A man broke away from the buffet line and joined her. He looked familiar, but I couldn't immediately place him.

I sidled up to the two of them and offered my hand, wanting to share my joy at the concert. "Hi, I'm Mira James. I'm a reporter for the *Battle Lake Recall*, and I was at the press conference the other day."

She reacted as if I'd offered her a smallpox blanket. "I'm here on my own free time," she said, backing up toward a wall. "I don't have to answer any questions."

"Oh no. I just came over to say hello. A friend of mine won backstage passes, which is why I'm here. She's over by the door." I pointed toward where Mrs. Berns was hitting up an uncomfortable-looking security guard, her last pair of sewn-in underwear dangling from the rear waistband of her shorts. At least I hoped they were her sewn-in underwear.

"Did you enjoy the show?" I continued. "I couldn't believe how awesome it was! I wish I'd brought my camera. I haven't had it out since the first day of the fair, when I was covering the butter sculpting. I was right up front for that, too, but this show was way better. Of course it was. No one got hurt here." I clamped my mouth shut. Have I mentioned I gush when I'm excited? One more good reason to avoid emotions.

Kate began distancing herself from me. "The concert was very good. I hate to be rude, but it's been a long day. If you don't mind?"

I thought she was going to leave, but instead, she turned her back to me and whispered to the man, who was digging into his plateful of buffet food. I glided back to Mrs. Berns, finally remembering where I knew him from. He was the same guy Janice had been speaking to at the bottom of the dorm stairs on Saturday, back when the police were still on guard. *He must work for the fair.*

When I reached Mrs. Berns, I subtly leaned over to yank the dangling underwear free, shoving them into her purse. "When will Neil get here?"

"I knew it'd just take one show to turn you into a DiamondHead," she crowed.

Suddenly, the room grew quiet, and we heard that sweet, booming voice of the sexy man in the black button-down shirt. His laughter filled the hall as he neared us, and it was almost enough to distract me from the agitated conversation Kate was involved in on the other side of the room.

Chapter 19

The previous night's dancing must have exhausted me in a cleansing way, because I slept like the dead, waking up around nine a.m. on the pull-out couch with a warm yellow sunbeam across my face. Kennie still slept on her bed across from mine, and I assumed Mrs. Berns was doing the same in the back bedroom.

I stretched like a kitty before I sneaked to the showers for a quick rinse and toothbrushing. Then I pulled on the navy-blue tank top and cutoff shorts I'd brought with me, returned to drop my toiletries and pajamas under the trailer so as not to risk waking the ladies, and set off to catch a Metro bus to the West Bank. My plan was to visit my old stomping grounds and exorcise some demons before covering the crown-passing ceremony later today. The balmy late-summer sun seemed behind my plan 100 percent.

This State Fair trip had been my first return to the Cities since I'd left for Battle Lake last spring. That was an easy fact to forget because I'd been isolated in the biome that was the fair since I'd arrived. It provided everything I needed—food, community, water, showers, bed. There was absolutely no reason to leave, and as I did, I realized the State Fair was just another small town, much like Battle Lake. That thought made me apprehensive to step outside the gate and into the gesellschaft that was Minneapolis / Saint Paul. I'd changed a lot since I'd left last April, but was it a change for the better?

I kept my face to the bus's window as it puttered down Como, heading west. Forty-five minutes later, I recognized the familiar businesses of Riverside Avenue. I'd worked in the neighborhood for almost ten years before escaping to Battle Lake. I pulled the stop cord and stepped out tentatively, not sure what I was expecting to find.

The area had been a hippie hangout when I'd left, a throwback culture with a flavor reminiscent of a 1990s Grateful Dead concert, peopled with a generation clinging to something they'd never known. The Riverside Café had taken up most of the block with its usually vegan and more frequently flavor-free dishes before it had closed last year. Chili Time Café had been across the street, patronized by college freshman dabbling in Marxism. It now stood empty. The scents of patchouli and Nag Champa incense had been replaced by curry and cigars, and the scarves and India print skirts were now suits and burkas, but the place still had the same energy. There was room to be different here. The diversity of color and appearance let me relax in a way I couldn't in a small town, a fact I'd forgotten in my rural isolation. My shoulders eased a little.

I strolled toward Perfume River, the Vietnamese restaurant I'd waited tables at before answering the siren song of Battle Lake. The outside was still painted salmon and yellow, two bay windows leading into a narrow restaurant that had room for only three rows of tables, seven tables deep. I pulled the door open and smiled to hear the same tinkling bell, the familiar scent of lemongrass and garlic washing over me.

I'd hoped my old friend Alison would be working the lunch shift, but she was nowhere in sight. I stood at the front counter and waited for someone to come from the rear of the restaurant, where the kitchen and wait station were. A teenage girl finally appeared, wearing the requisite black skirt, white shirt, and tie. I recognized the bow tie. It was the one we all fought over because it was the only clip-on and didn't constrict your throat like the real ones.

"Hello. Can I help you?"

"Is Alison working?"

She smiled prettily. "Sorry?" Her Vietnamese accent was faint.

"Alison Short? The manager?"

"Oh, she doesn't work here anymore. My family bought the restaurant in June. The food's still awesome, though. Would you like to see a menu?"

I peeked around her, peering at the kitchen behind the glass of the waitress station. I spotted one man chopping vegetables and another stirring a steaming soup pot. I didn't recognize either of them. "Maybe later. Thanks."

I shoved my hands in my pockets and retreated quickly. If I took a left, I'd end up in front of my old loft apartment above an art supplies store. If I went right, I'd find myself in front of the 400 Bar, which had been another favorite hangout. I'd danced to a lot of bands and drunk a lot of vodka there. The bartenders and bouncers had known me by name, and that was the shameful truth. I considered coming back to the bar later tonight, when it was open, to confirm with someone that I had in fact once lived here and was not disposable or easily replaced, but what does a person do at a bar if they don't drink?

As I sat frozen between two choices, a young woman walked toward me. She was about my height, with long brown hair. Her head was down, but there was something familiar about the way she carried herself. As she drew closer, I noted the short-sleeved white blouse she was wearing over a dark cotton skirt. She wore comfortable black shoes. Her only break from the uniform was a dramatic amber ring on the middle finger of her right hand.

When she passed me to go inside Perfume River, she didn't look up, and I didn't say anything because I'd suddenly realized who she was: me, a year ago.

Well, that was that, wasn't it? There was no longer anything for me here.

When a bus stopped in front of me with a pneumatic wheeze and huff of exhaust, I stepped in, pausing to glance around one last time before the doors closed behind me. I felt oddly unrooted, vulnerable, but also free. It was a lonely, scary feeling, like the bird who doesn't know what to do once her cage door is opened.

It was too much to fit in my head. As if in reflection of my mood, the sun crept behind the clouds and a deep rumble echoed along the sky. The humid temperature dropped noticeably.

I forced my thoughts to shift focus. I didn't like the unmoored feeling. More importantly, there was nothing I could do about it. What I *could* do was find out who'd killed Ashley Kirsten Pederson.

And if I succeeded, people would realize they needed me, right? I couldn't be so easily erased.

In a few hours Lana would be officially crowned Milkfed Mary, Queen of the Dairy, her beautiful young head enshrined in Grade A unsalted butter. Hopefully, she wouldn't also have it handed to her by the same person who'd offed Ashley. In any case, I'd been lax in not yet successfully tracking down Lana to question her about Ashley's murder and to make sure she felt safe herself.

I would fix that.

I'd also check in on Mrs. Pederson to see how she was doing and ask if she had any new information, including—if I could swing it without further damaging her—what poison had been used to kill her daughter.

Yes. The relief of a plan.

Chapter 20

The Dairy Building's doors should have been swung wide to the public, but the sign out front said OPEN SOON! and workers scurried in and out. I followed one of them into the building and kept to the perimeters so as not to attract attention. Those on the job were intent on their tasks, like ants working feverishly to beat a rainfall. I knew they needed this afternoon's ceremony to go smoothly. One slipup, and the Milkfed Mary pageant would be considered certifiably cursed, years of positive publicity for the dairy industry down the drain. Someone would be forced to develop a new, less-cursed gimmick, like a Prince Gouda, King of Dairy-Based Fooda, contest. See how hard that'd be? No, they needed to make certain the new queen was installed without a hitch.

"Excuse me," I asked a worker with an armful of carving tools. "What time is the ceremony supposed to start?"

He tried to look at his watch, but it was too buried under his armload. "Three o'clock. Then the butter carving starts at 3:15 sharp. Let's hope no one dies."

Very blunt. He must not have been from around here—and by "here," I meant the Midwest. I nodded my thanks and let him go past. I glanced around. The cavernous building was extra spick-and-span, but otherwise, everything seemed as it had when I first was here, five days previous. Including, I noticed, the sponsorship banner touting the Bovine Productivity Management group over the top of the carving booth.

I hadn't noticed it when I'd covered Ashley's ceremony because it blended with all the other signs strung about touting the dairy industry. Plus, I hadn't been looking for it. Now that I knew that Ashley may have been dating an older man with a Swedish-sounding name who worked for the pageant-sponsoring company, it became important. Yanking out my pad and pencil, I copied down the name, website address, and phone number.

Satisfied to have a focus other than my own life, I sneaked out the rear of the building, intending to return to the trailer to grab a jacket and my camera before returning to snag a good position for the crowning ceremony. The temperature had dropped precipitously since this morning, and the smell of ozone in the air promised a doozy of a thunderstorm this afternoon or evening.

An argument in a shadowy nook to my left attracted my attention. I adjusted to the outdoor light, but I didn't need my eyes to recognize immediately that this fight was ugly.

"I told you to shut the hell up about it," a man with his back to me raged. He was short, maybe five eight, with dark hair. "I'll get the goddamn money."

He was speaking to a woman, the side of her face and the wicked grip he had on her left arm visible to me. I stepped closer and coughed, alerting them both to my presence.

He clammed up, releasing her and marching off, sticking to the shadows and never turning to see who I was. That left Kate Lewis, the woman he'd been threatening, alone and facing me. She stepped out of the shadows, pulling down her sad, rumpled blazer and covering the bare belly peeking through her untucked shirt. They must have been tussling before I'd happened upon them for her to have been so exposed.

"Hi," she said, walking toward me. Her eyes were unfocused. She recognized me but wasn't immediately sure from where.

"Hi. We were both at the concert last night." I wondered if the man who'd just left was the same guy who'd been backstage with her. There was no way to be certain.

"Of course." She laughed nervously.

"Are you all right?"

"Fine." She blinked rapidly. "How are you enjoying the fair?"

She was obviously embarrassed, so I allowed her change of subject. "It's great. I'm having a wonderful time. You?"

"I love the fair." She patted her hair and tugged at her jacket again. "I'm afraid I have to run. Big day here, you know." She smiled distantly before disappearing inside the Dairy Building.

I waited until she was out of sight and then jogged out of the alley and into the main traffic, where the guy who'd been hassling her had gone. I hoped to see his face, but he'd been swallowed up by the crowd. I followed the flow back to the Silver Suppository. I grabbed my toiletries from under the front steps, where I'd left them this morning, and entered the trailer.

"Hello?" No answer.

Kennie's bed was unmade but empty, makeup stains on her pillow attesting to another late night. Actually, I'd never seen her without makeup, either before or after bed. I tiptoed to Mrs. Berns's bedroom. "Hello?"

The door was ajar, and I poked my head in just enough to see the corner of the bed. I didn't want any surprises. "Mrs. Berns?"

The visible slice of the bed was empty, so I risked opening the door a little wider. Still no one. I opened it all the way and was treated to the view of a neatly made bed and pristine room. Mrs. Berns had an admirable work ethic, even when on vacation. I was about to shut the door behind me when something caught my attention. A black shirt lay across the bottom of the bed, and I'd seen it somewhere before.

Actually, *on* someone before.

Someone quite famous.

I walked over and held it up, affirming that it was, in fact, the same black, ruffled-at-the-collar, sweated-in, chest-hair-framing shirt Neil Diamond had serenaded the State Fair in last night.

Oh my. A smile spread across my face. *Oh freaking my.*

Jess Lourey

I laid the shirt back where I'd found it after taking a quick sniff (music-man sweat and Paco Rabanne) and returned to the trailer's main room. Folding my bed back into a table, I set up my laptop. I might be in a "Summer of Love"–themed trailer park, surrounded by cowboys and farmers, but I could still connect with the twentieth century.

My computer hummed and clicked as I flipped my notepad open to review my most recent notes relating to Ashley's murder:

Janice Opatz sneaky. Ashley Pederson dating older man? Delrita cheating with Dirk who was cheating on Lana. Delrita says older man Swedish-sounding guy from sponsoring company. Kate Lewis acting odd at concert, hanging out with same shorter guy as Janice. Bovine Productivity Management is sponsoring company, www.bovineproductivity.com, St. Paul, 651-333-5255. Motives for murder: revenge (Lana)? Janice covering something up? Kate Lewis distracting attention from her embezzling? And how and when did Ashley swallow the poison and what poison was used—ask Mrs. Pederson if police know.

Not much there. When my wireless connected, I went straight to the Bovine Productivity Management site, wondering what sort of nefarious activities I'd find hiding behind that Orwellian name. The home page was a soothing montage of vibrant greens, earthy browns, and crisp whites. The words "sustainable," "healthy," and "help" were connected to "innovation" and "conservation."

Photos of men biking in front of cornfields and women smiling into cameras as they tended to immaculate herds of cows flashed across the screen. Something about this wholesome and well-oiled operation sparked my warning feelers. In my experience, companies that "helped" and "conserved" as much as BPM claimed didn't have enough leftover cash to pay for slick PR websites.

I moved my cursor over the "About Us" link and clicked.

> Bovine Productivity Management is a corporation
> dedicated to supporting dairy farmers in sustainable
> efforts designed to decrease costs and increase out-
> put. Our scientists are continually seeking ways for
> farmers to procure more milk from happier cows. We
> invest our time in improving cow feed, medicine, vi-
> tamins, and quality and quantity of milk. When dairy
> farmers achieve, BPM achieves.

That sounded good. Vague, but good, which I supposed was the intention. I clicked on "Our Products," and was rewarded with stulti-fying information about GrowGood, their patented fertilizer; Robusto and Cornucopia, the cow vitamins they produced; and ME, or "Milk Enhancer," their bestselling bovine growth hormone.

The website also offered links to their press releases, an investor information page, and a corporate-responsibility page with more of the blandly soothing language. It wasn't until I clicked on "Meet Our Family" that I found what I was looking for: a list of employees' names and job titles.

I counted forty-three, which was a good-size company in my esti-mation. Only ten were women. Of the remaining thirty-three, two had Swedish-sounding names. Per Olafsen was listed as the laboratory director, and Lars Gunder was the marketing manager. After not much thought, I decided Lana would have been far more likely to cross paths with Mr. Gunder, who would presumably be the contact person for the Milkfed Mary pageant. Too bad there weren't photos of either man so I could guess their ages.

I flipped open my cell and dialed BPM's number.

"Bovine Productivity Management. How may I direct your call?"

"Yes, is Mr. Gunder in?"

"I'm afraid he isn't. May I take a message?"

I thought quickly. Surprisingly, my brain recommended I tell the truth. Well, *part* of the truth. "Yes. My name is Mira James, and I'm a reporter for the *Battle Lake Recall*. I wanted to get some quotes from Mr. Gunder about the Milkfed Mary pageant sponsored by BPM. They're having a crown-passing ceremony this afternoon."

"You're in luck! He'll be there, and he'll be more than happy to answer questions before or after the event."

"Thank you." I hung up, scribbled a note in my pad, and called Ron to get Mrs. Pederson's number.

"What have you found out?" he grunted.

I was loath to tell him that Ashley appeared to be a boyfriend-stealing manipulator lacking a moral compass. He probably already knew it, but I wasn't eager to speak ill of the dead, especially the youthful dead. Where's the justice in not living long enough to fix your mistakes? "Not much. I'm following some leads."

"The older man?"

"I don't know anything for sure."

He paused, and when he spoke, his voice was pained. "She had a reputation around town."

"Ashley? You mean being snotty?"

"I mean being friendly with older gentlemen."

I raised my eyebrows. "This firsthand information?"

"No."

Then I had zero interest in speculation. "So you gonna give me Mrs. Pederson's number?"

"Are you going to ask her what poison was used?"

"If you'll admit to being too chicken to do it yourself," I said. "You're her friend. It'd be a lot easier for you to ask her."

"You'd be surprised," he said. "Hurry up and get me the full story." He rattled off the Pederson home number before hanging up without saying goodbye, as was his pattern.

"I'm working on it," I muttered, staring at the quiet phone. I took several breaths, steeling myself before making the difficult phone call.

I punched in the numbers.

"Ron?"

I'd forgotten I was holding one of his cell phones. His name must have shown up on her caller ID. Her voice was sad and distant.

"No, Mrs. Pederson. It's Mira James. I have one of Ron's phones while I'm at the fair."

She coughed. "You're still there? Did you find anything out?"

"I'm afraid not. That's why I'm calling. I have some difficult questions for you, but they might be helpful if you're up for them."

Her voice came out a little stronger. "Ask."

"Do the police know how Ashley came in contact with the poison yet?"

"Not really. Right now, they're assuming she ate or drank it, but it'll be a while yet before we get the official toxicology reports. The medical examiner said it must have been something she consumed right before she went into the booth, though, because cyanide acts quickly."

"Cyanide?"

"Yes." A sniffle. "The examiner believes that was the poison used, based on her . . . on the way she died. We're not supposed to release that information to the public until it's been confirmed."

I sat back, my brain whirring. "I'll forget I heard it. Does cyanide have a taste or a smell?"

"Apparently it has an odor like almonds, but not everyone can smell it. In small doses, depending on what form it is, it doesn't have any taste or color. Likely, Ashley drank it, but all the other girls who were in the dorm with her right before she left for the Dairy Building said Ashley only drank a diet cola, and she opened it right there in front of all of them. Lana specifically remembers because the can was a little fizzy, and Ashley was upset because she was worried it would stain her outfit."

That confirmed what Delrita had said about Ashley's last meal having been a diet soda. "How long after she drank it would the effects begin to show?"

"Not more than ten minutes, the medical examiner said."

"So it must have been something she came in contact with while she was in the dormitory with the other princesses, on the way to the Dairy Building, or in the booth itself?"

"That's what they think."

I triple-underlined the "talk to Lana" note I'd written. "Just one more thing, Mrs. Pederson. Do you know anything about an older man Ashley might have been seeing?"

There was a long pause on the other end. Her voice, when it came, sounded pinched. "She was seeing Dirk Holthaus. Only Dirk. They were very much in love."

I felt like a total ass for asking, and it struck me that Mrs. Pederson, like most mothers of teenagers, would have had little idea who her daughter was spending time with. In fact, I was willing to bet there was a lot Carlotta didn't know about Ashley. "Thank you. I'm sure you're right. How're you and Steven holding up?"

"We're still in shock, to be honest." Her voice cracked. "You'll tell me if you find anything out?"

"Of course. You'll be the first to know." It was a white lie, probably. I certainly wasn't going to share anything that would make her life more difficult.

We exchanged more small talk before ending the call. While my computer was still warmed up, I researched cyanide poisoning. Med-e-cine. com confirmed what Mrs. Pederson had said. It also explained Ashley's cherry-red skin after she died. Cyanide worked by inhibiting the body's ability to process oxygen, trapping it in the blood and not letting it reach the cells, thereby turning skin pink or red.

Cyanide was more easily available than I would have guessed. Apricot pits, cassava root, the burning of plastic, silk, or rubber all produced it. People in certain industries, like electroplating and photography, had access to the toxin. Also, those who worked in chemical labs. I made a note next to the Bovine Productivity Management page of my notepad. I didn't know how one went about asking a receptionist if her company created or used cyanide, but I'd put it on my to-do list.

Cyanide could come in a lot of forms, but gas and water-soluble salts were the most common. In Ashley's case, gas seemed unlikely as she hadn't been alone all morning, and she was the only one poisoned. A selective version made more sense. Swallowing only 300 milligrams of hydrogen cyanide salts would be enough to kill a person. More would do it more quickly. As to the symptoms of poisoning, it was likely that Ashley had experienced brief but intense pain, including nausea, inability to breathe, and seizures right before her death. That would explain the bricks of butter scattered around her body when the lights popped back on.

I rubbed my face. To hear that Ashley had suffered, even for a brief moment, was sobering. Even if she was a rudenik who made poor choices, she'd still been little more than a girl.

I was about to shut down my computer when, on a whim, I searched for Shelby Spoczkowski, 1977 Milkfed Mary, Queen of the Dairy. The odds that she still went by her maiden name were slim, but in a country where 50 percent of marriages ended in divorce, I could hope.

Apparently, it was my lucky day, because I stumbled across a realty website in Florida that listed Shelby Spoczkowski as their number one seller. They even posted a picture of her, but it was too tiny to tell if she was the same woman I'd seen on the Midwest Dairy Organization website.

I tried the realty office number, but the receptionist said she had no idea where Shelby had grown up. She offered me Shelby's cell phone number. When I tried it, I was directed to voicemail after four rings. Not ready to leave a message, I jotted down her cell number so I could try back later and glanced at the tiny clock in the corner right of my computer screen. The passing of the crown was starting in fifteen minutes. Time to skedaddle.

I scratched the ladies a quick note to let them know I wouldn't be back until late, made sure I had enough paper in my notepad, and knelt to grab my digital camera from underneath the main bench. It wasn't where I'd left it, so I searched in all the other likely spots. When I couldn't find it there, either, I scoured the trailer end to end, but it was no good.

Someone had stolen my camera.

Chapter 21

The realization made my skin clammy.

Relax, I told myself.

Mrs. Berns or Kennie had probably borrowed the camera. Still, on my way out, I made sure to lock the door, and I eyeballed all the windows. The ones at the front and back were open, but they were at least nine feet off the ground. When I double-checked the lock on the only exterior door, I noticed several scrapes on it, brighter than the surrounding metal, but I didn't know if they were new. I was out of time to worry, though. I was already late for the ceremony. A growl of thunder rumbled across the sky as I took off.

My plan—on top of finally talking to Lana, if I could catch her alone—was to amble into the Dairy Building, hang back, and see if I could spot Lars Gunder. Once I introduced myself, I'd no longer be able to spy on him, so I'd just play it cool and observe how he interacted with the princesses and Janice Opatz. Then I'd try to catch up with him after the butter carving began and see what information I could extract. That's where my plan got a little hazy, but I'd winged my way through worse.

When I neared the Dairy Building, I realized that taking precious time searching for the camera had put me at a serious disadvantage. The place was packed as tight as a church on Christmas, and the heavy raindrops that'd started to fall were only going to add to the crowd scrambling to get inside.

I searched my purse for my press pass. Thankfully, it hadn't gone the way of my camera. I held it up to the security guards stationed at the doors, elbowing my way to the front of the crowd. People glared, but I didn't let that slow me down. Bunch of rubberneckers, as far as I was concerned, come to watch another queen enter the Booth of Death. At least that's what I'd started calling it, and judging by the return of the security guards outside and police officers stationed nearby, I wasn't the only one worried about how this story was going to end.

I was able to squeeze all the way to the rear of the enormous building, about fifteen feet from the butter-sculpting booth. Actually, I was standing in nearly the same spot as I had been when the lights had gone out last Thursday. My heart chilled at the thought. Were we in for an encore presentation of a beauty queen murder?

I dismissed the idea out of necessity. I needed to talk to Lars and Lana, and besides, there were police officers stationed discreetly all around the room. We'd be fine.

My breathing calmed. I watched people buzzing around on the stage erected near the carving booth. I recognized Janice Opatz, wearing her signature red suit. She was arranging the blonde hair of a young lady decked out in a glittery, spaghetti-strapped purple gown. I guessed she was Lana Sorensen.

She was easily as pretty as Ashley, with wide blue eyes, a proud nose that didn't take up too much space on her face, and plump lips set in a serious line. I liked that she wasn't smiling. This was a sad occasion, even if she was benefiting from the tragedy.

A third person stood on the stage, his back to the crowd. He was a shorter man, maybe five nine. Lana, in her heels, was a good two inches taller. He was trim and slick in his three-piece suit.

When he turned, my heart hurdled a beat: he was the same guy who'd been at the dorm with Janice after last Tuesday's press conference and at the Neil Diamond concert with Kate. Was he also the same guy who'd threatened Kate earlier today?

I studied him from a safe distance. He had a quick smile, patting a tense Janice on the back with hands that I was certain were professionally manicured. Lana's body language suggested she was trying to keep her distance from him, though it was hard to be sure, crowded as they were on the small stage.

After a signal from a cameraman in front, the man grabbed the microphone. "Welcome. Thank you all for coming."

Janice and Lana assumed a post on each side of him. Behind and to the right, coming through the exit door nearest the Booth of Death, ten young women in ball gowns entered. Delrita was at the front, followed by Megan and then Brittany, and seven more pretty women I'd never met. They all appeared nervous, like kittens at a wolf party, and Brittany seemed to be crying. Megan elbowed her, and she wiped her eyes and stood straighter.

"I'm Lars Gunder, a representative of Bovine Productivity Management," the man at the microphone said.

My pulse quickened. Lars Gunder, PR guy for Bovine Productivity Management, and possibly Ashley's lover.

He continued. "We are proud sponsors of the Milkfed Mary, Queen of the Dairy pageant, which stands for everything our company is about: wholesomeness, a love of the dairy industry, support for farmers, and community. We, along with the entire state of Minnesota, were deeply saddened when Ashley Pederson of Battle Lake died shortly after being crowned the fifty-fourth Milkfed Mary."

He didn't register any change in emotion when referring to her. Either he was one coldhearted bastard, or he wasn't the older man Ashley may have been knocking boots with.

"Tonight's event is set up to honor her, and to pass on the crown, which is what we're sure Ashley would want. Janice Opatz, the queen chaperone and a woman who loved Ashley dearly, would like to speak."

People clapped halfheartedly, waiting for the real show to start. Janice approached the microphone. "Thank you for coming," she told us, her voice clear as crystal. "I knew Ashley Pederson well. She was a beautiful girl, inside and out. She cared deeply for those around her."

Delrita rolled her eyes so slightly that it could have been mistaken for a long blink.

"She was also a shining beacon of the dairy industry, bringing our message of calcium-enriched goodness, conservation, and sustainability to communities all across Minnesota. When farmers achieve, we achieve." Polite applause again broke out through the echoey building.

I was busy scribbling notes. Janice was parroting the BPM slogan. I wondered what exactly a sponsorship of the pageant entailed. Who paid whom how much money, and what benefits did they derive from the transaction? Outside, the rain picked up, thrumming a steady drumbeat on the metal roof.

"Ashley was taken from us far too soon," Janice continued, "but her legacy will endure through the good work that she started. Lana, will you please step up?"

The classically pretty young woman advanced to Janice's side and peered out at the crowd. She still wasn't smiling. In fact, she looked grim and more than a little afraid. Someone wearing a headset handed a crown to Lars, who offered it to Janice. A police officer at the edge of the stage whispered into his shoulder unit.

"It is with a mixture of sadness and pride that I crown Lana Sorensen of Carlos, Minnesota, the reigning Milkfed Mary, Queen of the Dairy," Janice called out. "Congratulations, Lana!" More applause rang through the building, louder than before.

Lana tipped her head forward to accept the crown and graced the audience with a tight smile. She stepped to the microphone, and her strong, Minnesota-accented voice filled the building. "I didn't want it this way."

She turned and lifted her skirts to step down the stairs and off the stage as the crowd began whispering excitedly. Was this a revolt? The Great Dairy Rebellion?

Janice and Lars exchanged worried looks, but visibly relaxed when the same assistant who'd handed over the crown approached Lana with a winter coat. With no more pomp, Lana was led from the stairs at the side of the stage, past the booth, and behind the blue curtain that guarded its entrance. Workers emerged from the shadows and quickly disassembled the stage, giving us an unbroken view of the glass-sided gazebo, eleven butter mountains spinning quietly inside. The crowd that had seconds ago been humming their surprise went silent.

I had the distinct feeling we were all witnessing a virginal sacrifice when the door to the booth opened and Lana entered, beautiful and pale, followed by the same woman who'd sculpted Ashley's likeness. Part of me wanted to put a stop to it, to cry out how ridiculous it was that we were letting this happen a second time, but I knew an outburst would only get me kicked out. As Janice had said, the show must go on.

The crowd held its collective breath as Lana placed herself in the designated chair in the center of the booth.

The sculptor, appearing shaky but determined, sat behind the central slab of butter, quickly producing a bread knife and a clay ribbon tool. Through the open doors behind us, a flash of lightning lit up the preternaturally leaden sky. We all glanced back at the torrential rains, glad we were indoors, and then returned our attention to the booth.

The central floor of the butter-carving booth lurched and then began slowly turning.

Chapter 22

Lana and the sculptor began to rotate, both of them blanching for a moment for likely very different reasons. The first rotation was uneventful, and then the second, and then the third.

When it became apparent that both winter-jacketed women were going to remain safe, everyone in the Dairy Building heaved a collective sigh of relief. No one would die here today.

The ten princesses-in-waiting were ushered into the crowd, where they began to hand out Milkfed Mary trading cards and reassure us with their healthy, calcium-rich smiles. I was given an Emily and a Lana. Emily was from International Falls and next fall would attend the University of Minnesota at Duluth to pursue a career in agronomics. Lana was from Carlos, which I already knew, and was enrolled at the University of Minnesota, Twin Cities, in the fall, majoring in math and English.

She wanted to work as a high school teacher when she graduated. Thank god for martyrs.

I slid both cards into my back pocket, curious as to whether there had once been an Ashley trading card. That puppy would be worth some money. I kept one eye on Lana and one on Lars as I ruminated. He watched the sculpting for half an hour, answering reporters' questions as they came up to him, his body language oozing a precise balance of solicitude and charm. I still wasn't ready to introduce myself.

Outside, the storm abated, and suddenly, a sliver of sunlight appeared amid the gloom. It had been one of the quick and intense late-summer storms common to the upper Midwest.

When Lars finally sauntered toward the nearest exit, I squeezed through the crowd and followed at an appropriate distance. If he was simply going to his car, I'd run up to ask questions. If he stopped by the cyanide booth to refresh his supply, I'd take him out at the knees.

He did neither.

Instead, he peeled off his jacket as he strolled to the east and then north, stopping to remove his tie.

"Daddy!" Two little girls dashed out from the Kidway, a cordoned-off section of the fair devoted to rides for children five and under. The girls splashed through puddles and latched themselves to Lars's legs. Neither child appeared to be older than four, and both had sandy brown hair curling haphazardly around their heart-shaped faces.

A tiny woman with a large bag over her shoulder and a stick of pink and blue cotton candy in each hand followed the girls and stretched up to give Lars a peck on his cheek. From my position twenty feet away, I noticed both adults wore wedding rings, so I used my amazing deductive powers to mark them as husband and wife. I had a hunch I was following the wrong guy with a Swedish-sounding name.

He relieved his wife of the bag, hoisted the smaller daughter on his shoulders, and took the other by her hand. I followed them around the rides for forty-five minutes, beginning to feel more and more like a heel. They were the sweetest foursome. When the younger child fell and skinned her knee, he scooped her up and found a bench to settle her on while he fished a first-aid kit from the bag. She sniffled as he cleaned and dressed her wound. Then he walked his three ladies over to the bathroom and waited outside.

Weighing Mrs. Pederson's grief-drenched voice against the faces of his daughters, I decided it was now or never. I walked rapidly toward him. "Mr. Gunder?"

He turned, a mildly surprised look on his face. "Yes?"

Up close, his skin was as smooth as a baby's. His eyes were cerulean, but the hefty bags underneath gave them a gray tinge.

"Hi. You don't know me. My name's Mira James. I called you at work earlier today and left a message. I'm a reporter with the *Battle Lake Recall*, and I wonder if you'd mind answering a few questions about Ashley Pederson?"

His mouth tightened around the edges, but he kept his delivery cordial, slipping back into the supersmooth PR voice he'd used at the ceremony. "Not if you're quick. I'm here with my family and like to keep them separate from my work." He tapped his chin with a finger. "Battle Lake is Ms. Pederson's hometown, if I'm not mistaken." He made an expression of mild sadness. "I'm so sorry for your loss."

"Thank you. Had you met Ashley?"

"Of course. I know all the girls in the pageant. It's part of my job as marketing director at BPM. At least, it is this year. This is the first time we've sponsored the pageant."

"I'm sorry for you as well, then. Has Ashley's death generated a lot of bad publicity?"

"Too soon to tell, but I shouldn't think so. It's an unfortunate situation, obviously, but it's not tied to our company."

I nodded. "What exactly does your company do?"

"Support farmers. We help them to grow their stock in a sustainable fashion, getting the most productivity out of their cows as possible."

"That sounds interesting," I lied.

He glanced around, obviously trying to get rid of me before his family came out of the bathroom. "It really is. If you'd like, I can give you a tour of the factory tomorrow."

What was I going to say? "That'd be awesome. Thank you."

"No problem. Just show up before noon and ask for me at the front desk."

He didn't tell me where they were located, and I didn't ask because I already knew. "Great. Thanks for your time."

He nodded and excused himself as his wife and daughters walked toward us. I took off toward the Dairy Building to finally garner a meeting with the elusive Lana Sorensen.

Chapter 23

Turned out it took a crazy long time to carve a head out of butter. It was nearly nine o'clock before Lana exited the booth, whole and alive but looking like she'd just spent six hours in a rotating refrigerator with no bathroom breaks.

The press, who'd earlier packed the Dairy Building, were no longer around. In fact, not many people remained, at least up close to the booth, and Lana and the sculptor's descent was anticlimactic. Out of habit, I stayed back and watched as Janice strode up to Lana in front of the blue curtain and patted Lana's head. The motion seemed more possessive than affectionate.

After every one of Lana's hairs was in its approved location, Janice gave a curt nod to the sculptor and led her charge away. They beelined to the dormitories. I continued to hang back, waiting until they were out of sight to follow them up the stairs. Janice's gravelly voice floated down.

". . . very well tonight. But would it have killed you to smile?"

Lana murmured something in return, and Janice spoke again. "Well, it's done now, so I don't suppose it matters. Just remember, if you say one word, the whole thing is lost. And who does that benefit? No one. But it'll hurt plenty."

My foot slipped down the face of a stair, and I banged my shin, drawing an abrupt halt to the conversation on the top floor. So much for stealth. I pattered quickly back downstairs and toward the center of the barn. Blending in with the crowds and the cows, I kept one eye on the entrance to the second floor as people milled in front of me.

Sure enough, Janice appeared, casting a suspicious glare around the Cattle Barn. I ducked behind a milking machine display. When I looked up again, I caught her red jacket slipping outside, purse in her hand. I waited for ten full minutes before darting back upstairs, cringing at the bruise I could feel swelling on the front of my leg.

I knocked on the closed door at the top. "Lana?"

"Come in."

She was the only girl in the dorm. She was sitting in front of a vanity wearing sweats, still in the heavy makeup from the ceremony. Next to her rested an uneaten peanut butter sandwich on white bread.

She'd been leaning forward to remove her contacts when I entered. She glanced at me without interest before returning to her task. "Did Janice send you to keep watch on me?"

"No. My name is Mira."

"Lana." She reached for a pair of glasses as thick as hockey ice and slid them onto her nose. They transformed her from a nubile beauty queen into an earnest schoolteacher. "What can I do for you?"

I'd heard of people who rehearsed conversations beforehand. I wrote myself a mental note to become one of those people someday. "I'm a friend of Delrita's." The sideways lie felt sticky. Lana struck me as a straightforward, likable person.

"She's not here." She indicated the empty room.

"I know. She told me that Ashley stole your boyfriend."

Lana reappraised me, her eyes as big as moonstones behind her glasses. "You're that reporter from Battle Lake. Delrita told me about you."

She possessed a natural shit-cutter. I'd had to work years to develop mine. Now I *really* liked her. "Yeah, that's me. From what I gather, Ashley was generally a pain in the ass, but she was all her mom and dad had. Do you know what happened to her?"

Lana turned to fiddle with a pot of lip gloss in front of her. "I know she was poisoned, but I don't know who did it, if that's what you're asking."

I didn't respond, and after a handful of uncomfortable seconds, Lana filled in the space between us. "She did steal Dirk, I suppose, but he didn't put up much of a fight. Anyhow, he wasn't worth killing anyone over. Besides, where would a farm girl like me get poison?"

"I don't know where *anyone* gets poison." She didn't respond, so I continued. "Can I ask you something?"

"You already have."

I smiled. "This is even more personal. You don't seem like the beauty queen type. You've got the looks, but you seem way too no-nonsense for the job."

She laughed, but it was a melancholy sound. "I ran to help out my family. I never cared if I won or not."

"Help your family how?"

"To make my mom proud. To bring good press to the farm." She shrugged. "The usual."

"Why do you think Ashley entered the pageant?"

Lana sighed. "I think she's one of those girls who just needs attention. She'd shrivel up and die if she didn't have it."

I didn't point out that Ashley's fame hadn't done her any favors in the staying-alive department. I was just happy that Lana was opening up. "I heard from a few people that Ashley was seeing an older guy, probably someone from Bovine Productivity Management. You know anything about that?"

"Yeah. She was fooling around with Mr. Gunder."

"You sure?" I ran back through what I'd witnessed the last couple hours. "He's married with kids."

"Sure as I have eyes on my face." She blinked the magnified googlers for effect.

"Is that what you and Janice were talking about when I came up here? The secret that you shouldn't let anyone know about?"

Her enormous blue eyes turned chilly, and I lost any edge I had won. "That's none of your business."

"I'm sorry," I said. "I really am. I'm just trying to help Ashley's mom. I promised her I'd get to the bottom of this."

Lana studied me, finally arriving at some quiet decision. "Look, one thing has nothing to do with the other," she said, her voice soft. "The secret Janice was talking about is not connected to Ashley's death. I promise you that."

Knowing possibly less than I had when the day started, I thanked her and returned to the trailer to type up a draft of the second Ashley article I'd promised Ron. There was no sign of Kennie or Mrs. Berns, so I got right to work.

The Passing of the Crown

Ashley Pederson secured Battle Lake's place in the state history books when she was crowned the 54th Milkfed Mary, Queen of the Dairy, making Battle Lake the home of more Milkfed Marys than any other city. That pride turned to sorrow when Pederson was poisoned during the opening ceremony of the Minnesota State Fair.

At a ceremony on Tuesday honoring Pederson, Janice Opatz, Milkfed Mary chaperone, had this to say: "[Ashley] was a beautiful girl, inside and out. She cared deeply for those around her."

Lars Gunder, a representative for Bovine Productivity Management, the sponsor of the Milkfed Mary pageant, said, "We . . . were deeply saddened when

Ashley Pederson of Battle Lake died shortly after being crowned the 54th Milkfed Mary."

Lana Sorensen, Carlos, Minn., native and first runner-up in the pageant, received the title of Milkfed Mary in a somber passing of the crown.

The article was embarrassingly short.

Chapter 24

Wednesday morning, Mrs. Berns and Kennie finally caught me.

They'd stacked beer cans on the floor under my bed, and so when I tried to sneak out like I had the previous mornings, I made a huge clatter. Mrs. Berns rushed out of her room, hair askew and face smudged with sleep, and Kennie sat up in her bed and stared triumphantly at me. Well, as triumphantly as someone can stare when one of her eyes is mascaraed shut.

"Thought you'd get away again, missy?" Mrs. Berns cackled. "Leaving every morning before we're awake and being asleep like a rock when we get in?"

I was counting the beer cans at my feet. "It looks like you two are doing just fine without me."

"That's not the point," Kennie piped in. "This was supposed to be a fun ladies' week."

"I didn't get that memo."

"Consider yourself informed in person," she said, rolling out of bed. "Mrs. Berns and I have made some exciting discoveries at the fair, opportunities very few people know about, and we're going to share them with you today."

I stacked the beer cans into a garbage bag to bring to the recycling bin. "Can't. I have appointments. Some of us are working here."

"Tonight. We're meeting right out front of the International Bazaar at five o'clock. You'll be free then," Mrs. Berns said confidently.

She was right, of course. My only plans were to check in on Delrita this morning as she posed for her butter carving, and then head to the tour of BPM before noon. The truth was, I wouldn't mind hanging out with Mrs. Berns after that, but Kennie was a lot of work on a good day.

Catching my hesitation, Mrs. Berns sweetened the pot. "I found the super spiciest food on the planet right here at the fair. I'll buy supper, and then we'll show you what else we discovered."

Ah. She knew me too well. Food so spicy that it made my eyes water and my nose feel like it'd been bored with a drill dunked in battery acid was my new vice, now that liquor was taboo. I hadn't found anything to sate it at the fair, not even the spiciest hot sauce at the Jamaican booth. And if Mrs. Berns was getting along with Kennie, who was I to judge? Besides, what choice did I have? These two knew where I lived. "Fine. Five o'clock, in front of the Bazaar."

"You won't be sorry!" Kennie trilled.

"I already am." I was halfway out the door before I remembered. "Hey, which one of you pinched my digital camera?"

"Huh?"

"My camera. I kept it under this bench, in a soft case, and now it's gone. I scoured the whole trailer looking for it."

"I didn't take it," Kennie said.

"Me neither. Last I saw it, you were coming back from Ashley Pederson's fresh corpse, telling me about how you had seen something funky in a photo and you were going to enlarge it on your computer. Did you ever do that?"

A simultaneous explosion of memory and fear met in my brain, creating a sulfurous smell. "You *sure* neither of you has my camera?"

They shook their heads. "You think somebody stole it," Mrs. Berns said, "somebody who wanted to know what you saw when you snapped Ashley's last minutes?"

She was reading my mind.

I nodded. "But I don't even know what I saw."

"Who else knew you took those pictures?"

"Who didn't? I told Ron Sims, plus a reporter from the *Pioneer Press* that I met up with at the press conference . . ." My mouth went dry. "I think I mentioned something to Kate and Lars backstage at the Neil Diamond concert, too."

"Who's Lars?"

"He works for the company sponsoring the Milkfed Mary pageant, and there's a good chance he was sleeping with Ashley."

Mrs. Berns whistled. "I like a good thrill myself, but you got a death wish, honey. Why you like to swim with the sharks, I'll never know. You better watch your back."

I would have answered her, but I was already out the door, bag of clanking beer cans in hand, to change out of my pajamas and brush my teeth before heading over to watch Delrita and the sculptor spin in the booth.

Tall, flaxen-haired Delrita Taylor was now the first runner-up in the Milkfed Mary, Queen of the Dairy contest. She didn't draw as big of a crowd as the first and then second queen, but a steady group of fairgoers moved in and out of the Dairy Building. As I watched Delrita rotate slowly in the refrigerated booth, I wondered what crazy Minnesotan mind had invented the idea of whittling a person's head out of butter. If you were debating which dairy product would make the best medium for head carving, sure, I could understand choosing butter, but how'd you even arrive at that point in a conversation?

The intricacies of the dairy world escaped me, but imagining them freed my brain enough to reprioritize my list of duties for the day: I still didn't know a thing about the sculptor. As the last person to see Ashley alive, in fact the one who'd been trapped in a tiny spinning room with her at the moment she'd died, Glenda Haines was a likely suspect. I made a note to speak with her after today's session, something I was sure the police had already done. The fact that she was still at work spoke to their belief in her innocence, but I wasn't going to leave any butter pat unturned.

A familiar voice to my left caught my attention. It was Janice, conversing with a woman her age who was accompanied by two small children. Janice was viciously squirting disinfectant gel on her hands as she spoke. I sidled closer, hoping to eavesdrop, but her sixth sense warned her I was near.

"Mira. How are you?" Janice's eyebrows arched, making her look both years younger and pissed. She dropped the gel into her purse and massaged it into her hands. The acrid smell assaulted my nostrils.

"Fine, thank you. Delrita's doing great up there."

"Thank you," the other woman said, holding out her hand. "I'm her mother."

Janice's eyebrows dropped, and she relaxed her body language with some effort. "If you'll excuse me? I have work to do."

As Janice stalked off, I noticed for the first time that she had a small chunk of hair missing in back. Her shoulder-length, helmetlike tresses were dark and glossy, making it hard to distinguish one area from another, but there was definitely a tiny ragged spot where one layer had been sliced shorter than the rest, about a centimeter across. I wondered if Janice knew about her shitty haircut, but she was out of sight before I could ask.

I turned back to Delrita's mom and took her proffered hand. "Pleased to meet you. You must be proud of your daughter."

"Very."

"Where're you guys from?"

"Hibbing originally, but Delrita lives in White Bear Lake now."

I was surprised. "Milkfed Mary contestants aren't all newly graduated seniors?"

"Nope. They need to have graduated high school and can't be more than twenty-four years old. Delrita's twenty-two, so she's the oldest one this year."

Knowing Delrita was seven years younger than me made me feel old, not to mention cheated. She really *could* have bought her own beers the other day; she'd been using my money, not my ID.

"And who are these two?" I asked, indicating the giggly, towheaded children with her.

"My grandkids. Delrita's nieces." She tousled the hair of the nearest and smiled. "The whole family will be in and out at some time today, including my husband. We had to hire extra help to run the farm while we were away, but this is important. We're all thrilled to bursting about Delrita's placing in the pageant."

It was the second time she'd made the point, and when I gave her my full attention, I read her earnestness. She was a simple-looking woman wearing worn blue jeans and a shapeless yellow T-shirt with a smiling cat on the front. From the little I knew of family dairy farming, it was one of the most time-consuming jobs on the planet, requiring early mornings, late nights, and constant attention to your herd. Delrita's mom's calloused hands supported my theory that she was a hard worker. To have her daughter up there getting all this attention, the picture of milk-fed goodness, must be a highlight.

"You should be," I said. "Will you excuse me? I have to get to an appointment. I just wanted to stop by and say hi to Delrita."

"Nice to meet you."

"You too." I turned, shooting Delrita a wave as I passed her. She grinned and waved back just before the booth turned her away from me.

That's when I saw she was missing a curl of hair from the exact same spot as Janice.

Chapter 25

I made a note to ask Delrita about the hair weirdness later. She was scheduled for a long session in the booth, and I had to catch a bus to Bovine Productivity Management. Heading out of the building, I was surprised to run into a crowd on the outside larger than the one inside, and they were all holding signs.

MEAT IS MURDER.

FREE THE COWS.

HAVE YOU HAD YOUR GLASS OF CHEMICALS TODAY?

They appeared to be the same bunch I'd literally run into the day Ashley had been murdered. I tried to circumvent them, but it was impossible to leave the Dairy Building without wading through the protesters. As I pushed forward, head down, a brochure was shoved in my hand. On the front was a brown-eyed, sad-looking calf over the words "Can I have some of that milk?"

I looked up and recognized the sign holder as the same guy I'd collided with when leaving the Cattle Barn the other day.

"Hello," I said to him.

He ignored my greeting. "The average glass of nonorganic milk contains eight drops of pus."

My nose wrinkled. "Um, gross."

"Factory-farmed cows spend their lives in cramped quarters with barely enough room to turn around. They're force-fed antibiotics and growth hormone that end up in our food and our water supply, creating the perfect environment for a superbug strong enough to wipe out the human race, and causing both girls and boys to reach puberty prematurely."

He was tall, probably six five, and wiry. His clothes hung off him, but he was clean, and he appeared well meaning. Still.

"You see those cows over there?" I asked, pointing at the Cattle Barn behind him. "They look pretty happy to me."

"Some small farmers still respect the land and their animals and grow sustainably," he said grudgingly. "We're not here protesting *them*. We're speaking out against the corporate dairy industry, as exemplified by Bovine Productivity Management."

Now we were cooking with Crisco. "BPM? The sponsors of the Milkfed Mary, Queen of the Dairy pageant?"

"Yeah. That's why we're here." He indicated the Dairy Building. "They're pretty corporate, huh?"

"The worst." Could I pull out my notebook without him noticing?

He started warming up to his subject. "They've created some of the most toxic antibiotics in the industry, and their Milk Enhancer has some dangerous side effects."

"Like what?"

He ran his fingers through his hair and grimaced. "We can't be sure. They guard their secrets well, but we've got it on good authority that they're doing terrible things. They conduct a lot of their experiments right here in Saint Paul, at their local lab. Cows go in, but they don't come out."

We were talking about the lab I was visiting in about an hour. Interesting. "Thanks for your time."

"Wait, let me show you some pictures." He pulled out photos of scrawny-looking cows packed together in mud up to their knobby knees. If cows had knees.

"They basically don't have room to turn around. Corporate cows don't get to eat their natural diet of grass. They're fed grain, antibiotics, and noxious protein made from ground-up dead animals, including other cows." He took a breath and plunged back in. "When they calve, their babies are taken away from them and fed an artificial diet of formula so humans can have that milk, which our bodies are not designed to digest. You know how your throat gets gummy when you drink milk? That's your body telling you it wasn't made for you."

I swallowed. As a point of fact, I hadn't drunk a glass of milk in years. The faint animal smell always turned me off. I loved my cheese and ice cream, though, and I didn't want to hear any more rank details about my diet. "Well, thanks for your time. I didn't catch your name?"

"Aeon. Aeon Hopkins. There are alternatives to dairy that are good for your health, good for the environment, good for cows. One glass of rice milk contains more calcium than your average glass of cow's milk, and it's easily digestible as well as delicious."

"All right, Aeon. Thanks." His little speech had me feeling queasy and unsettled. I pushed my way through the protesters, finally reaching some breathing space.

The weather had bounced back from yesterday's storm to the same sultry climate that'd opened the State Fair. As I made my way to the south gates, I was thankful that I'd worn a sundress instead of the one pair of pants I'd packed. Already, the deep-purple cotton clung to my back, and the humidity curled the baby hairs escaping from my ponytail. I passed an ice cream booth and stared longingly at someone licking a cone of toasted almond fudge, but all I could think of was salty pus. *Cheese and rice.* If that man had ruined my taste for ice cream, there was going to be some payback.

I hopped the next bus, letting a breeze from the cracked window wash over my moist neck. Choosing the right bus—actually, buses, since I needed to transfer three times—to reach the headquarters of BPM had been no small task, and when, an hour later, I was dropped off at the edge of Saint Paul near a deserted-looking industrial area, I wondered if I'd wasted my time. I had no goal other than to size up Lars Gunder as Ashley's possible lover and find out more about BPM and its products, but I hardly expected him to spill romantic or company secrets. Heck, I hadn't even been able to coax the guy at the Scotch egg stand into divulging his recipe.

I was here, though, and so I might as well see this through.

I recognized the front of the Bovine Productivity Corporation from their web page, though their official image had Photoshopped out the barbed-wire-topped, ten-foot wall surrounding the gigantic facility. I pressed the speaker button next to the front gate, peeking through the iron bars at the scrubby brush surrounding the building. On BPM's website, the bushes had been grand oak trees. I wondered what other false fronts the business had.

When I identified myself, I was buzzed in and strode up the front sidewalk and into the main building, which sprawled like an urban high school. The interior was straight out of *Brave New World*, all cold white walls and pristine floors. An immaculate receptionist, looking like she may have been a Milkfed Mary herself in the not-too-distant past, smiled up at me as I entered. Her teeth were artificially white, and her eyes stayed flat, not reflecting her smile.

"Welcome. Can I help you?"

"I have an appointment with Lars Gunder." I shifted from one foot to the other, feeling like bacterium in a petri dish in my sweaty, sleeveless sundress and flip-flops. My hands were clenched as I waited for some sanitation system to detect and then eject me. Red lights would flare, sirens would wail, and long metal pincers would emerge from behind a secret panel, snag me by the neck, and lift me off the ground while a leather boot on a stick appeared to kick me out.

"Of course." She spoke softly into a phone and then suggested I have a seat, holding her brittle smile all the while.

No sirens.

Two white leather chairs flanked a glass table in the waiting room. I sank silently into one, or at least tried to, but my wet thighs bleated loudly against the surface. It was in everyone's best interest to pretend my body hadn't just made that noise, and so I didn't bother glancing apologetically at the receptionist.

Instead, I leaned forward, riffling through both of my magazine options: *Farm Journal* and *Dairy Farming Now.* Fortunately, Lars's arrival saved me from learning more about teat salve and the hoof-split crisis. I shook the hand he held out, glancing surreptitiously back to make sure I hadn't left a stain on the chair.

"Thank you for coming, Mira. I wasn't sure if you would."

"Wouldn't miss it," I said. "Quite an operation you have here."

"Thank you. This main building is where we do some of our testing as well as house our corporate employees. Wait until you see the lab."

I followed as he slid a card into an electronic lock, opening two automatic metal doors that led off the foyer. A whoosh of air greeted us. It smelled like rubbing alcohol, dry dog food, and something that caused an instinctual fear reaction in me. At first I thought it was the smell of the doctor's office when you were about to get a shot, or that weird tang someone who has intense stage fright gives off, but neither was it exactly.

I couldn't put my finger on it, so I ignored it. I found that by the time we'd taken four different turns and were in the bowels of the face-less, white-halled building, it was hardly noticeable, and my heartbeat returned to normal.

"Ever get lost in this place?"

He chuckled, but like the receptionist, there was something robotic about his attempt at good humor. "You get used to it. You see those guys in white coats?" He stopped, pointing at the glassed-in lab to our right, the first windowed room we'd passed. Inside, three men worked over a series of massive microscopes arranged on a stainless-steel table. They wore protective goggles, face masks, and thick rubber gloves. They were surrounded by whirring machines, delicate-looking computer equipment, and stacks of testing materials. In one particularly intricate operation, a blue liquid bubbled from one end of a glass piping unit to another, trying to escape the flames poised below.

"They're about to make history," Lars whispered.

"What're they doing?" I asked.

"Updating ME. That's Milk Enhancer, our best-selling product. In its current form, it doubles milk output on an average cow. These scientists are days away from changing the formula to *quadruple* output."

I unconsciously adjusted my boobs under my still-damp sundress. "Doesn't that hurt the cows?"

"Not at all. And think of all the hungry people in the world who could be fed if your average cow produced four times as much milk. This project is my baby. I'm currently negotiating to get the newest version of ME sent overseas."

I didn't like the sound of that. "Do you test it on real cows first?"

His reflection in the glass raised an eyebrow. "Of course. We have a full testing lab here."

"*This* isn't the testing lab?"

"Different kind of testing. You are the curious one, aren't you? I like an intelligent woman." He rested his hand on my shoulder and massaged lightly. When I glanced over, uncomfortable at the physical contact, he smiled flirtatiously, turning on the full charm.

The tightness at the corners of his lips indicated another emotion altogether, but only because I was watching for it. I could see how another person, like an eighteen-year-old, attention-hungry farm girl, would hear only the flattering words. "This lab isn't set up to accommodate animals, but we have a building on the grounds that is," he continued. "By running the product on high-quality dairy cows before releasing it to the public, we ensure farmers the best results, no worries."

I thought of Aeon and his claims that the products weren't safe. "Run into any hitches testing ME?"

"None." He abruptly dropped his hand from my shoulder. "Let's go look at the manufacturing facility and the packing warehouse."

He led me through a maze of corridors to the rear of the building, where we stepped outdoors and through another security gate before entering the blue-collar area of the plant. In the rear, out of sight from the street, were several warehouses, a behemoth of a manufacturing plant, and a distribution center. Lars stopped at a small building to grab us bright-yellow hard hats before showing me around the other buildings, smiling and waving at the hundreds of workers busily producing, boxing, and transporting cow products.

All the rear buildings we'd entered had sturdy, reinforced doors but were not walled-in like the main structure. The only exception was a small building surrounded with razor wire.

"What's in there?"

Lars smiled his oily smile, but it was beginning to wear at the seams. "That's our product-testing lab I spoke about earlier. Can't go in there. We'd interrupt important stuff."

I motioned toward an out-of-place piece of equipment. "Why does a testing lab need a bulldozer?"

"They've got to park them somewhere." Before I could point out that there were much more sensible places to store it other than inside the razor-wire fence—say, in the giant building marked GARAGE across from us—he grabbed me by the elbow and steered me into the next warehouse, the fourth one we'd entered on our tour. It was packed floor to ceiling with boxes, workers in blue shirts swarming around like busy bugs, driving forklifts and moving product. They treated us as if we were invisible. Made me wonder how many visitors they got.

We stood off to the side, out of the way of most of the traffic, and Lars numbed my brain with sleepy facts about how many boxes were packaged each day, how many pounds of stock moved through the place, and what innovations they'd made in product shipping. Soon, all his words ran together like a buzzing drone, oddly soothing in its banality: ". . . to 122 countries . . . cows six times more productive than they were twenty years ago . . . by stimulating the mammary glands and hormone level, which then produces . . . harmless . . . thoroughly tested . . . progress."

He insisted I take notes in case I wanted to write an article about BPM. I obliged, furtively scribbling the layout of the place and specifically the testing lab's location. That took all of five minutes, but his lecture continued interminably. When I was about to bleed from my eyes from boredom, his pocket buzzed. He smiled apologetically before pulling out the phone.

I watched his face turn gray as he listened to the person on the other end of the line.

"I see. When?" He grimaced. "Yes. I understand." He snapped the phone shut, his posture rigid. "I'm afraid something unexpected just popped up. I have to cut this short."

"You'll help me find the exit first, right?" I thought I was joking. Of course he'd walk me out of this maze.

"Obviously." His light tone from earlier was entirely absent. He walked briskly ahead, much more quickly than he'd moved on the entire tour.

I wondered what terrible news he'd just gotten.

He marched out of the warehouse, across the open courtyard, and to the gate surrounding the byzantine main offices. There seemed to be a commotion to my right, at the testing lab, but I couldn't do more than glance over—I saw a second bulldozer coming out of the side of the lab and, behind it, a blurry pile of brown—or I'd have missed my chance to slip inside the gate he'd charged through.

I ran to catch up with Lars as he stalked into the main offices. Once inside, the antiseptic white of the halls smothered me like cotton. I couldn't imagine having to work in this lonely, sanitary building every day, particularly after the bustle and brightness of the warehouses and manufacturing centers out back.

"Lars, could you slow down some?"

"Sure. Sorry." He pulled back a little, but not much, and the sucking clop of my flip-flops was the only sound as we hurried along the fluorescent hallways.

"So how much does it cost to be a sponsor of the Milkfed Mary pageant?" I asked. I'd let him do his PR patter, and now I was hoping he'd answer the questions I'd really come about.

"I'm not sure of exact figures."

"What does BPM get in return?"

"Positive publicity, certainly, but it's important for us to give back to the community, and that's priceless." His answer was rote, a sound bite he was used to handing out.

"I see. And did you spend time alone with any of the candidates?"

He stopped dead in his tracks, facing away from me. He didn't immediately turn, and I was afraid of what his face would look like when he did. I had crossed a line. When he finally swiveled, however, he was the picture of composure. "I think your tour is done."

"I don't know how to get out of here." He'd taken a left and then a right when we'd entered the main offices, which put us in a white hallway that looked like every other white hallway in this massive building.

"You strike me as the type who can find her way." He smirked and strode off, disappearing behind a door marked PRIVATE.

I glanced up and down the endless, ominous hallway, and suddenly, my chest felt like someone was sitting on it. *Don't be paranoid*, I told myself. *You're in a place of business, and there's people here, even if you can't see them.* I tried not to let other thoughts pollute that mantra as I flip-flopped quickly away, but it was hard not to notice that the interior of the main building resembled a mental institution.

I tried the door Lars had disappeared into. It was locked, and no one answered when I knocked. Rather than stand still and let my burbling panic boil over, I chose to keep moving. I'd run across an exit or a person sooner or later.

I took a right, then a left, and another right. The doors were numbered, but they didn't follow a pattern I could suss out. I spotted a change in lighting ahead, indicating an outside window, and my confidence level rose. It occurred to me to wonder where all the BPM employees were. The warehouse had been humming with activity, but these halls were like underground tombs. Far off, I thought I heard a sad moo followed by the agonized squeal of a monkey, but I wrote it off to my imagination.

Still, this place made me undeniably nervous, and I started to get the suffocating feeling that I remembered from the Haunted House so many years ago. In light and layout, they had nothing in common, but the trapped feeling they imparted was the same.

I picked up my pace, nearly running, only to be greeted by a peculiarly inset door. The change in light I thought I'd spotted was just a trick of my eyes, shadows from the door playing off the white walls. I leaned against the wall, breathing deeply and trying to calm my heart. I was considering yelling until someone came to me when I heard voices coming around the corner and down the hall to my left. My heart leaped with joy. I was about to attach myself to whoever was approaching when I caught their words.

"It's bloody disgusting, is what you should have told him. We're scientists, not butchers. Maybe the USDA *should* find out about it."

"And maybe you want to spend the next decade in jail, reading about your kids graduating from college or getting married instead of being there to watch it."

"You think it's that bad?"

"I think if anybody finds out, we're as dead as the . . ."

That was all I needed to hear. The only thing worse than possibly going to jail was having a stranger overhear you confessing to the bad things that would get you sent to jail. I needed to make myself scarce. I swiveled in place and jiggled furiously at the nearest doorknob, relieved when it opened.

I stumbled in, off balance, and fell forward as the automatic hinge on the door closed it behind me, taking all light with it. I whimpered in blind terror because before the door had swung shut, I'd seen the terrible secret it hid: freshly dead animal carcasses piled five feet high.

Chapter 26

The stench was overwhelming. I thrust out my hands to catch myself, and they plunged into soft fur pulled tight over cold, atrophied flesh. I swallowed a scream and jumped up and back, wiping my hands on my dress, trying to rid them of the traces of death.

The room was so dark I couldn't tell if my eyes were open or closed. The dominant color before the door had closed had been black, white, and red, the soft hides of cows matted with grime, their eyes staring glassily at nothing. I thought I'd seen an exploded stomach, a gory mess where a cow's udders should be.

Like a zombie, I backed up to the door until I felt the smooth, cool handle in my back. My heart was in my mouth, and all I wanted to do was flee.

Unfortunately, the doorknob was turning under my hand. I cowered behind the door as it opened. The light from the hallway shone over the grisly display in the center of the room. I clapped my hand over my mouth to keep from crying out. It was a small space, no more than twenty feet by twenty, filled with carnage.

The same two voices I'd heard in the hall spoke.

"Jesus. You were telling the truth."

"You think I'd lie about this?"

"You know what the USDA'll do if they find out we've been testing animals in this building? You know how many codes that violates?"

The man grunted. "Got no choice. Olafsen said we gotta speed up the experiments, both the type and number of animals, and the testing lab just isn't big enough."

My heart was splitting my chest open with its beats. I knew the name. Per Olafsen, BPM laboratory director.

"And so what the hell are we supposed to do with these?"

"Get 'em out of here. Move 'em to the grinder."

"I went to six years of college so I could drag dead cows down a hall?"

"No, you went to six years of college so you'd know that a wheelbarrow'd work much better. Let's go out to the warehouse and see what we can find."

"Damn USDA . . ."

The door swung shut. I was again immersed in darkness, the only live animal in the room. I counted to twenty, my brain floating above my body so fear didn't overwhelm me. When I reached twenty-one, I cracked the door and peeked out cautiously. Empty. I stepped into the bright, horribly white hallway and let the door sigh closed behind me.

Swallowing my bile, I glanced down to assure myself that my hands and knees were not covered in blood from where I had fallen into the pile of animal corpses. My extremities looked normal. Cold, but normal.

I had to get the hell out of here. I forced one foot after the other and kept taking rights until I arrived at the viewing window of the lab Lars had taken me by on the outset of the tour. Sucking in a deep breath, I noticed for the first time the white cameras discreetly nestled near the ceiling. Surely, somebody had viewed me enter and exit the dead room, but I couldn't turn back time.

The three scientists inside the lab still leaned over their microscopes on the stainless-steel tables. They could have been building a nuclear death ray for all I cared. I just needed to escape before the scream percolating in my belly reached my lips. I took the next two rights and found myself at the door that led to the antiseptic lobby, which was the picture of warmth compared to the grisly graveyard I'd just left.

"How was your tour?"

I jumped at the voice, then smiled wanly at the receptionist, trying for normalcy on the off chance my gruesome detour had not been witnessed. "Fine. Don't these white walls make you feel a little off-center?"

"I like them. Everything's so clean and safe here."

I nodded. "That works out well for you, then. Thanks."

As I stepped into the healing sun of a wonderfully unsanitary day, I realized what that unidentifiable odor I had first detected beyond the automatic doors had been: the scent of terrified animals.

I yanked out my phone as I stumbled toward the bus stop. It took various dead ends as I continued to search across the three return bus rides, but I finally reached the correct person at the USDA and reported what I'd seen.

They said they'd look into it.

The dead animals at BPM were probably not an anomaly at a plant that tested drugs on living creatures, but stumbling onto them had unsettled me deeply. I welcomed the protective arms of the State Fair when I finally reached it: the bustle, the smiling families on vacation, the air redolent with the smell of fry oil and the burned-sugar smell of cotton candy, the warmth of the sun. It was well past lunchtime, but I was pretty far north of hungry.

I stopped at the trailer to get a change of clothes before heading to the showers for a full-body scour. I tossed the purple sundress, one of my favorites. I couldn't scrub the smell of death off it. When I was as clean as I could get without an exorcism, I headed to the Cattle Barn, the path becoming as familiar as my driveway.

My plan was to pet some cows and visit with the Otter Tail County people who were exhibiting their animals to get a story for the paper but also find out what they knew about Ashley and Bovine Productivity Management. The second goal was a long shot, but if nothing else, I found myself looking forward to hanging out with happy, *live* cows.

I was on Judson Avenue, poised to enter the Cattle Barn, when a commotion up the road caught my attention. I figured it was Aeon and his gang continuing their protest, but then I heard a scream and saw people jumping into buildings. In seconds, I could see directly down the street with not a single person in my line of sight, so I had a clear view of the charging bull barreling toward me, its head down and massive horns curling at the edges.

It snorted and growled as it pounded closer.

What the hell?

Is someone filming a commercial? Am I dreaming?

The immobilizing force of surreality kept me anchored to the spot even as the bull kicked up his enormous hoofed heels and pawed angrily at the ground. He stampeded toward me, his horns as wide across as my arm span and much thicker. He tossed his head and stared me down as he charged, white showing in his rolling eyes.

I couldn't move.

Chapter 27

His grunts were ferocious as he bore down, and other than peeing my pants a little, I was paralyzed. All my flight response had been used up in the horror room at BPM.

The few slippery seconds it took my frazzled nerves to react were all the bull needed to cover the three hundred yards separating us. When he was close enough to smell, my brain finally sent a message through to my nerve endings and I tensed to move, but it was too late.

If I hadn't been jerked roughly from the side, I'd have been decorating the beast's horns.

"Why didn't you run?" Aeon asked, panting, his expression shocked. We were leaning on the inside doorway of the barn.

I started to tremble as I realized I'd almost been gored. "I don't know. It didn't seem real." Thirty seconds late, my reactions fully caught up with me, and I slumped to the ground, my legs too shaky to support me.

He ran an unsteady hand through his hair. "I told you to watch out for the dairy industry."

I appreciated his attempt at humor, even though I was at risk of shock-vomiting on his shoes. "I have a hunch that one wasn't a good milker anyhow." I laughed weakly at our lame jokes. "But in all seriousness, we should call security. He could hurt someone."

Aeon nodded at the people screaming and running for high ground, staying just ahead of the rampaging bull. "Looks like someone already did."

We watched as three men with electric prods raced past from one direction, three from another. They slowly directed the brute back the way he had come as a seventh guy stood by with a handgun. The scene was ripe with tension.

This immediate section of street had been cleared by the creature's initial pass, but small groups were moving forward to catch a glimpse of the action, like storm chasers on the heels of a tornado. One angry lunge of the bull and he'd be on the idiotic rubberneckers in seconds, smashing them like mosquitoes.

The seven herders seemed to know what they were doing, though, and kept leading the animal back, away from the crowds. After an interminable half an hour, the bull was coaxed into a trailer at the end of the block, and people swarmed outside, buzzing with the collective high of disaster averted.

"Where'd he come from?" I asked.

"There's a rodeo here tonight," Aeon said darkly. "One of the bulls must have escaped."

"Let me guess. You're going to tell me how cruel the rodeo industry is." My delayed adrenaline rush had passed, and my legs had stopped quaking.

"It is. But that's not my thing right now." He looked me up and down. "You sure you're OK?"

"I'm OK." Thoroughly cured of my cow crush, but OK. "Thanks for saving me. What're you doing here, anyway?" I asked him. "I don't see your sign."

"My sign?"

"Your protest sign."

"It wasn't sewed on." He smiled genuinely. "I can walk around without it."

I smiled back. "Good to know."

"Anyhow, I gotta run. Take care."

After one last searching look to make sure I was OK, he took off in the same direction the trailer carrying the bull had gone. I collected myself and then walked toward the rear of the Cattle Barn to seek out the Otter Tail folks. The area was still vibrating with excitement, and people whispered as I walked past. I imagined they were sussing out how someone too stupid to jump out of the way of a charging bull was allowed out without a babysitter.

"I didn't think it was real," I mumbled, confirming their suspicions.

I speed-walked to the rear of the barn, where most people had missed seeing exactly which silly girl had played impromptu matadora. When I located the Otter Tail County stalls, all three were empty of people but full of cows. I waited for ten minutes until two grizzled men and a broad-shouldered teenager in T-shirts and jeans showed up.

"Nice animals you have here," I said, indicating the two black and whites and the brownish-reddish one. My brain was still a little jangly or I would've come up with a much better greeting.

The tallest guy appeared to also be the oldest. His gray hair put him at about sixty, but when he smiled, his eyes crinkled merrily and took ten years off my estimate. "Thank you. You a farmer?"

"No. I'm a reporter from the *Battle Lake Recall*."

"Ayuh. How's old Ron Sims doing?"

"The usual. Taking long lunches and trying to run the world from behind his desk."

The tall guy chuckled. "That sounds about right. I'm Jim, this is my grandson Dan. We're from over by Fergus. Jack here is from Underwood."

"Pleased to meet all of you. I'm Mira." I pointed at the ribbons nailed to the fronts of the stalls. "Looks like you came off pretty well. What'd you guys win?"

"I've got dairy cows here, Holsteins, but you probably knew that," he said kindly. "Lucinda won a blue ribbon, but Jenny didn't place this year."

I pulled my pad and paper out of my purse. "All right if I use some of this in an article? Ron has me covering Battle Lake as well as all of Otter Tail County's presence at the State Fair."

"That's fine. And Dan here has a grand prize–winning Araucana over in the poultry barn that he wouldn't mind showing off if you want to head there next."

I was scribbling furiously. I wrote *lizard? duck?* next to the word "Araucana." "You must be very proud."

Dan beamed but didn't respond.

"Jack, your cow won something, too, right?" Jim asked.

"This one here's a beef cow," Jack responded, "a Limousin, and a red ribbon will have to do for him."

Thoughtfully, I stopped writing, my competitive spirit rising to the top. "Do they have any housecat exhibitions? I've got a real beauty at home."

Dan snorted, a failed attempt to hold back a laugh rather than a sniff of judgment. "Just livestock."

"Bummer." Tiger Pop would have to settle for being grand kitty in my own little world. "Say, did you hear about Ashley Pederson's death? She was from Battle Lake."

Darkness fell over their faces at my painfully awkward segue. "I know Steven, her dad," Jack said. "His heart's broken. Saddest thing I ever heard when I found out his daughter died."

I nodded. "The police say she was poisoned."

"I don't know who'd do that," Jim said, shaking his head. "She was a sweet girl, and all of us Otter Tail farmers were so proud of her. She represented us well."

He either hadn't heard the rumors or was choosing to be respectful speaking of the dead. I liked both options for him. "Her family didn't have any enemies, did they?"

Jim's eyes widened. "Hold on. This isn't *Law & Order*. You're talking about Battle Lake. Worst thing that'll happen is you lose some fingers in a farming accident. We look out for each other."

"So what happened to Ashley?"

They shook their heads and studied their feet. The cow nearest Jim bent its leg and leaned on him, a friendly gesture like a dog resting against his owner. Jim pushed the cow away, firmly but kindly. It was odd for me to see people so comfortable with huge animals. I tried a different tack. "Do you guys know anything about Bovine Productivity Management? They're the company sponsoring the Milkfed Mary pageant."

This got a reaction. All three men shuffled, and Jim spit on the cement. "We prefer to farm the old-fashioned way," he said. "One year, only once, I needed the money bad enough to try their Milk Enhancer. Never again. The milk tasted funny, salty and sweet at the same time, and I couldn't keep up with the milking. Hurt my cows."

"I heard worse stuff about what that ME does," Dan said, speaking up for the first time. His granddad shot him a look, and he moved his weight from one leg to the other nervously. "Nothing I know for sure, though."

"Ayuh," Jim said. "You should ask the swindler over at the BPM booth."

"Bovine Productivity has a booth here?"

"Absolutely. We can't afford most of their stuff, but they figure it doesn't hurt to try. Ask him about their Milk Enhancer."

My talk of BPM and Ashley had brought down the congenial mood we'd started with, and I felt bad. "Thank you for your time." I was walking away when something occurred to me. I turned and addressed Jim. "When your cows have calves, do they get to drink their mom's milk, or do you feed them formula?"

He patted the back of his cow. "Formula's expensive, so I let them nurse as God intended. They eat only organic grass and feed for the same reason. Mind you, small family farmers like me are a dying breed. The agribusinesses are choking us, squeezing all the milk and meat they can out of an animal with their chemicals and corporate farms."

Dan and Jack nodded in agreement.

"Thanks." As I walked away, I wondered what else Aeon had been right about. If most of the milk we drank was stolen from the babies it was intended for, did that also mean that every glass of milk really did have eight drops of pus in it?

My stomach did a greasy flip as I thought about all the cheese I'd eaten since I'd arrived at the fair. Maybe I'd need to sample dairy-free life, I thought as I caught sight of the BPM booth. It was on the far side of the cavernous barn, in the middle of a long line of agricultural product stalls. BPM had more signs than the rest, so many that I was surprised I hadn't noticed it on a previous trip. I strode up, introduced myself to the fiftysomething, heavy-browed man behind the counter, and asked him if ME really worked.

Not bothering to ask why I wanted to know, he beetled his bushy eyebrows and pointed to the cow tethered to his booth. "See for yourself," he said.

Her udders were engorged and popping with veins. She stood lightly on her back feet and munched on the feed in front of her. "Doesn't all that milk hurt her udders?" I asked.

"Not at all. Cows love to make milk. It's what their bodies were created for."

As he came around the front of the counter, I noticed there was something oddly feminine about him. It wasn't his height or build—he came from some hearty stock and was a good five inches taller than me. His hair was close-trimmed, too, and his arms and hands were as hairy as a hobbit's.

I couldn't put my finger on what was giving me that impression, and so I pulled my stare away from his body and watched as he leaned over to squeeze a teat. The cow recoiled as if she'd been poked with a hot iron. White milk whizzed out, hitting the ground with a ricocheting force.

"Wow. Impressive." I made a note to try to break her out and set her free before the fair was over. "Do you have any materials I can take with me?"

He handed me a stack of brochures, which I intended to throw away as soon as I left the building. They wouldn't tell me anything the BPM website hadn't. I neared the entrance of the Cattle Barn, sidestepping manure deposits and keeping a wary eye out for escaped behemoths.

Nothing left to do except discover what the Milkfed Mary sculptor knew for sure.

Chapter 28

I scanned the street for bulls before darting out. I stuck close to the buildings but hit a vulnerable, open area near the go-kart pit. Rather than risk it, I picked up speed and sprinted the last two hundred yards to the Dairy Building.

It was stuffed full of fairgoers milling around, pushing against each other, lowing, looking for food. I didn't know if humans had always behaved so much like cows or if the fair just put an agricultural spin on everything.

Well over a hundred thousand people attended the Minnesota State Fair on any given day, so while you got a lot of the blonde, blue-eyed farmers in town for the livestock and agriculture exhibits, you also ran across the Goth kids who gathered to check out the animals and ride the rides, world-weary city people as giddy as schoolchildren at the idea of immersing themselves in a simpler time, and recent immigrants and out-of-towners who wanted to experience Minnesota Nice firsthand.

Children tugged at their parents, leading them to the merry-go-round or the nearest snow cone vendor, shiny young people on first dates stared in awkward terror as farm animals calved in front of them at the Miracle of Birth Center, and people generally gathered in good cheer to celebrate music, food, and the state's agricultural roots. It was Disneyland with cows, made more festive by its ephemeral status. From start to finish, the Minnesota State Fair lasted only twelve days, always ending on Labor Day.

Of all the joys of the fair, the food was the most legendary. When a sunburned guy strode by with a creamy white sundae smothered in chocolate sauce, my militant antidairy resolve weakened. What if the ice cream at the State Fair was only made with the milk from happy, organically fed Minnesota cows, like Jim raised?

Yes. *That* was the reality I was going to accept.

The fact that I hadn't eaten since breakfast sealed the deal. I waited my turn in line at Dairy Goodness. Yum. Nothing tasted quite so good as compromised principles.

The humid air melted the ice cream quickly, which was just how I liked it. Melting ice cream has worlds more flavor than hard frozen. I licked and smiled, my tummy encouraging my mouth to keep up the good work. The cone was almost demolished when I reached the Milkfed Mary booth on the other end of the building and noticed that it was empty of people. Real people, anyhow. It held Lana's likeness carved in butter, and now Delrita's poised next to it, both of them looking like yellow cartoon renditions of generic, smiling, big-haired females. I grimaced at the empty booth. Had my gluttony cost me a chance to speak to the sculptor?

I moved over to the blue curtain, tossing my napkin and cone wrapper in a trash can.

"Knock knock?" I said to the curtain.

"Be out in a minute!" a pleasant female voice answered, and sure enough, sixty seconds later, I was face-to-face with Glenda Haines. She was a petite woman with strong hands and a lined face. Her winter coat was slung over her arm.

"I start sweating the second I step outside of that refrigerator," she said. "My body knows it's still summer, even if I refrigerate it for half a day."

I held out my hand. "I'm Mira. I'm a reporter for the Battle Lake newspaper, in Ashley's hometown. Would you be able to answer a few questions?"

She closed her eyes and kept them closed, a tiny frown on her face. When she reopened them, she had tears filling the corners. "I'm trying to move past that awful incident."

"I'm very sorry, I really am, but I told Ashley's mom I'd see what I could find out. She's devastated."

Glenda sighed. "Fine. But I'm starving. Let's go to JD's and I'll tell you the little I know."

I didn't have much time until I was supposed to meet Mrs. Berns and Kennie, but I wasn't going to let this opportunity slip. I followed her to JD's Eating Establishment, whose slogan was "Definitely Nothing on a Stick!" Their little diner offered a red countertop and stools. I saved Glenda a seat while she grabbed a cheeseburger and fries. When she returned, I eyed her fries hungrily. The ice cream cone had been pretty small.

"How long have you been carving the Milkfed Mary heads at the fair?" I asked.

She bit into her burger, and grease oozed down her chin. It smelled delicious, but I refused to rethink my position on eating red meat. After all, *I* was red meat, too, and I'd already waffled on one stance today, no matter how weakly or briefly it'd been held.

"This is my first year."

This triggered an alarm bell. If she was new to the operation, she might be the weak link, someone who could easily be paid off to look the other way as Ashley was poisoned.

Or to poison her. "Who did the carving before then?"

"June Gerritt. She's the best, the queen in our field. All of us butter sculptors dream of reaching her level. That woman makes butter come to life under her fingers. And have you seen the hair on her carvings? Stunning. Voluminous. *Creamy.* I could spend a whole lifetime studying under her and not become that good. God doesn't spread his gifts out as equally as we'd like." She crunched on a fry emphatically. "Anyhow, when I got the call to fill in for June, I thought I'd died and gone to heaven."

"So you're just temporary?"

"Yeah. June broke her arm a week before the fair opened. Don't know how."

June Gerritt's coincidentally being rendered unable to work the same week as a Milkfed Mary was murdered in her booth was momentarily less interesting to me than the underground world of butter artistry that I'd stumbled onto. "How many of you are there? Butter sculptors, that is?"

"More than you'd think. Between state fairs, weddings, corporate retreats and all, we keep busy. But the Minnesota State Fair? That's the top of the heap, let me tell you. Actors have their Broadway. Country singers have the Grand Ole Opry. Seed artists have the Corn Palace. Us butter sculptors have the Milkfed Mary booth at the Minnesota State Fair."

I chewed on that. "So Ashley's death must have been pretty devastating."

She set her burger down and placed her hand on mine, her eyes beseeching. "It was the worst day of my life. The very worst day. I had a new snowsuit all ready to go, and I was as nervous as a bride on her wedding night as I traipsed up those stairs into The Booth."

I could hear the capital letters on her words. She was a bit of a ham, but harmless, I'd decided. No killer described butter-carved hair as "voluminous."

"I followed right behind Ashley, who looked a little peaked," she continued. "I mentioned that to the police already, you know. No, that girl didn't look right, but she was a professional, and she kept that smile plastered on her face right up until the lights went out. As soon as they did, I heard her begin to thrash and gag. I felt around for her, but it was as dark as the devil's heart in there."

"Did she throw up?"

"Yes, but I didn't know that for sure until the lights came back on. So I hear the coughing and gagging, and I'm reaching around for her, and she swings her arms and knocks me over. Before I could get to my feet, the lights snapped on, and she was there on the floor, turning the oddest red color."

"What'd you do next?" I prodded.

She looked away from me, picking up a french fry before putting it down, uneaten. "I ran out to get help. I'm not proud of the fact that I didn't stay and try CPR or something, but the police told me I couldn't have done anything for her. Once their skin starts turning color, they said, the cyanide's already got them in its death grip."

"The police told you what kind of poison it was?"

Her mouth widened in an O. "I wasn't supposed to spill. Darn it."

I nodded. "I wonder where somebody'd get cyanide."

She nodded in agreement. "I know! This is Minnesota!" She said the last part as if the idea of poison being in the state were as ludicrous as the pope stealing a pair of high-tops. *He's the father of the Catholic Church! Banana pants!*

"The police have any leads?"

"Not that they told me. I'm just an artist." She shrugged. "Police don't take us creative types real seriously. Going back into the booth after Ashley died was scary, but it was all disinfected and clean. I think I did a pretty good job on Lana."

She ate the fry this time, chewing as she spoke. "Delrita was hard. She's got those round cheeks, which can be difficult to re-create in butter. Too much and it looks like she's smuggling acorns. Not enough, and it doesn't resemble the subject."

"You're doing good," I assured her. "Beautiful. Say, you wouldn't happen to have June Gerritt's phone number?"

She pulled out her cell. "I've got her on speed dial what with all my questions. Here you go."

I wrote down the number. "I really appreciate your time, Glenda."

"My pleasure. You're going to stop by to see Brittany's carving tomorrow?"

"Wouldn't miss it for the world," I said as I took off to meet my roomies. And if I'd had the foresight of a hamster, I would have instead run in the opposite direction.

Chapter 29

As I strolled toward the International Bazaar, I wondered how I was going to locate Mrs. Berns and Kennie. The front entrance spanned a block, and there were two large side entrances. The entire area was swarming with people, pawing through the silks and spices and standing in line for Minnesota-ized fried rice, baba ghanoush, and tostadas.

We should have been more specific about our meeting location, I thought, right up until the main Bazaar entrance was in sight. That's when I realized those two Battle Lake ladies wouldn't, *couldn't*, blend into any crowd. They were both dressed like flirty cowgirls in the flouncy gingham miniskirts professional square dancers wore. Mrs. Berns was attired in head-to-toe green and Kennie in pink, but they otherwise wore matching cowboy hats, neckerchiefs, snap-front checked shirts, and cowboy boots. They looked like they'd walked straight out of a *Lawrence Welk* episode.

When I neared, two short-haired women in comfortable shoes were inviting them to a parade later that night. "It *does* sound like a happy parade," Mrs. Berns was saying earnestly, "but we have plans with our friend Mira here. Maybe another time."

The women nodded and left, stealing glances over their shoulders at the two Battle Lake cowgirls.

"Why are you both dressed like that?" I asked.

"You'll see." They giggled in unison. It was an alarming sound.

Mrs. Berns grabbed my hand. "Before our memorable evening begins, let's get that spicy food I promised you."

She led me and Kennie toward the restaurants edging the Bazaar. We strode past the International Grill, Island Noodles, and West Indies Soul Food before stopping in front of the Caribbean Shack. That's when I sorrowfully realized that I wasn't going to get my fire-food fix tonight. "Thanks, Mrs. Berns, but I've been here. Their food is only Minnesota spicy."

"Out front here, maybe, but we've got a special seat in back." She winked at the lean man behind the counter and squeezed the top of her arms together in the universal, saucy "see my cleavage" gesture. Unfortunately, her girls were closer to her knees than her shoulders and had no way of responding to the command. The counter guy chuckled good-naturedly as he waved us inside his workspace, through a side door that led behind the customer counter, and toward the rear. Two women took his place out front.

The back room was as clean as the laboratory I'd visited earlier, only with soul and delicious, hearty smells. Here, the stainless-steel counters held pots of rice and dried red beans, spices arranged in alphabetical order, and sealed pots of homemade jerk sauce. I also smelled some spicy heat in the air, the promise of a raucous chili pepper, something that'd clear my nose and jump-start my heart.

"Have a seat," he said, indicating three chairs for us. His voice was melodic, rising and falling like the sea in the middle of each word. "You'll have the usual, then, Mrs. Berns?"

"Three of 'em."

He yanked out three plates, flipping them in the air before setting them on the counter, lifted a steaming lid off a pot on the stove, and scooped out three servings of red beans and rice. The food smelled as comforting as hot tea on a cold night.

Replacing that lid, he opened another, and every corner of the back room was filled with the tangy scent of jerk seasoning. The smell was both sweet and peppery and made my nose tingle like I needed to sneeze. He handed us each a steaming plate, which we balanced on our knees.

"Thank you," I said, accepting a fork. In my experience, jerk wasn't overly spicy, but the food looked delicious, and I was starving.

"Not yet," he said, and reached into the refrigerator. He pulled out a gallon jar of what looked like chopped onions laced with bits of carrot, both floating in a brine. When he removed the lid, I stood, drawn to the piquant, vinegary smell.

"What is it?"

"Onion relish." He smiled. "It's not for little boys."

"Then you'll be happy to know you've got three real women here," Mrs. Berns said around a mouthful of rice.

"Make that two." Kennie removed her neckerchief and mopped her brow, which was dripping makeup-colored sweat. "This here is hot enough as is."

"Lots, please." I held out my plate and didn't take it back until it was generously covered with the white-and-orange relish. I sat back down and took a bite. The soft and warm rice and beans hit my tongue first, with the cool onion relish tickling the top of my mouth.

I moved it all around before biting in.

The first taste sensation was the zip of the vinegar as I sank my teeth into a surprisingly mild onion. The second was the soothing earthiness of the beans. The last, coming out of left field, was a flash so hot it made my eyes smoke. I started coughing. "What's in here?"

He laughed. "Red Savina habaneros. The spiciest pepper known to man, and now, to woman."

"Is it in the beans and rice?" I asked. The heat in my head made it difficult to speak. Little bundles of dynamite were popping off, starting in my nose and working their way to my brain, clearing one area before blasting another.

"See here?" He indicated the orangish-red bits in the onion relish. "This is the pepper."

Tears ran down my cheeks as the heat rush began to subside, leaving euphoria in its wake. I felt alert and alive, like I could see in the dark and read people's minds. I held out my plate. "More, please."

He looked at Mrs. Berns in mock sadness. "Ah. She is as bad as you said."

She smiled around her fork. "I warned you."

He spooned a second layer of onion relish on my plate and cracked us each a can of diet cola. I rarely drank soda, but the combination of fiery food and sweet carbonation was too much of a treat to pass up.

"Can I get some ice?" Kennie asked. Most of her foundation had melted into her collar, but her eyes glowed unusually bright. Pepper wuss. She hadn't even tried the onion relish and was sweating her face off.

Taking a cooling chug off my can, I had a sudden vision of Ashley drinking her last diet cola, the only food or drink anyone saw her partake of during the window of time in which she'd been poisoned. Lana had witnessed Ashley open her can and then pour it over ice.

Could the cyanide have been in the cubes?

The pepper-induced thought was revelatory. It would explain why no one else had been poisoned. If I was right, who'd supplied the ice? I made a mental note to look into that, turning back to my homemade, soul-cleansing food.

Later, after our bellies were full and heads completely cleared, Mrs. Berns gave the booth owner a generous tip, and the three of us made our way to the west end of the fair. We passed the Haunted House on our way, something I'd taken pains to steer clear of since I'd arrived. Avoiding it was hard, since it was situated right next to the International Bazaar, but with a map and a little creativity, it had been possible. I didn't want to freak out Kennie and Mrs. Berns by exposing my neuroses, though, so I simply looked away as we walked in front of the mansion and pretended I couldn't hear the screams, though my palms grew wet and my stomach bubbled.

Delayed reaction to the spicy food, I told myself.

Mrs. Berns was eyeing me suspiciously, so I took control of the conversation. "Where're we going now? You'll have to tell me sooner or later."

"First, put this on." Mrs. Berns fished in her purse and pulled out a Care Bear pin. Funshine Bear, if I wasn't mistaken, and he was about an inch and a half tall, yellow, with a smiling sun on his belly.

I stared at the pin, not understanding. "What do you mean?"

"You gotta wear it to get in, dummy," Mrs. Berns said.

Too many questions. Head full. Play dead.

"Here, I'll do it." Kennie grabbed the pin from Mrs. Berns, inserted the pointy end into the strap of my second sundress of the day, and snapped it tight. "Perfect, though I still think Grumpy Bear would have been a better fit for her."

Again, that shared snicker that turned my blood cold.

"You have to tell me something about where we're going, or I'm not taking another step." I stood firm in front of a barn.

Mrs. Berns nodded at it. "It has something to do with what you see up there, Mary."

Mary? Was she becoming senile? I glanced up at the green, blue, and white sign that read SHEEP AND POULTRY. Because I knew Mrs. Berns so well, I made a leap from sheep to Mary, who had a little lamb. "Sheep and lambs aren't the same thing."

"Close enough," she said, throwing up her hands. "And I told you something, like you asked, and that's all I'm gonna say. Besides, we're almost at our destination."

My head spinning, we navigated two more blocks through the crowds and then past what I thought was the westernmost edge of the fair—the Swine Barn. When we kept walking, I said, "I don't think there's anything back here."

Rather than answer, they kept moving forward as the crowds thinned. Though it'd be another two hours before the sun set, the night was still hot and the road was dusty from animals crossing. I wished I had brought some water.

We veered sharply to the right and walked another four hundred yards to stop in front of a pole barn colored a dull brown. Few people were around, yet both Mrs. Berns and Kennie instantly tensed up, scanning the perimeters as if we were about to exchange top-secret spy information.

"What is it?" I whispered. They shushed me and slipped between the barn's metal doors, tugging me in behind them and closing the doors tightly.

We had arrived.

Chapter 30

"Fair Bear badges?" a gruff voice asked.

The room we found ourselves in was close and dark except for a slit of light between the doors opposite the entrance. The buzz of a crowd leaked through the crack, and the air smelled like manure and close-packed bodies.

Mrs. Berns and Kennie produced Care Bear pins from their oversize purses, so I flashed Funshine. The doorman ushered us in through a sealed door, and then between metal gates, down some sort of animal run, and out into an amazingly well-lit barn.

The smell was stronger in here, musky and pungent. Platform benches ringed the interior, cascading down to the middle, where they encircled a large corral with half a dozen sheep milling around. The benches were packed with men, women, and children, most of them wearing blue jeans and snap-front western shirts, and more than a few in cowboy hats and boots, just like Mrs. Berns and Kennie. The crowd was rumbling, as if something exciting were about to happen.

"What is this?"

"Welcome to the Mutton Busting competition!" Kennie whooped.

I looked over at the sweet little fluffy balls of sheep in the corral and back at the audience, staring avidly at animals. "Is it like cockfighting?"

"Not at all," Mrs. Berns said. "We just ride 'em. We don't make them fight each other."

"We?"

"Well, not technically." Mrs. Berns eyeballed Kennie. "The mayor here exceeds the weight limit, and why the hell would I want to ride a sheep? Fortunately, Kennie had a burning desire to be a Mutton Busting clown. I'm her manager. Turns out I like her just fine when I can tell her what to do." Mrs. Berns smiled broadly.

I began piecing together odd, unconnected observations I'd made the last few days. Kennie and Mrs. Berns getting along. Kennie complaining about soreness, then giggling conspiratorially with Mrs. Berns. Both of them smelling like beer and wool when they stumbled in late at night. "And the Care Bears?"

"Fair Bears," Kennie corrected. "This here is a secret operation under the radar of the State Fair Corporation. Only Fair Bears know about it, among other fair secrets."

I glanced around at the be-Wranglered audience, most of them looking like hardworking farmers in their thirties and forties, all of them leaning forward eagerly to watch as petite men and women walked among the little white puffs of sheep on the floor, deciding which one they'd ride. Everyone wore a Care Bear pin on their shirt.

"I'm in."

Mrs. Berns whooped. "Thought so. Go save us a seat while I get Kennie's clown makeup on." Mrs. Berns and I exchanged an insider smile when Kennie wasn't looking. Clown makeup was all Kennie ever wore.

I found a spot toward the front. The air was ripe with the smell of agitated livestock, and the air was dusty. The sheep all wore twelve-inch numbers on canvas squares tied to their backs and appeared completely oblivious to the ignominy about to be visited on them.

Probably for the best.

When one of the riders chose a sheep, they pasted a number on their back that matched the canvas number on the sheep. Then they moved to the sidelines to await the beginning of the competition. Once all the sheep were claimed, "We Will Rock You" blared over the speakers.

I wondered how an event this large and noisy could ever be a secret. People walking past the building had to hear the hubbub, though muted, emanating from the walls. As if in answer to my question, Kate Lewis appeared across the floor. She wore a brown hoodie and was hunched over, but she was still recognizable.

She got the attention of and then whispered fiercely to a young cowboy, who leaned against the ring and generally ignored her until she slipped him something. He glanced at his hand and nodded once without looking at her. Then she took off. I couldn't see what they'd exchanged, but I had a hunch.

When Mrs. Berns returned, her beautiful, wrinkled face flushed, I asked her if people bet on the Mutton Busting.

"Of course. We're Minnesotans, not Mormons."

Pieces of the puzzle were starting to come together. It made sense that Kate would be betting on the show if she were in serious debt, as implied by her embezzling. As an emcee strolled to the middle of the ring, microphone in hand, I had a second thought that canceled out the first. "Mrs. Berns, do the sheepboys here have access to bulls, too?"

"You betcha. Rodeos, mutton busting, cow roping. All that good stuff goes together."

I knew that I hadn't been the target of the escaped beast today. Wild, charging bulls weren't exactly precision instruments, and there were easier ways to hurt someone. Besides, I couldn't think of a single reason for anyone at the fair to want to attack me. But releasing it *would* bring more attention to the fair, and as Chaz the *Pioneer Press* reporter had told me, there was no such thing as bad attention when you were trying to make money.

If my hunch was correct, I hadn't just witnessed Kate place a bet on a sheep. No, I'd seen her pay off the guy who'd released the bull. On impulse, I asked Mrs. Berns to save my seat and hurried over to the cowboy Kate had just spoken with.

"Hi," I said.

He didn't look up. He took his laconic, lone rider image very seriously.

"Who's your money on?" I asked.

"Number 23," he said, indicating a little man with blue cowboy boots and a matching hat who was circling his sheep. "He's won the last two competitions."

"Thanks for the tip. Say, if I wanted to release a bull into the State Fair and make it look like an accident, who would I talk to?"

He finally looked up. His eyes, visited by fear and then settled by anger, gave me all the answer I needed.

He tugged his hat low and marched off.

I returned to my seat next to Mrs. Berns, feeling satisfaction at having solved another small mystery. And my discovery established that Kate was a desperate woman, one willing to go to extreme measures. I needed to track her down and ask her some questions.

But no time for that now. The mutton busting was about to begin, and Kennie was prancing into the ring in all her clown glory.

The crowd went wild.

Chapter 31

In the end, I decided one Mutton Busting event in a lifetime was more than enough. Turns out sheep don't really like to have people on their backs, no matter how skinny they are. It scares them, and they poop when they're scared.

Kennie and Mrs. Berns both had business to attend to after the event, so I ambled back to the trailer on my own. Since no one was around, I settled for firing up my computer and researching one Aeon Hopkins, cow rights activist.

I couldn't help but wonder how anybody knew anything before the internet as I sorted through the 323,000 hits initially displayed. I narrowed the search, slapping a pair of quotation marks around his name, and was rewarded with a manageable twenty-four matches.

The first site I pulled up was called Mad Cows, Mad People (MCMP). The page layout and graphics were rudimentary, bright and garish colors competing against horrific animations of tottering cows being led to slaughter. I clicked the "About Us" link and was brought to a description of an organization that opposed everything Bovine Productivity Management represented:

> The goal of MCMP is to fight to have animals and the
> earth treated with respect. We believe that animals
> are not on the earth for human gain and that they
> have worth in and of themselves. MCMP believes civil

disobedience, protests, referendums, and force are all acceptable means of spreading our message.

According to the staff page, Aeon Hopkins was the director.

I returned to the search page and discovered that the next three hits were far less flattering. All of them linked Aeon's name with eco-terrorism, the first tying him to the bombing of a California lab that experimented on monkeys; the second covering a trial where he'd been charged with breaking windows and spray-painting "Puppy Killers" all over a college building that housed beagles used for invasive testing; and the third connecting him to the liberation of calves being raised for veal.

Only one article delved into Aeon's past.

Apparently, civil disobedience ran in his blood. He was the son of Chandra Hopkins and Chad Jacobs, the founding members of GreenFreedom, an international group legendary for their outrageous animal- and earth-liberation acts. The most famous incident had involved chaining thirty people to the deck of an oil rig out at sea until the company agreed to pay retribution for a recent oil spill that had destroyed miles of coastline and killed thousands of seabirds, but there were hundreds more examples.

The rest of my research didn't reveal anything else remarkable, but I couldn't help ruminating over the relative mildness of picketing a state fair. Aeon's gig here seemed tame for someone of his counterculture status, unless there was a grander scheme, say the murder of a Milkfed Mary? I pushed the thought away as soon as it appeared. Aeon had saved me from a bull goring today. That didn't seem like the move of a coldhearted killer.

I yanked out my notebook and flipped to the page with June Gerritt's number. It was almost nine o'clock. I hoped I wasn't calling too late.

She picked up on the second ring. "Hello?"

"Hi. You don't know me. My name is Mira James, and I'm covering the Minnesota State Fair for my local newspaper, the *Battle Lake Recall*. Do you have time to answer a question or two?"

"I suppose, but I'm not there this year. I broke my arm."

"That's what I'm calling about." I doodled as I spoke. "This is the first fair where you haven't been the head carver, right?"

She clucked. "It's true, and what a year to miss. That poor Pederson girl died right in the booth."

"Yeah, I know. I talked to your replacement, Glenda, today. She's still pretty shook up."

"But she's doing a good job. I stopped by to look at her first two carvings. Beautiful work."

"I agree," I said, crossing my fingers to protect me from the consequences of my lie. I wasn't an appreciator of butter art. "Can I ask how you broke your arm?"

"No suspicious circumstances, if that's what you're wondering. I fell off my shoe crossing the street. Damn clogs."

Well. That was about as innocent a way to incapacitate yourself as could be. "Sorry to hear that. Thanks for talking to me, though. I hope you heal soon."

With my phone still in hand, I decided to follow up on another lead. Three rings, then four. Then five. I glanced at the digital clock across the trailer. It was after ten in Florida.

"Hello?" The connection was scratchy, and it sounded like the woman speaking was in a crowd.

"Hi. Is this Shelby? Shelby Spoczkowski from Minnesota?"

A pause. "Hold on." When she came back on the line, there was still some static, but the crowd noises had disappeared. "Who is this?"

"I'm a reporter covering the murder of Ashley Pederson, recently crowned Milkfed Mary."

"I heard about that." A click followed by an inhale came down the line. She'd lit a cigarette. "You're reaching pretty far back for a story, though. I haven't been connected to the pageant since the seventies."

"You moved to Florida afterward?"

"Not right away. I stayed around home till I met my husband. He moved us to Florida and then dumped me for a Barbie doll with fake boobs." A deep drag on her cigarette. "Back then, I didn't know a soul out here. But you didn't call to ask about my personal life."

"No. I wanted to ask you what you know about Janice Opatz."

A few beats of quiet, then: "The only Janice I know was Janice Klepper. She was involved in the Milkfed Mary pageant the same year as I was."

"Are you still in touch with her?"

"Not really. Is she in trouble?"

"No, not at all. I just want to make sure I get the facts straight on everyone. Janice was your first runner-up?"

There was wheezing on the other end of the line, and it took me a second or two to realize she was laughing. "What's so funny?"

"Oh, you had to have been there, I guess. Janice wasn't first runner-up. She wasn't even a contestant."

My blood thundered in my ears. "What?"

"Janice's older sister was the first runner-up the year I won. *Barbara* Klepper. Blonde, blue-eyed, the whole package. Too bad she was a snake. Slept around with everyone's boyfriend, including her sister's. Janice idolized Barbara, followed her everywhere, begged her way into being a gofer for the pageant chaperone so she could spend more time in her sister's shadow. Janice refused to believe it when she found out Barbara had done the dirty with her boyfriend."

Apparently, boyfriend stealing was a bit of a tradition in the Milkfed Mary crowd. "How'd Janice find out about the cheating?"

Shelby paused in her smoking, and I heard a stamp and a click as she put out the first and lit the second cigarette. "I told her, actually. Felt sorry for her. She was a bit of an odd duck and had the strangest quirks. For example, she'd rub her hands together endlessly when she was agitated, like she was washing them but there was no water? She just about wore her skin off when I told her about Barbara. She wouldn't hear it, of course, and she was so ticked off at me for bad-mouthing her sister that she put warm Nair on my eyebrows that night while I slept. I never felt a thing, and when I woke up and washed my face, my eyebrows came off with the water."

She started her wheeze-laugh again. "It felt like the end of the world at the time. Funny what's important to you when you're young."

"Did she get fired from her gofer job?"

"She didn't own up to taking my eyebrows until after . . . the incident. By then, everyone was feeling too sorry for her to punish her."

Synapses were firing in my brain, trying to connect random bits of information. "The incident?"

"It was awful." Another drag off the cigarette, this one deeper than the previous ones. "Janice's sister, Barbara? She hanged herself the day after we all got crowned. There was a rumor she was pregnant and didn't know what to do, but that might have just been a rumor. You know how those things go." Her voice trailed off.

My blood grew heavy. "Holy hell."

"Yeah. The pageant directors felt so bad for Janice they let her stay on. I heard she ended up as the chaperone a couple years later, after the original one retired."

"Yeah." I almost wished I smoked. "Wacky world."

"Yeah." I could hear Shelby's thoughts tumbling on the other end, reminiscing.

"Well, that's about all I needed to know," I said, still reeling.

"I can't have been very helpful." She took a final drag off her cigarette. I didn't hear her light another.

But she had been. "It's been nice to talk to a woman with some perspective on the Milkfed Mary pageant. I appreciate your time."

"No problem. Take care."

"You too."

I hung up, trying to figure out where this information about Janice fit. It seemed like it was an important piece in the puzzle, but really, it just told me that she'd had a hard life and was unstable in her past and a liar now. That wasn't much to go on.

I clicked over to my email in an effort to rid my brain of negative thoughts.

It worked. I was greeted with a sight that made my heart beat with equal parts trepidation and excitement: another email from Johnny.

Dear Mira:

Battle Lake's not the same without you. I went to the library yesterday to get a book on canning salsa, and the place was too clean. Curtis says he's responsible, but I see the ladies from the Senior Sunset doing the actual work. We need to talk—I've got something on my mind. Miss you.

I read the first and last lines seven times each. I didn't care what was in between.

Johnny was breaking down my defenses.

In fact, it was amazing I'd held out this long. After all, I lived in Battle Lake, the land where few dared to be single. Around there, a guy and a gal called it fate when they ended up at the same bar two nights in a row, true love if they liked the same bands and smoked the same brand of cigarettes.

But what had Johnny meant by "we need to talk"? My heart trip-thudded. Needing to talk was never good. Wasn't a general misunderstanding better than a direct confrontation, especially when it came to potentially intimate relationships?

I wrote several replies, ranging from flirty to gushing to neurotic. I deleted every single one. I didn't know exactly what I wanted to say and didn't trust myself not to mess up any forward progress we'd made.

I chose instead to read a novel until I grew sleepy, eventually putting head to pillow, where I was met with nightmares of charging bulls, landfills stacked with cow corpses, and lying, hanging beauty queens.

Chapter 32

Brittany was next in line to have her likeness sculpted the following morning, but before I went to see her, I needed to call Chaz Linder to follow up on Kate's money problems. To my surprise, the reporter answered, though his voice sounded cottony with sleep.

"Hello?"

"Hi, Mr. Linder. This is Mira James. We met at the Milkfed Mary press conference at the State Fair last Friday."

"Do you know what time it is?"

I did. The digital clock had told me just before I stepped outside the trailer to sit on the front steps so my call didn't disturb Kennie and Mrs. Berns. "Six thirty a.m."

He paused. When I didn't offer any more, he said, "That's really early."

I glanced around. The campgrounds were bustling. Since my fellow campers were mostly farmers, they'd already eaten breakfast and were already getting down to the business of the day. Animals needed to be fed and stalls cleaned out. I'd gotten swept up into this world of farm time, and frankly, it made sense. Get to bed early and attack the morning. You missed all sorts of temptations and were introduced to new opportunities.

From his tone of voice, though, Chaz didn't agree.

"Sorry," I said. "It won't happen again. I'm calling to ask you a couple questions about Kate Lewis, if you don't mind."

He cleared some sleep out of his throat. "Fine."

"She's being charged with embezzling?"

"Yup. I take it you don't read the *Pioneer Press*. We came out with an article yesterday stating that the attorney general is officially investigating her." He yawned. "Seven of her coworkers have been subpoenaed to testify. I think next week, actually."

"How much do they think she embezzled?"

"No one knows. She's been the final word on the books for over ten years. Hold on." I heard the squeak of bedsprings, footsteps, and the sound of a briefcase opening. "It was her regular trips overseas that got someone's attention. The AG thinks it was one of her employees who blew the whistle, disgruntled because their boss was living the high life while everyone else was working their fingers to the bone.

"Here's the kicker, though." His voice picked up as he warmed to his subject. "If not enough money comes in this year to cover questionable purchases Lewis made on the fair's behalf, the corporation will have to file for bankruptcy. So even if she's found guilty, it doesn't help the fair out. They still need to come up with the money to pay their bills—it doesn't matter if it was one person who dug them into the hole."

"Bummer." I was scribbling in my notepad, which was balanced on my knee. "So it wouldn't be out of line for Kate or someone in her corporation to do something dramatic to bring people to the fair?"

Paper rustled on the other end. "I know where you're going with this. But doesn't murdering a Milkfed Mary seem an extreme maneuver?"

"You tell me. How many people have their fortunes tied up in the fair?"

"More than a few." He sounded fully awake now. "So tit for tat. Any new information on Ms. Pederson's death?"

"Nothing official." I'd never been much of a sharer, even as a kid, and so I withheld the fact that Ashley may have been dating Lars Gunder and that Janice Opatz was as warped as wet wood. There was something I *could* share that might benefit us both, however. "But I was thinking. Is it possible the poison that killed Ashley was put in her ice cubes? According to the police, the last thing to go in her mouth was a diet cola that witnesses saw her open, so the drink itself probably wasn't tampered with, but we don't know where the cubes came from."

"Hmm. I'm not sure if they've looked into that angle, but who knows? I've got some connections in the police department. I'll float that idea over there and call you back if I find anything out. And you call me if you find anything more. Deal?"

"Deal."

I had a feeling both of us had our fingers crossed.

Chapter 33

Brittany's head carving drew a decent-size crowd. I hadn't seen any other kind at the fair, to be honest. The place was bustling from when it opened at 6:00 a.m. until it closed at midnight, and every corner of the fair (except the Haunted House and game stalls) brought back memories of an easier, happier time, even for those of us who'd never experienced such a thing.

Families shared fresh-cut french fries and rode the bumper boats and Ferris wheel, couples of all ages rode on Ye Old Mill to sneak kisses in the tunnel of love, and the JFK Remembered exhibition was a permanent display.

Even the futuristic touches, like the alternative-energy presentation, were connected to basic human needs of hearth, community, and food. I wondered if a person could take up permanent residence at the fair. Who wouldn't want to live like this all year long? Probably they'd need to serve some healthier food, but otherwise, I bet a lot of people would be on board.

I left the Dairy Building to kill some time before Brittany was done posing and I could talk to her. No protesters gathered outside, no rampaging bulls threatened, so I wandered and drank in the sights for a few hours. I was leaving Saturday, which meant I had less than three full days remaining here.

It also meant I was going to see Johnny soon, which sent a tingle to all the right places.

Walking past the Deep-Fried Nut Goodies on a Stick booth on my way back, it occurred to me (generously, I might add) that Brittany would love one. I stood in line to make my purchase and decided I might as well buy one for myself while I was there. Wouldn't want to make Brittany feel uncomfortable eating in front of someone who had nothing.

By the time I returned to the Dairy Building, I was down to one deep-fried Nut Goodie—I figured it would be a waste of perfectly good grease to eat mine cold—which I handed to a grateful Brittany as she materialized from behind the blue curtain.

"Man, thanks!" she said in her high-pitched voice. "I'm starving. All that butter in there just makes me think of eating." Rather than ask what kind of food was under all that powdered sugar and batter that I'd handed her, she dug right in. I admired an adventuresome eater, and as I watched her chew, I guessed she was the only Milkfed Mary who appeared truly milk-fed. She was five six, probably 150 pounds, which was healthy by normal standards but on the outside range of acceptable in the beauty pageant industry.

Like most people who didn't waste time starving themselves, Brittany was good-natured. "Jeez, this is delicious! Is this a candy bar in here? Yum!"

"Not just any candy bar. A Nut Goodie." It was hard watching someone else eat it, even if I'd just devoured one, and I promised myself I'd have another later to ameliorate the situation. "How'd the carving go?"

"See for yourself." She pointed at the slowly rotating booth behind us. Inside now were three butter heads and only eight unfinished blocks of butter. I recoiled. Since when had I started considering a block of butter to be "unfinished"? Would I start seeing regular butter everywhere as not yet done? *This butter is just sticks! I want my money back!*

"You look lovely," I said. "Your butter head *and* you. The sculptor is turning out great work." If you liked generic female faces beneath voluminous yellow hair circa 1970, that was. The sculpting job would probably be a lot easier if the contestants were allowed to have terrible disfigurements, like missing noses or a patch over their eye so you could easily distinguish one finished product from another. As it was, Lana's, Delrita's, and Brittany's pretty heads looked nearly identical to me.

"Yeah, we were kinda bummed it wasn't Mrs. Gerritt. Everyone wants her to be the one who carves their butter head. But this new lady is nice. She made my teeth really even, huh?"

Sure enough, when Brittany's head came around, her yellow teeth were perfectly square and aligned, if twice their natural size. It was hard not to think of pancakes, chunky golden butter teeth melting off the top of the stack, when looking at them. "Nice. Do you want to sit down and finish that? I wanted to ask you a few questions if you don't mind."

Brittany glanced around. I guessed she was searching for Janice Opatz, who was nowhere in sight. Shrugging, she led me outside to a rare empty bench. "Whaddya wanna ask?"

"You know I'm trying to find out what happened to Ashley, right?"

She nodded.

"I'm not having much luck. Have you heard anything?"

She munched thoughtfully. "All of us kinda decided it must be someone from her hometown who did it." She glanced at me quickly. "No offense. It's just that none of us knew her long enough to have wanted to kill her, is all."

It was true that the majority of murder victims knew their killer, yet I didn't have any Battle Lake natives on the suspect list for Ashley's death. The State Fair just felt too far away from home to look in that direction. If one of Ashley's classmates or dance-line partners were going to off her, why would they bother doing it so far from home? "I heard she was pretty snotty."

Brittany shrugged. "Most of us just got out of high school. We're used to snotty girls."

"What about Lana?"

She wiped her mouth. "How do you mean?"

"I know that Ashley stole Lana's boyfriend. Wouldn't that make a person madder than usual?"

Brittany leaned toward me, an earnest expression on her face. "You'd never say that if you really knew Lana. She's a sweetheart. She looks out for all the rest of us. And we all feel so bad for her, you know?"

I shook my head. "I don't follow."

"With her mom losing the farm. Mrs. Sorensen's had a tough go of it ever since Lana's dad died. That was a couple years before the pageant, I guess, and Lana and her mom did their best, but a few weeks ago they found out the bank's foreclosing on them. That's not even the saddest part, though. You should hear Lana talk about her father. She was a total daddy's girl. First they lost him and now they're losing the family farm. It's terrible sad."

I sat back. This insight into Lana's dire financial situation was new. I mentally flipped through my encounters of the last week until I reached my conversation with her. She'd said she had run for the Milkfed Mary title to help out her family. "To get good press," I think were her exact words. It looked like first runner-up hadn't been enough of a help.

"You think it'll make any difference to her family farm now that she's the official Milkfed Mary?"

Brittany shrugged. "She gets the scholarship now, if that's what you mean. She didn't know how she was going to make it to college this fall without that. And she gets $10,000 in cash, but not until she's successfully completed her reign."

"Hmm." I filed that piece of information to examine later and pursued a loose end that had been nagging me since Delrita had hidden Dirk and me upstairs. "Who's got offices up in the dorms, where you guys sleep?"

"Janice has one. The other one belongs to that marketing guy from the cow place."

"Lars Gunder, from Bovine Productivity Management?"

"Yeah, him." She nodded happily. "He seems like a nice guy."

I raised my eyebrows. Replacing high school home economics with "Identify a Creeper" classes might be the way to go. "Any idea why he'd have an office upstairs, and why Delrita, but not Janice, would have a key to it?"

Her eyes widened. "No. Why?"

I smiled. Her innocence was disarming. "I was hoping you'd know."

"Uh-uh. I think the pageant's sponsoring company always gets that office, no matter who they are, but I can't imagine why Delrita would have a key. That's weird. Maybe she borrowed it from that Lars guy, or he gave her a spare in case he lost his?"

Her guesses just raised more questions. I was about to ask her who was on deck to get their head carved tomorrow when she leaned forward to set her empty Nut Goodie container on the ground.

As she did, I saw that she had a lock of hair sliced unevenly from the back of her head, exactly where Delrita and Janice had.

Chapter 34

"Brittany," I said, my blood chilled, "do you know you have a snip of hair missing from the back of your head?"

Her hand shot up in alarm. "Where?" She felt around the back of her layered and curled shoulder-length hair.

I guided her hand to the spot. "Feel that?"

"Oh yeah. Weird." She teared up. "Does it look horrible?"

"No, it's not bad. A person wouldn't notice it unless they were looking for it." It was the truth. The stump was only two inches long and no wider than a comb. I didn't see any reason to alarm Brittany by telling her that Delrita and Janice shared the same "mark." I needed to check the other Milkfed Marys but quick and see if they had a similar hair deficit. "When are you all going to be together again?"

"Who?"

"The Milkfed Marys."

"Oh. Miss Opatz wants us all there for Megan's head carving tomorrow morning for a photo op. Should be fun!"

"Thanks." I'd check them all then.

Brittany mentioned she had an interview on MPR in an hour to prepare for, and I needed to go to the 4-H and Agriculture Horticulture Buildings to interview the Battle Lakeans there displaying their goods, so we parted ways.

I was on the way to the 4-H building when I unexpectedly bumped into Alison Short, my old manager at Perfume River. She was with a guy about her age who I didn't recognize. Seeing her familiar face in these surroundings was disorienting. She looked the same—cropped blonde hair, a gap between her two front teeth, short and sturdy German build. "Alison!"

"Mira? They let you out of Battle Creek!"

I smiled. "It's Battle *Lake*."

"Whatever." She gave me a hug. "It's good to see you!"

"You too. I stopped by Perfume River the other day, but they said you didn't work there anymore."

"Yeah, new owners. They told me I could keep working, but only as a waitress. They wanted family to run it. I decided to move on. I'm a day manager at the Seven Corners Grandma's now."

I knew the restaurant. It was near my old apartment. "How do you like it?"

"It's fine. The pay is good, and there isn't much trouble during the day." She punched my arm lightly. "How about you? Life good up nord wid the deer and wood ticks, eh?" She smiled wickedly, but because she was one of those naturally kind people, her jokes never stung.

"About what you'd expect." *Oh, except for the dead bodies.* "I'm working at the library and do some writing for the newspaper. That's why I'm in town. Battle Lake has a lot of local people in the fair, and I'm covering them."

"Fantastic!" Alison's friend gave her sleeve a tug, pulling her attention away. "We need to get going. We're meeting some friends at the Space Tower." She grimaced, and then her face lit up. "You wanna come with?"

It was tempting, but I had an article to research. Plus, I was still agitated from seeing Brittany's missing chunk of hair. "Can't. I have to work."

"Later then. Lissa's having a party tonight. You remember Lissa? She's still at the Riverside Plaza, same apartment. You should come!"

Her invitation raised mixed emotions. I liked being invited, but my West Bank life had been characterized by booze and bad choices. Still, seeing old friends might erase the feeling of rootlessness nagging at me since visiting the area on Tuesday. "I'll see. I'll try."

"OK. Great to see you!"

As they walked away, I called the library on a whim. I think I wanted to feel needed.

It was answered on the third ring. "Battle Lake Pubic Library, Curtis Poling here."

"*Pubic* Library?"

"Dammit, where are my glasses! Ida, did you move my spectacles? I can't read the card here without 'em."

"Curtis? It's me, Mira. What are you reading?"

"Oh, the ladies made a bunch of cue cards. Said my telephone-answering skills were poorly lacking. I have one to read when I answer the phone and then one for each possible question a caller could ask. The damn print is so small, though, that I gotta squint to see what's written. Ida! Woman! Find me my glasses!"

I held the phone away from my ear while he cooled down. When he'd subsided to angry muttering, I asked him how things were going.

Deep sigh. "When I started, I thought this was an easy job, but I didn't know there were so many stupid people in the world. You know how many dumb questions I get each day?"

I had a hunch. "Goes with the territory. You haven't burned the place down yet, right?"

"Not yet, but if one more person asks me how often the weekly magazines come in, or if I can find them some dang blue book about a bear, or what other names Mark Twain wrote under, I might just try."

"I'm sorry, Curtis."

"Not your fault," he grumbled. "And it's not all bad. I just like to complain sometimes." In the background, I heard a chorus of female voices agreeing with him.

"I sure appreciate you helping out," I said.

"And the whole town appreciates you taking Kennie Rogers off our hands." His chuckle was dry. "How's that working?"

"About like you'd expect, only I think she has a new venture she'll be bringing back with her."

"Hold on. What is it?" He sounded apprehensive. That was an appropriate reaction.

"Mutton Busting. Turns out she makes a really good clown at a sheep rodeo."

"She makes a really good clown as a mayor, too." The chuckle again. "How about Mrs. Berns? You tell her we miss her."

I smiled. The Senior Sunset folks were a tight-knit bunch. "She's fine, and I will. So everything's good back home?"

He was quiet for a moment, and when he spoke, he reminded me why everyone should have elderly friends. "As good as it can be without you here. No one can run the library like you. Whole town misses you."

My eyes felt surprisingly hot all of a sudden. "Thanks. I'll talk to you Saturday, when I come back."

I hung up quick before my emotions got the better of me. The Ag-Hort Building was in sight, and the 4-H Building just two blocks on the other side, but I needed to head back to the trailer and grab the notebook I'd forgotten before I conducted my newspaper interviews. I strode with my hands in my shorts pockets and my head down, still feeling warm and fuzzy and a little teary as I pulled into the campgrounds.

I stopped short when I spotted my trailer.

A man knelt next to it, toward the front by the hitch, and even with his back to me, it looked like he was searching for something. A cowboy who'd dropped his spurs? But this guy was far too spiffy for that, wearing a suit and dress shoes.

When he stood and turned, my heart felt gripped with icy tongs.

It was Lars Gunder messing with my Airstream, and he'd seen me see him.

Chapter 35

My hackles rose instantly. I hadn't liked the guy even before he'd stranded me in the hallways of BPM and left me to stumble into that horrible room. It might be his marketing background; I was always suspicious of guys who sold other people's stuff for a living. It was so parasitic. Plus, he was likely a cheater who preyed on young women.

My apprehension was connected to more than that, though—more even than the possibility that the USDA had followed up on my call and told him I was the one who narced. My distrust of him was primal.

"Mira! This your trailer?" He stood quickly, slipping something into his jacket pocket. He brushed his hands on his pants and smiled, lighting up his bland face. The sun shone through his thinning hair, exposing his scalp. I wondered why I hadn't noticed before that he was balding.

I stepped closer, but not too close. "Yep. What're you doing here?"

He marched over and held out his hand, which I reluctantly and briefly shook. "I hope you don't mind. The campground director told me which lot you're staying at."

"What're you doing here?" I repeated.

He studied me for a moment and then glanced off quickly. "I have something to tell you." He clenched his hands before shoving them in his pockets, blinking rapidly. He was playing the role of nervous informant perfectly.

His tone of voice and exaggerated nervousness made my bowels feel crunchy. This whole moment was very wrong, and I couldn't look at him without seeing the dead hooves sticking out from the bottom of that pile and hearing his scientists talking about ramped-up animal testing.

Two lots over, a couple argued about how much money they'd spent at the beer stand. Cries of joy from the Midway echoed around the campground, and the smell of smoky barbecue wafted on the air. There were literally thousands of people around. He couldn't hurt me here, but everything about him made me want to run.

"Mira." He stepped in closer, like he wanted to whisper to me. His eyes glistened. I tried to step back, but my feet were trapped in tar.

"Well, hot dog, and I was telling Kennie we should be sorry for you." Mrs. Berns's voice carried across the expanse from the entrance of the campground to where Lars and I were standing, dancing too close in the bright day. "Lonely girl on her own at the State Fair, I thought, but here you are making friends and influencing people."

Lars jerked back, momentarily surprised, and quickly recovered. He threw a dazzling smile at Mrs. Berns. "We were talking shop, I'm afraid. I'm Lars Gunder, marketing director for the Milkfed Mary pageant sponsor. And you are?"

"Hungry." She turned to me. "You ready to get some chow?"

It took me a beat or two to realize she was deliberately extricating me from a situation that was making me visibly uncomfortable. "Of course."

"Wait." Lars held up his hands. "Before you ladies go, let me help you to sleep better."

"What?" we asked in unison.

"Your trailer." He nodded at the silver hulk. "It isn't balanced."

"I bet Kennie's end is sagging," Mrs. Berns grumbled. "Am I right? Is the front lower than the back?"

He chuckled and led us over to the hitch. "See this leveler here? It's not your front or back that's uneven. It's your side. A couple cranks,

196

like so, and you should be all set." He stepped back. "Check it out. Even steven."

"Thank you," I said. The fear I had experienced moments ago felt distant and a little crazy. All the fried food must have been clogging my intuition. "Was this what you were going to tell me?"

He nodded without meeting my gaze. "That's it. I'll see you around."

As he walked away, Mrs. Berns leaned toward me. "There's a snake oil salesman if I ever did see one."

"I think you're right." I shivered, shaking the last of his energy off me. "He's married with two kids, two little girls, but there's a possibility he was fooling around with Ashley right up until she was murdered."

"You don't say," she said thoughtfully, wrinkling a proud nose that was already wrinkled. Her eyes were as clear as glass. "If you told me he worked at a cyanide factory, I'd say you had your Milkfed Mary killer."

I watched his back disappear into the crowd. "If only it were that simple. It could just as easily be a hundred other people. Take Kate Lewis, State Fair Corporation president, suspected embezzler, and likely releaser of wild bulls. Killing Ashley would bring the media spotlight to the fair and dig her out of her financial hole. She seems too nice, though."

Mrs. Berns crossed her arms. "Nice people murder, too. Any one of us with enough reason could be a killer."

I looked over at her. "When'd you get so wise on murderers?"

"You been around as long as me, you pick up on stuff. Speaking of Kate Lewis, I met one of her employees at the Mutton Busting last night. She's a rider, semipro. I got to talking to her, and it turns out she's a receptionist at the offices here. Why don't we go ask her what she knows about her boss?"

"People don't just tell you if their boss is a murderer."

"They don't tell just *anybody*, but they do tell their sheep sisters. Come on."

Chapter 36

The satellite office of the State Fair Corporation was an unpresuming structure housed on the fairground's northwest corner. The building was one-story gray brick with no sign out front, and I'd probably walked past it a hundred times.

"You'd think they'd advertise what they are."

"Probably don't want to be bothered," Mrs. Berns said. "Come on inside and meet Eustia."

The woman behind the counter looked as though she'd been separated from Mrs. Berns at birth. Mrs. Berns was ten or so years older, if depth of wrinkles and posture were any guide, but they both had tightly sprung apricot curls, assertive noses, and tiny bodies. They also both dressed with their own little pizzazz, though Eustia's ran toward the wild-fingernail-art end of the spectrum, whereas Mrs. Berns was more about accoutrements, usually in the form of decorative weaponry.

"Is it difficult to type with those?" I asked after introductions had been made and mutton-busting camaraderie exchanged. Eustia's fingernails were long enough to curve downward and painted red, white, and blue.

"Not as hard as wiping my rear." She cackled. Surely, she was Mrs. Berns's long-lost sister.

"I was telling Mira here that you know all about Kate Lewis," Mrs. Berns said, leaning on the counter. "Said you might be willing to give us the skinny about her embezzling."

Eustia glanced toward the entrance. "I don't remember saying that."

"Come on now. Do I have to crack out the tequila again?"

"Oy, not the tequila," Eustia groaned. "My head's still pounding from the other night."

Mrs. Berns whispered, "Look here, Eustia, we just want to satisfy our curiosity. What you say in this office won't go outside of it."

Eustia sighed, glancing worriedly at the door again. "You swear?"

"Cross our hearts," I said.

"Well, get closer, and if anyone walks in, you two are just looking for directions." She lowered her voice to a raspy murmur. "Kate's from your neck of the woods, you know. Graduated high school in Fergus Falls. Isn't that by Battle Lake?"

"Just up the road," Mrs. Berns said.

"After she graduated, she attended the community college there, then transferred to the university in Minneapolis. Ended up with a business degree, an MBA to be specific, but fat lot of good it does her. Doesn't keep her husband from abusing her. The more he yells at her, the sadder she gets, and the more he yells at her. Before I got transferred here, I was her personal receptionist. Sat outside her office listening to those two fight, either over the phone or when he'd stop by her offices."

"What's he do?" Mrs. Berns asked.

"Besides nurturing his gambling addiction? Oh, he works for the State Fair Corporation, too. Maintenance man. That woman married beneath her, but I don't mean because of his job. That man's a waste of skin, simple as that."

Mrs. Berns nodded. "Sounds like the truth."

I remembered the man that Kate had been arguing with in the alley behind the Dairy Building. "Is her husband short?"

"I'd say so. Not more than five seven, though he wears those silly inserts. Looks like he's always gliding down a mountain, even when he's standing stock still."

Could have been him but could also have been Lars. "So, do you think she was embezzling?"

"I don't need to think what I know. I saw the books." Eustia crossed her arms and leaned back, no longer whispering. "She started by skimming a little off the top, but when that wouldn't satisfy that bastard husband of hers, she'd make $10,000 disappear in a couple of months. I think they flew around the world so he could gamble where the laws were more lenient. Big trouble, that. You get in over your head quick. It was only a matter of time before the authorities caught up with her. I should have turned her in much earlier, but I felt sorry for her."

So Eustia was the whistleblower. "Think she's going to jail?"

Eustia nodded. "For sure. We're just hoping she doesn't drag the fair down with her, and I think she feels the same way. I believe she always planned to pay it back. She loves this fair more than anybody, and if it weren't for her husband, she'd never have harmed it. Too late to worry about that, though. Her ass is in the shit can, and last I saw her, she was a desperate woman."

"How desperate?"

Eustia scrunched up her face, which caused her bejeweled glasses to slide off her nose, where they were caught by their chain. "Between you, me, and the wall, I think she let that bull out the other day. She wanted to get more press for the fair. If it breaks even this year, she won't have hurt it permanently. We'll recover next year. But if ticket sales don't cover enough of the unpaid bills, we're going under."

"That's stupid," Mrs. Berns said. "Releasing dangerous animals is no way to attract people. Why, if I wanted to get some rubberneckers in, what I'd do is . . ." She slapped her mouth shut.

I finished her thought. "You'd murder someone?"

"I was going to say I'd have a wet T-shirt contest."

I rolled my eyes. "Nice save."

Eustia didn't have anything more to share, and she and Mrs. Berns devolved into talking shop. With nothing to add to the mutton-busting conversation, I thanked Eustia for her time and excused myself. I needed some fresh air.

My wandering didn't clear my head, but it brought me past the Ag-Hort Building. I figured I might as well do some more article research as I couldn't do what I really wanted to do—check the Milkfed Marys' hair to see if they were all marked—until tomorrow, and I needed some mental space before I could connect the dots on Kate. Something was there, something that I was missing, a piece connecting her clearly to Lars Gunder and the two of them to Ashley's murder.

I stepped out of my head and into Ag-Hort.

It seemed busier than it had been during Henry Sunder's book launch, but saying something was busier at the fair was like calling someone more dead, or pregnanter.

The main exhibit in the building changed every day. Today the focus was on honey, and the entire north end of the cavernous building was given up to displays of honey-sweetened baked goods, specialty honeys, cooking with honey demonstrations, glass-encased miniature apiaries, and beeswax sculptures.

A woman leaned out of the stall nearest me, its front counter creaking under the weight of hundreds of jars of bee nectar, a rainbow of yellows and browns and even some red. She looked a little like a bumblebee herself, with her fuzzy blonde hair streaked with gray and wearing a black-and-gold-striped T-shirt. "Care to try our basswood honey?" she called out.

I stepped over and read her name tag. "Mrs. Lieber? Susanna Lieber?" She was exactly the person I'd come to see.

"Yes?" She didn't recognize me, and her expression said that she felt bad about it.

"Don't worry—we've never met. I was just reading your tag and recognized the name. We're both from Battle Lake. I work for the *Recall*. Ron Sims, the editor, has me at the fair covering locals. Your family owns the honey business south of town?"

She held out her hand. "Pleased to meet you. Yup, we have Honig Lieber's Honey Farm. Three of our honeys won grand prize ribbons this year!"

"Was the basswood one of them?"

"You betcha. Here you go."

I accepted the small plastic spoon she handed to me. The dot of honey on it was the palest yellow, almost clear, and it smelled like flowers and sunshine. I licked it off, savoring the mild spread of sweetness and light. I almost moaned it was so delicious. "That's wonderful. What makes it basswood honey?"

"The hives are located in a basswood forest."

I was skeptical. "So it's mostly basswood, but might have other stuff mixed in?"

She laughed. "We make it as scientific as we can. Look at this." She directed my attention to a row of ten honeys, arrayed from lightest to darkest. "Our basswood bees produce the super-light stuff. Buckwheat honey is the darkest, and it has the most antioxidants. Honey is healthy."

"Yum. Do you guys carry anything besides honey?"

"Beeswax candles." She pointed. "My sister is over there if you want more info about those."

I thanked Susanna and moved on to her sister, who was womanning the beeswax stall on the opposite side of the honey room. I was fascinated by the comb pattern in her candles and the intricate shapes she could form from the wax. I listened to an impromptu candle-making lesson before tracking down Georgina Schmitz, Battle Lake's reigning jelly-making queen, in the adjacent preserves room.

Georgina was displaying her famous crab apple jam as well as golden raspberry jelly, apple butter, and wild grape jelly. I didn't put up much of a fight when she made me sample each one. I wished I had my camera so I could snap a photo of the sunshine gliding in a high window and through a stacked pyramid of her wares. The sunbeam lit them up into the deepest peach and jeweled purples, an edible pirate's treasure.

After speaking to all the Battle Lakeans in Ag-Hort, I sauntered over to the 4-H building, my belly full of homemade sweetness.

Battle Lake was also represented well in this arena. The town boasted one of the largest 4-H groups in the state, and the participants had various projects on display, from homemade rocket ships to quilts to farm dioramas made from tinfoil, toothpicks, and tempera paints. I interviewed any of the kids who happened to be near their projects and convinced one of the leaders of the Battle Lake 4-H to email me the photos she'd taken so I'd have visuals to go with the article.

After the 4-H Building, I headed to the animal barns. I'd already inspected the Otter Tail County cows in the Cattle Barn, but still had stops to make in the Swine, Horse, and Sheep and Poultry barns.

It was in the latter that I discovered that Dan's prizewinning Araucana was in fact a chicken. According to the placard in front of the champion bird, the breed was both tufted and rumpless. "Sorry," I whispered to it. It couldn't be easy to breed with those bona fides.

It actually wasn't bad looking for a bird. The tufts of feathers near its ears were regal, like one of those giant, ruffled collars that Victorian royalty wore. True, its butt was a sad little downward slope lacking definition or tail feathers, but when it was facing away, you could hardly notice.

I was leaning in to determine once and for all whether chickens had ears when I realized that I'd voluntarily walked into a structure almost entirely given over to poultry.

Normally, avian critters and I didn't mix. When they dive-bombed my windows, or swooped close to my head, or pooped on my shoulders, I knew the truth: birds were malicious, calculating creatures with a tremendous aerial advantage.

Yet, peering around at the clucking, quacking barn inhabitants, it occurred to me that for the first time in my life, I wasn't scared. For sure it didn't hurt that all the birds were locked in cages, but even better, I knew that if they were out, they couldn't fly because they were chickens. If one of them happened to break free, all I had to do was run or kick it, and I'd be safe.

I closed my eyes in relief as a tremendous weight lifted from my shoulders. Why hadn't I tried immersion therapy before? I knew how demented my bird phobia was, but that shouldn't have turned me away from them. Instead, I should have *leaned into* the fowl world.

Ah. The liberation of finding out you're no longer afraid.

"Wanna pet her?"

"Eep!" I yelled, glancing over to see Dan had pulled a neighboring Araucana out of its cage. The sound that had escaped my throat was a wet and choking squeal.

The chicken cocked her head, mirth and malevolence in one beady eye. She blinked, and a dollop of poop fell out of her rumpless.

"No, I do *not* want to pet your chicken," I said, backing away. So much for overcoming my fear. "Thank you for the offer. I'm allergic."

"To chickens?"

"All birds. Feathers. I'm allergic to feathers." Suddenly, my world began to close in. Who had I been kidding? Birds were terrifying. I was outnumbered.

"She lays green and blue eggs."

"Tell her I mean no harm."

He cocked his head, subconsciously mirroring the chicken's gesture. "Huh?"

"Tell her I'm sorry I had eggs for breakfast, and that I won't let that happen again."

"You OK?"

"Thank you. Yes, I'm totally OK. Time to go."

He put the chicken back in its cage. "Have you had a chance to see the sheep yet? They're on the other side of the barn."

I didn't even have the presence of mind to question that organizational choice because I was being approached by two black-headed ducks with bright orange eyes and a ring of fluff like a massive boa around their necks. They were waddling toward me with malicious intent, and I was fairly certain they were packing tiny shivs under all those feathers.

"Some other time. Thanks!"

I turned and tried to walk calmly away, but I imagined I could hear the leathery *thwup-thwup* of charging duck feet, and so instead I ran, pretending I was running toward something instead of fleeing.

When I reached the sunlight and scared a flurry of pigeons into the air, I actually cried out.

Chapter 37

Later, after I'd sent the "Battle Lake at the Fair!" pieces to Ron, I was calm enough to venture outside my trailer.

In the course of writing the articles, I'd decided that I would attend Lissa's party that evening. Part of me believed I needed to put the old me to rest before I could become the new me, and I desperately craved a fresh life, one without alcohol and people who clung together out of boredom and convenience rather than friendship. In Battle Lake, I had true friends, like Curtis and Mrs. Berns, or Nancy and Sid and Jed, whom I could count on. That was new to me, and a big deal. I wasn't used to having people I could rely on to pet sit or bring me soup and bagels if I was sick.

I might be the first person to complain about living in a small town, but the truth was Battle Lake was a good place to heal. I couldn't imagine residing there long term, but the comfort and safety were helping me to move to a new sort of peace, one defined by the choices I made instead of the life events thrust on me.

And saying goodbye to my empty, drunken, loose past would feel great. Maybe it would even free up some psychic space and make more room for Johnny.

I splurged on a cab to the West Bank. The Metro Transit system at night felt about as safe as walking naked through a prison. Sure, a lot of people connected to Battle Lake had been murdered in the last five months, but at least we knew the killers by their first names. All part of the small-town charm.

I paid the cabbie thirteen dollars, plus a two-dollar tip, and stepped onto Cedar Avenue in front of Palmer's Bar, which was rocking as usual. When I'd left the Cities last spring, the trend among college students and suburbanites was to prowl upscale bars expensively decorated to look like dives. Well, Palmer's was the real deal, having more in common with *Star Wars*' Mos Eisley Cantina than a Hard Rock Café. Inside, the drinks would be stiff, Hamm's would be flowing on tap, and the jukebox would be stacked deep with an eclectic mix of local bands, blues, and acid metal.

Directly across the street, reggae and a domestic fight filtered out of the Holtzermann, a rabbit's warren of apartments snaking above the stores lining the opposite side of Cedar Avenue. I'd never met any-one who knew the actual number of apartments that comprised the Holtzermann, or where it began or ended. A person could easily get lost in the crisscrossing halls, the dead ends, the studio apartments that were actually carved-out closets from the two-bedroom next door.

I'd once attended a party there, above the West Bank drugstore. During the course of the evening, a fire had erupted in the kitchen, probably started while someone was cooking drugs. Rather than calling the fire department and risking getting caught, the guy who rented the place put out the licking flames with an extinguisher.

But the fire had opened up enough of the thin wall to show through to the other side, where we discovered a dusty and worn but fully intact theater in the heart of the Holtzermann, all entrances and windows to it completely boarded up and plastered over. We'd spent the night crawl-ing in and out of the hole in his kitchen and acting silly on the stage.

The West Bank was a strange place.

I bypassed both the Holtzermann and Palmer's, skirting around the bar to the Riverside Plaza, the ugliest apartment complex west of the Mississippi. The imposing structures comprising the complex, each a different height, looked like enormous cinder blocks with multicolored panels placed randomly. Instead of brightening the appearance, the dingy peach, powder-blue, and Easter-egg-green panels served to age the entire building. I'd been told that the front of the complex had been featured in the opening shots of *The Mary Tyler Moore Show*, the idea being that Mary Richards lived inside. If that was true, it was a surprise anyone ever moved here, thinking that this was the best Minneapolis offered.

Lissa lived in the McKnight building, the tallest in the complex. It had thirty-nine floors and more than four hundred apartments, but only five elevators. A swaying man in work boots was urinating in the one that was open.

"Going up?"

"No thanks," I said. "I'll take the stairs." The building hadn't changed.

Lissa's apartment was on the seventh floor, number 711, which was an easy number to remember even though my senses had been hazy every time I'd stumbled to it. I followed the geometrically patterned 1960s carpet and stopped at the red diamond in front of her door. I could hear laughter inside, and people singing along to the music.

I recognized the tune—"Waitress in the Sky," by the Replacements. Alison and I used to crank that song at Perfume River. It was the anthem of waitresses on the ground, and listening to the lyrics, I couldn't remember why. I knocked.

No one answered, so I opened the door and walked in.

The music grew louder. Lissa had inserted special light bulbs with stained-glass patterns in all her lamps, giving the room a muted, warm glow. The front space, her living room, was packed with chattering partygoers, clinking drinks in their hands, and behind, in the kitchen, guests were laughing and leaning in close.

I didn't recognize anyone.

I put my hand on the doorknob at my back. This'd been a bad idea. I started to twist, and the knob twisted back. The door opened, and in strode Alison.

"Mira! You made it! Lissa, come over here. Mira's here!" Alison draped one arm around me and waved across the room with the other.

Near the stereo, a dark head popped up, and I spotted Lissa's familiar kohl-rimmed eyes and bloodred lipstick framed in a Bettie Page haircut. She finished her conversation and wove through the crowd toward us.

"Mira!" She gave me a hug. "Where you been? I haven't seen you around for a while."

"I moved."

"No shit. When?"

Alison laughed. "Last winter. Remember? I told you about it when I quit Perfume River."

"Actually, I moved last spring." I smiled wanly.

"Same difference," Allison said, accepting a joint someone passed her.

"Well, good to see you," Lissa told me. "Hey, Alison, did you hear about Bill getting busted?"

"Again? What for this time?"

"Selling weed, what else? Hey, Mira, grab me a drink, will you, and get one for yourself. If you go in the kitchen, you'll see there's hard liquor and a keg. Choose your poison. Oh, and there's a ten-dollar cover. You can pay Glen. He's the guy in the tie-dye." She steered Alison toward the stereo.

I found myself standing there, alone in a crowd. The Replacements were now singing "Little Mascara." On the other side of the room was the entryway to a brightly lit kitchen full of liquor. Ten dollars could buy me the feeling of fitting in. I'd get a little tipsy, enjoying that warm tingle as it spread to my fingers and toes, and realize that I knew more people than I thought here. I'd strike up a conversation with that guy whose band I'd seen at the 400 Bar last year, or that chick who'd always come into Perfume River on Wednesdays for lunch and order Imperial Tofu, hold the onions. We'd realize we had tons in common.

As the evening grew late and the drinks flowed, we'd get looser and pledge our undying devotion to one another while we hashed out what was wrong with the world and how we'd fix it if given the chance. In between, we'd dance wildly and loosen our clothes, smoke whatever was passed our way. When Lissa and Alison would cross my path, I'd hug them and tell them it was OK that they hadn't written or called, that we'd be friends forever. Even if we never showed it, we'd just *know*.

"Hey, you OK?"

I blinked, holding on to the wall for support. Next to me was a long-haired guy with a giant nose as hooked as a claw.

"I think I need some fresh air," I told him.

He appeared concerned. "You want me to get one of your friends?"

"I don't have any friends here," I said. "Thanks anyway."

I opened the door and stepped into the hallway. Following the geometric pattern back down the hallway to the stairs, I passed a loc'd pair making out in front of the exit door. I chose the elevator, pinching my nose against the sour pine scent of urine-soaked carpet and used my elbow to push the button for the first floor.

Outside, I hailed a cab, which dropped me off in front of the State Fair. Following a familiar path, I was back at the Airstream in no time. Warm light spilled out when I cracked the door, along with the comforting smells of hot cocoa and buttery, microwaved popcorn.

"Mira! You're just in time," Mrs. Berns called out. "Kennie and me are putting together a care package for the Pederson family, and then we're going to play some gin rummy. Care to lose oodles of money to an old lady and a crazy mayor?"

I smiled so wide that it pushed back the tears. "More than anything."

Chapter 38

Over popcorn and cards, I'd started to develop a theory about the Milkfed Marys' hair mystery, and both Mrs. Berns and Kennie had assured me it made sense, not that they were a reliable gauge of sensibility. I'd need to wait to see all the Milkfed Marys together with their hair down to test my theory, and it turned out that wasn't gonna happen until the daily State Fair parade taking place later in the afternoon.

I found that out when I turned up to Megan's butter carving the next morning and learned that the entire Milkfed Mary crew's scheduled appearance had been canceled so they could attend a community event in Saint Paul, followed by a last-minute interview set up at the KSTP station. Megan was going to miss out on both, but one of the princesses had to stay at the fair and hold down the butter fort.

I thought I could at least check out Megan's do, but she was rotating in the booth with her blonde hair in a ponytail and with the collar on her jacket turned up, so I was SOL. Glenda was having a bear of a time sculpting the perky hairstyle, which required her to balance butter in midair with all the skill of a civil engineer.

I hung around for the entire carving of Megan's head, staking out a comfortable bench near the east wall where I could read and people watch. In the end, Megan's carving took four hours, a third less time than the previous ones because her face was rather bland, making her the perfect subject for the milquetoast medium. When she stepped out of the booth, I had a quick chat with her and discovered she knew nothing of any significance.

"That's creepy about Brittany's hair, though." She shook her head in disbelief, her ponytail swishing from side to side.

"She told you?"

"Yeh. We were all talking about it at the dorm last night."

This might save me some time. "Anyone else missing hair?"

"Delrita and Brittany, that's it. We all checked each other. Felt like we were looking for ticks. I think it's that princess from Olmstead County who did it. She's such a ho-bag, I can totally see her cutting off people's hair." She put her left hand to her right wrist, then stopped as a look of frustration crossed her face.

"What's up?"

"My aquamarine bracelet. It was a graduation present from my boyfriend, and I hardly ever take it off. I couldn't find it anywhere this morning. I keep feeling for it out of habit."

This was a new twist, but it supported my current theory about where the hair had gone. "Yeah? Anyone else missing jewelry?"

"Not that I know of."

"Can you ask the other princesses for me? I'll be at the parade today."

She snorted. "Am I supposed to flash you a sign if I find out something? We'll be on a float, you know."

"A thumbs-up will do."

She wrinkled her button nose. "OK. If I remember."

After my dish with Megan and a final scan of the Dairy Building to make sure no suspicious, cyanide-toting characters were in attendance, I headed back to the trailer to grab my wallet, which I must have left behind after losing $12.55 to Mrs. Berns in a feverish, if one-sided, gin rummy marathon.

I smiled as I passed the Kidway. In no hurry to be a mom myself, I still loved the squeal of kids having fun. I was yanked out of my reverie when Delrita crossed my line of vision, disappearing behind the towering Giant Slide, a two hundred-foot-plus permanent fair structure.

She'd ducked behind one of the walls hiding the metal supports. I dashed after her, curious why she wasn't with the rest of the Milkfed Marys at the community event. A screech of outrage made me draw up before I cleared the corner of the slide wall.

"You're a liar!" someone said. The voice was familiar, but I couldn't place it without a face. "You just wanted to ruin my career, and you've done a mighty fine job of that, thank you."

Delrita responded. "This isn't about you. I didn't even *know* you before the pageant."

"You promised you'd keep the secret. I had to leave the girls unchaperoned to come here and talk some sense into you. Why can't you just keep it all under wraps for seven more days? Then we can both go our own way."

"Because I don't like the lying." Delrita's voice was solid with conviction.

A snort. "Didn't bother you when you signed on."

"That was then. Things have changed."

The accuser laughed, an ugly, threatening sound, and that's when I definitively identified the speaker: Janice Opatz. "I'll say they have."

"Mommy, I want to go." The little girl's voice sounded scared. "Please, Mommy."

Delrita and Janice had a child back there? I stepped forward. "Mira?"

"Delrita?" I found myself eye-to-eye with her, and at her heels were the two towheaded girls Delrita's mother had introduced to me as Delrita's nieces at her butter-carving session. And here they were calling Delrita "Mommy."

"This is just great," Janice hissed. "Now the whole world will know. Good work, Delrita."

I ignored Janice and spoke directly to Delrita. "You have kids?"

"Two," Delrita said firmly. "Emma and Eleanor, will you say hi to Mira?"

Emma, the oldest, held out her hand. Eleanor ducked her face into her mom's skirt. "I'm pleased to meet both of you." I returned my attention to Delrita. "Does this mean what I think it means?"

"That I'm not eligible to be a Milkfed Mary? Yeah."

Janice puffed up. "It's in the rules, clear as a bell. Section 14, article 3, subdivision 7: 'A Milkfed Mary contestant must not have been married or have had any children, even if given up for adoption, prior to winning her title. If she gets married, becomes pregnant, or has any children at any time before the termination of her reign, she will forfeit any title and all winnings, including scholarships and endorsements, associated with the pageant.' Delrita knew the rules, and still she entered the contest. She's a liar."

Big tears started to stream down Emma's cheeks.

"You're upsetting the girls, Janice. And it's just a stupid contest," I said. I stopped myself from voicing what I was really thinking: *You'd think the dairy industry would be more supportive of breeders.*

"A contest I never should have entered," Delrita said, "and one I'm formally withdrawing from today. I made a mistake, and I'm tired of living the lie. I'm proud to be a single mom, and I'm proud of my babies." She hugged them both close.

I had a thought. I turned to Janice. "Was this the secret you were threatening Lana not to tell, up in the dormitory on Tuesday?"

Janice seemed ready to breathe fire. "A few of the girls knew. We decided it was in their best interest to keep Delrita's situation private. If the reputation of one Milkfed Mary is sullied, she tarnishes all the girls' standing. The contest becomes a joke."

"That's bull," Delrita said. "First of all, I only told Ashley, and that was in confidence. She told *you* because she was a worthless brownnoser. Lana overheard Ashley snitching to you and told me. And *second*, you weren't ever worried about any of us. You were worried about your job, plain and simple. I'm not going to ask anyone to lie for me anymore, which is why I've resigned. It's history." She looked over at me. "You can help me spread the word. I'm a mom, and I'm proud of it. Feel free to print that in your paper. Come on, girls. We've got some sliding to do!"

Delrita lifted Eleanor and rested her on her hip, grabbed Emma's hand, and led them off. I was left with an abruptly deflated-looking Janice.

She started to massage her hands and stopped, reaching into her purse for disinfectant. "I just wanted to protect the pageant, that's all," she mumbled. "It symbolizes something important in this immoral world: old-fashioned farm values. Was it so bad that I wanted to protect that?"

I studied her face, which had become sagging and gray without her characteristic controlled anger to plump it. "The pageant is important to you, isn't it?"

She nodded. "It's my life," she said simply. Then she turned and walked away.

I almost felt sorry for her until her missing chunk of hair drew my attention, reminding me of my theory. I was pretty sure that Janice Opatz wasn't exactly what she appeared to be, and the parade in an hour would prove it, if Megan didn't forget her job. I scurried back to the Airstream to grab my wallet. Mrs. Berns had scrawled me a note:

We've got a day full of Fair Bears' duties. Don't wait up. Bought you a fresh Nut Goodie.

Indeed, the green-and-red wrapped candy was serving as a paperweight to the note, but as I looked at it, a horrible realization dawned: I wasn't hungry for a Nut Goodie. By my count, I'd eaten seven of the battered, deep-fried candy bars since my arrival at the fair, and while my mouth was willing, my stomach and dimpling ass were currently on strike.

Ever the optimist, I shoved the candy in my purse for later and searched for my wallet. It wasn't on the table next to my laptop where

I'd left it, so I got down on all fours. A little scrabbling around, and I uncovered it just underneath Kennie's unmade bed. It must have fallen from the table where we'd played cards.

In that position, a black shape farther back under Kennie's bed became visible. I flattened into an army crawl and pulled myself forward, fully expecting to discover a pile of dirty underwear or some old food. Instead, my searching hand made contact with my missing camera.

I pulled myself and the camera out and sat on my heels, dust bunnies in my hair, and turned the camera around. It was definitely mine, or at least the newspaper's. It was unlikely Mrs. Berns or Kennie would have tossed it back there, and besides, I'd already checked that location when I first noticed the camera missing.

I flicked on the power switch, grateful to discover the battery still had juice. Selecting the "View Photos" function, I wasn't surprised to see that all the pictures of Ashley had been deleted, leaving only a series on Luna and Tiger Pop frolicking in my vegetable garden back home.

My heartbeat picked up as I realized what that meant: Somebody had stolen the camera, destroyed the photos of Ashley, and then returned it. The trailer had been broken into at least twice, and by somebody who didn't want evidence of what the camera had captured at Ashley's ceremony. I stood quickly, brushed myself off, and scoured the trailer for any more signs of a break-in.

Nothing.

I fired up my laptop next to see if anyone had monkeyed with it. A search of the history showed that no new sites had been visited. If the thief who'd broken into the trailer was interested in what I was doing online, however, they'd know I had been researching Aeon, cyanide, and the 1977 Milkfed Mary pageant.

A cold tickle of fear whispered down my back. I needed to warn Mrs. Berns and Kennie about our malefactor, and we'd have to make double sure to lock all windows and the door before we left.

With my computer on, I decided to check my email. I had only two messages. The first was from Ron:

Got 'em.

Short and sweet, like the man himself. Well, half like him. The second email was from Johnny, the third I'd received since our disastrous post-concert evening:

Hey, Mira! You wouldn't believe the bounty that's coming in at the farmers' market. When you get back, we'll have to do some canning. Oh, and the band got some good publicity at the fair. The *Pioneer Press* is running a full-page article on the Thumbs next week. Good stuff! I've decided to stop back at the fair. See you tomorrow? Johnny

Tomorrow.
He was coming tomorrow.

Chapter 39

Knowing this raised a different kind of fear in me, one that ran deep. Sighing, I decided that this was as good a time as ever to start the new life with the new me, the one where I was defined by my actions instead of my reactions. I hit "Reply" and typed quickly, my first email to him ever:

> Thanks for the email, Johnny. That's fantastic news about your band! You guys are going to make it big. Canning sounds great. I'm looking forward to seeing you tomorrow. I'd like to finish what we started.
>
> Mira

I immediately pulled the "Send" trigger before I chickened out.

I'd never been so direct with Johnny, so open about how I felt about him. I really did want to finish what we'd started after his show at the Leinie Lodge. I wanted him to kiss me long and hard. I wanted to melt into Johnny like I was butter and he was hot toast. I wanted to kiss so long that our lips pruned. I wanted to roll in the grass with him like we were wildcats tied together at the waist. I wanted all that and more.

There.

It was out there.

And it was the truth.

Then a thought occurred that squeezed my heart in a bad way: Had my email been too obtuse, too vague? Would he think I wanted to finish what we'd started in my garden, tying up the tomato plants? Or finish what we had started at the library, where we were renovating the children's reading space? Or even finish what we'd started in dialing back our relationship to friendship mode? *Frick.* I was the worst flirt. I should have just told him he needed to kiss me and be out with it. I couldn't retract the email, though. It was hurtling through cyberspace, probably already on his laptop and maybe even being read.

I shut down the computer, grabbed the camera, and headed to the daily State Fair Parade, certain that everyone could spot my dork flag flying. The streets of the fairgrounds were packed with couples strolling hand in hand, laughing and leaning into each other. How did they make it look so easy? Did I have a cellular disorder, a genetic man-repellent visible only under microscope or by watching me stumble through a conversation with a decent guy?

Agh.

Fortunately, the sounds of a marching band signaled the beginning of the early-afternoon parade and saved me from further self-flagellation. I elbowed my way to the front and turned my camera on so I'd be ready when the Milkfed Mary float sailed past.

I didn't need to wait long. Their float was blue spangled on white, pulled by a car that featured a plywood cow cutout on each side to disguise it. On the back of the float, ten beauty queens in ball gowns waved prettily at the crowd. I was pleased to see Delrita had stuck to her principles and was nowhere in sight. Megan was on the far side of the float, so I made a mad dash across the front, wondering briefly how embarrassing it would be to get run over by a cow car going twelve miles per hour.

"Megan!" I yelled. The parade route was loud with cheering and clapping. "Megan! Over here!"

She separated her name from the rest of the cries and glanced my direction. I caught her attention, giving her an expectant look. She flashed a rueful grimace and held up her hands to indicate that she hadn't found out anything. I let the float pass, snapping photos as long as I was there. I retreated to the shade of an oak tree once the Milkfed Marys were out of sight so I could look over the photos.

"Hey, did you get what you were looking for? That was some crazy high-risk photography, running out in front of a moving float like that."

I'd been so engrossed in studying the photos that I hadn't seen Aeon approach. I stared into his bright-blue eyes, which appeared sad, tilting down at the corners. Maybe it was the dappled sunlight under the tree throwing shadows.

"Hi, Aeon. How're you doing?"

"Been better. You eaten yet?"

"As a matter of fact, no."

He crammed his hands into his pockets. "Care to get a late lunch with me?"

"Let me guess. You're a vegetarian."

"Vegan, actually. But you don't have to be. The Blue Moon has great wood-fired pizzas with rice or regular cheese."

I reminded myself that Aeon was still on my suspect list, a hard fact to remember when he was being so nice. "Deal."

"Hey, I got a joke for you," he said, as we strolled to the diner.

"OK," I said.

"Knock knock."

"Please." I rolled my eyes to play it cool, but the truth was, I loved knock-knock jokes.

"Come on. Knock knock."

"Who's there?"

"Interrupting cow."

"Interrupting cow wh—"

"MOOOO!"

I laughed. The kids at the library story hour would love that one. "You actually have a sense of humor! So how come you're so serious all the time? A jury might go easier on you if you cracked more smiles, you know."

He stopped in front of the restaurant and looked down at his shoes. "You researched me and found out about the ecoterrorism stuff, didn't you?" His voice had an odd lilt.

I crinkled my forehead. "Yeah, but that's not what I was talking about. I was just teasing you."

He didn't respond. Instead, he entered the restaurant, ordered his pizza, and sat at a table. I did the same, joining him though I wasn't sure he welcomed my company anymore.

In the rear of the diner, an episode of *Gilligan's Island* was playing on the big screen. We both pretended to watch, neither of us talking even as our pizza and grape sodas were delivered.

"Look," he said, putting his rice cheese pizza down and finally speaking. "Breaking the law isn't my style. It's what The Originals did, and it took me a while to find my own direction."

"The Originals?"

He nodded. "My parents. Chandra and Chad. They founded GreenFreedom, but you probably know that already, too."

"I did," I mumbled around my pizza. "You call them 'The Originals'?"

"They're the original counterculture hippies, hell-bent on civil disobedience and insurrection. I was raised in that environment, and it rubbed off on me. All of it, the good and the bad."

My interest was piqued. "What was the bad?"

"The idea that I needed to destroy something to get attention. I understand activists who believe there's no other way to get heard, but it's not my style." He shook his head, his face impassioned. "I found that out the hard way, with the bombing and the vandalism."

I took a sip of my icy-cold pop. "Did you go to jail?"

"Nah. I had good lawyers. And my parents were so excited that I was turning out just like them. They wanted to see me do more of the same, but I couldn't. For me, two wrongs just don't make a right."

I munched thoughtfully on my pizza. "So the group you're in now, Mad Cows, Mad People, isn't radical?"

He laughed. "We try, but we stay within the bounds of the law. Our message is one of education."

I felt a kindred spirit in Aeon, though he was more organized than I'd ever be. He seemed like a gentle soul, if a lost one, and I wanted to pay him back for taking me into his confidences. "Hey, I need a sounding board for some theories about the Milkfed Mary murder. You interested?"

He nodded, and over more pizza and organic apple pie, I told him what I knew about Janice's peculiar past and Kate's embezzling. I threw in my trump card. "Lars might have been involved, too. There're rumors that he was seeing Ashley, and I bet he'd go to great lengths to keep that news from getting out."

Aeon cocked his head, his expression unreadable. "But it did get out."

"Lars might not know that."

"Regardless, you're still left with the big question: How would anyone have pulled off the poisoning? The papers said that Ashley wasn't alone all morning, and the only thing she ingested was a diet cola that several witnesses saw her open."

"But we don't know where the ice cubes came from." I'd promised Mrs. Pederson and Glenda Haines that I wouldn't spill that cyanide had killed Ashley, so I kept it vague. "A lot of poisons can be turned into a gas, which could then be frozen in an ice cube."

He sat back, and I waited for him to tell me how stupid that sounded. Instead, he said, "That makes Lars a much more likely suspect than Kate or Janice, given his access to chemicals and a lab."

"Yes!" I said, grateful that he agreed with my logic. "I think so, too!"

"You should tell the police."

"I already blabbed my suspicions to a reporter."

"Who?" Aeon asked, sitting forward.

"Some Chaz guy at the *Pioneer Press*. He was covering the press conference Kate held last Monday."

"You told him everything you're telling me?" He raised both eyebrows.

"Oh no. Just my theory about the poison in the ice cubes. I don't know if he'll even go to the police with it. He didn't seem too impressed."

Aeon rubbed his neck as he contemplated what I'd told him. "Then you have to. I'd do it anonymously, though. From a pay phone. Take it from someone who knows, you don't want the police to have your name connected to bad news."

"Amen," I said. "I'll go do it now."

"I'll come with."

"Fine."

We bussed our table and headed north and east, toward the only pay phone that I knew of, the one near the 4-H Building. We were inside the booth when I remembered that I'd lost all my change to Mrs. Berns in cards. "Let's run back to the Airstream. I'm sure she won't mind if I borrow some quarters. They were mine to begin with."

"Not a problem. I wouldn't mind seeing your trailer."

An odd tone in his voice made me glance over, but all six five of him was loping along innocently, a quirky smile on his face, his sad blue eyes guileless.

"It's not as cool as it sounds," I said. "The guy I'm borrowing it from pimped it out to look like a 1973 rumpus room."

He flashed me a peace sign. "I can dig it."

"You'll have to. Here it is."

"Cool." He pointed. "Hey, looks like someone left you a note."

I looked where he was indicating, at a scroll stuffed in the handle of the door. The rolled paper popped open when I yanked it out.

Aeon watched me as I read. "What is it? Everything all right?"

"No, it isn't," I said quietly. "This changes everything."

Chapter 40

"Who's it from?"

"It's not signed. Look." I held out the note, which read:

If you want to find the truth about Lars Gunder, go to his office tonight. You'll find a report that says it all.

Aeon whistled, low and long. "Wild. You recognize the handwriting?"

"No. And it's written in block letters, so I don't think I was meant to. And how in the heck would I break into Bovine Productivity Management?"

He looked around. No other fairgoers were visible, but we were surrounded by trailers, the nearest one only ten feet away, pink flamingo twinkle lights decorating the windows. "Maybe we should go inside. Whoever left the note might still be around."

"OK."

We advanced into the Airstream, where I made a quick scan of all the corners to make sure we were alone. Everything looked as I'd left it. "I think I need to call Bovine Productivity Management and find out if Lars is coming back to the fair tonight," I said.

"Not a bad idea." Aeon shook his head as he looked around. "You weren't lying about this place. How do you attach shag carpeting to a ceiling?"

"The miracle of hot glue guns, I believe. Make yourself at home while I call."

Aeon was forced to stoop to move around, but he politely walked the twelve feet to the other end of the trailer, by Mrs. Berns's bedroom door, to give me a sense of privacy. He played with the love bead curtain that hung outside the nonfunctioning bathroom while I dialed.

"Hello, Bovine Productivity Management."

"Hi, this is Mira James, with the *Battle Lake Recall*. I toured your facilities on Wednesday?"

"Of course." I imagined her voice was chilly, thinly veiling her contempt at me for accidentally stumbling into the carcass room and forcing BPM to revisit their security policies, resulting in piles of memos and meetings for all employees, and potentially, hopefully, an unexpected visit from the USDA. "How are you?"

"Fine. I had some follow-up questions to ask Mr. Gunder. Do you know if he'll be at the State Fair this evening?"

"I'm afraid not. He left this morning for Duluth. He and his family are taking a long weekend. Such a lovely time of year for that. Is there something I can help you with?"

"No, thank you. I'll try again next week." I ended the call and turned to Aeon. "He's out of town until Monday."

"Perfect. This'll make it easier."

"Make what easier?"

"Breaking into his office."

I held up my hands. "Are you out of your mind? That place is better protected than the White House. And anyhow, what happened to Mr. Follow-the-Law?"

"Mira, you gotta understand something. Mad Cows, Mad People has been tracking BPM for the past year. That company is the worst perpetrator of animal cruelty in the business."

I grimaced. I hadn't even told him about the mountain of poor dead animals I'd stumbled into. He'd probably spontaneously combust with anger. "I believe you, but what's that got to do with us?"

"If we could take them down, we could help millions of cows plus help preserve the environment. You're right that I won't risk anyone getting hurt, but there's no harm in peeking inside a little room at the top of the Cattle Barn. I don't think it's nearly as well protected as you seem to think."

"What?" But my stupid mistake came clear to me before the word even left my mouth.

"Lars's office. The note must be referring to the one he has here at the fair. A person'd have to be nuts to try to break into BPM."

Of course. "I forgot about his office here. Wait." I eyed him suspiciously. "How'd you know about it?"

"Like I said, MCMP has been following BPM for a year. We know a lot about them."

I considered our options. "How are we going to waltz past ten Milkfed Marys to get to that office? Or should we just have them stand guard?"

"I've got a better idea." Aeon smiled. "How about we sneak in when all the princesses are at the fireworks display tonight?"

He knew his stuff, which made me crabby. I hated it when I didn't get to be the boss of my plans. "Fine," I grumbled. "But I'm only going along because I've already been inside that office."

His smile widened. "So then it's not really breaking and entering?"

"Correct." I didn't try to hide the smile I had in response. "It's 'returning.'"

"Fair enough. What do you want to do until the fireworks start?"

"Know how to play gin rummy?"

Chapter 41

It was nearly dark when we left the trailer, at least as dark as possible on the neon-lit fairgrounds. I'd won back most of the money I'd lost the night before. Aeon was an agreeable loser, and I got to see deeper into the laid-back, non-crusading, knock-knock-joke side of his personality.

"What time are the fireworks supposed to start?" I asked.

"Ten o'clock sharp. The Milkfed Marys should all be backstage by now at the Grandstand, getting ready to introduce the event."

"It does look dark up there," I said, indicating the second floor of the Cattle Barn ahead. "Are you any good at picking locks?"

"It's one of my many talents," he said, his tone almost sad. "My parents taught me young."

I looked at him sideways. "You guys ever do anything normal, like go to the zoo or play on the swings?"

"Zoos are the worst kind of prisons for animals. We had a tire swing in our backyard."

"Good talk." We stood in front of the barn. "You ready, Freddie?"

"Ready. This should be a breeze, by the way. Old locks are the easiest to crack."

We sauntered into the now familiar building alongside about fifty other people. As usual, the traffic was constant. Inside, fair workers were delivering a late meal to the farmers with animals on display. They each received a Styrofoam container of what looked like beef stroganoff, corn, bread with a square of butter, and 2 percent milk. The cows didn't seem to mind that the farmers were munching on their relatives and byproducts, but personally, I'd never be able to look at beef or dairy products the same after this week.

Our plan was to nonchalantly stroll up the dormitory stairs as if we were expected, and that's just what we did. If anyone was wise to our subterfuge, I didn't notice because I was too busy looking innocent.

The door at the top was locked for the first time in my experience. Aeon directed me back down to the stairwell bend to keep an ear out for any unexpected arrivals while he got to work. Within minutes, he called me back up. He had the door open.

The dorm was a little eerie at night, like a strange Goldilocks fantasy where all the beds were empty but the bears might return any minute.

"Let's make this quick," I whispered as we tiptoed across the expanse of the dormitory to the offices on the far side.

"You don't have to tell me twice."

"Wait," I said. "Can you unlock Janice's office first? I need to check something." I hadn't tipped my whole hand to him. It just wasn't in my nature.

"I thought we were supposed to be quick."

I smiled but didn't tell him what I was after. "What I need in there will only take me a second."

He pinched his lips but didn't argue. I watched, fascinated, as he knelt in front of Janice's door and brought out a soft leather pouch of what looked like metal toothpicks in various sizes. When he said that old locks were the easiest to pick, I'd envisioned him flipping a tiny tool out of his Leatherman, not unrolling break-in gear as calmly as if he were pulling a handkerchief out of his pocket.

"You always carry picklocks?"

"You and I lead different lives, Mira."

The words felt condescending, and I reacted defensively. "Probably, but that doesn't explain you carrying around a full set. What else are you packing? Plastic explosives? Guns?"

He stopped in midpick and turned, standing to face me. He held his hands over his head, and his voice was much gentler. "You can search me. Wait, I've got a better idea." He turned all four of his pants pockets inside out. "I've got a wallet with seven bucks, some gum, a healthy dose of lint, a Swiss Army Knife that I've carried around since I was ten, and up until just now, the picklock set. I like to be able to get in and out of anyplace, always have, but I wasn't lying about being a pacifist."

We stared at each other for a few seconds, him patient and me undecided. Soon enough, I realized we had come too far to turn back, so we might as well keep working together. I trusted him less and less with each passing moment, though.

"I'll assume you don't have any dynamite taped to your ankles. Can you open that lock or not?"

"Watch me," he said, grinning, and sure enough, he had Janice's door open in under thirty seconds. He held it ajar for me and went to work on Lars's door after I slid through.

Aeon had the only flashlight, which he'd need to use sparingly given the number of windows on this side of the building. Fortunately, the moon was nearly full and the streetlights outside reflected through the floor-to-ceiling windows, giving me enough faint light so I could see around the interior of Janice's office well enough to read the letters on her desk.

That's not what I'd come for, though. I was after something bigger and stranger.

I took stock of my surroundings. The office was small, no more than ten feet by ten, and it was dominated by a huge, old wooden desk placed in the center. Two metal filing cabinets as tall as me stood beside the desk, pushed against the wall Janice's office shared with Lars's. On the opposite wall was a door that must have led to a closet. To my right, a dull leather couch hugged the cheap paneling, leaving only a ten-inch channel between it and the desk.

I riffled through the drawers of the desk and the filing cabinets, but that search yielded only paper. There wasn't anything untoward behind or under the chair or couch, or in the cushions.

That left only her closet.

Pulling open the creaky door, I stared at a spare power suit that looked an awful lot like a hanging body in the shadowy light. I squelched my fear and pushed the outfit aside. Nothing in back, including no secret door, which I always checked for when searching places I wasn't supposed to be. My pulse hammered with the urgency of my search. If even one of the princesses came back early and discovered Aeon and I snooping around, we'd be in deep trouble.

My last hope was the top shelf of the closet, which was stacked with shoeboxes, each with a year written on the end in thick black marker. I couldn't quite reach the bottom of the shelf, and so hopped and pulled, hopped and pulled, until I wrenched a box loose, this one marked "1998." One more hop and it was out, but it slipped from my hands while I was hauling it down.

The top came off, and an explosion of jewelry and human hair showered down on me.

Chapter 42

"Ew! Ew!" I danced around, shaking off the disembodied hair. The chunks landed on the ground with soft thuds, like mice falling from the sky.

"What is it?" Aeon asked, running into the office. "What's wrong?"

"Nothing. Well, something, but nothing I didn't expect. Janice has boxes of trophies in her closet."

"Come again?"

I knelt down and began gingerly tucking the earrings, bracelets, and other baubles back into the box. I was less eager to touch the hair. Each chunk was taped at one end, making it look like a homemade paintbrush. On the tape, Janice had penned information about the source of the hair. I currently held *Alicia, 1998, 4th runner-up* in my hands.

"Earlier this week, I was talking to some of the Milkfed Marys. Megan, one of the runners-up, mentioned that one night she woke up to see Janice leaning over Ashley's dormitory bed. At first, I thought it was connected to Ashley's murder, but then I noticed that three of the Milkfed Marys were missing a chunk of hair from their heads. Janice, too. See?"

I held up another brown-hair packet, this one labeled *Janice, 1998, no grays yet!*

"Jesus. So all these boxes are full of hair and jewelry she stole from past Milkfed Marys, plus her own hair?" He shuddered. "That's messed up."

I shrugged. "And mostly harmless." I didn't mention Janice's rough life or that I'd lost my dad about the same age as Janice had lost her sister. If she needed tiny baubles and hair trophies to keep her sane, who was I to judge?

Glancing back at the stack in the closet, I pointed out to Aeon that they started in 1978. "I'm pretty sure Janice stole my camera after I let slip last Saturday that I'd photographed something odd about the back of Ashley's head during her ceremony. I realized yesterday that I'd captured a bald spot on Ashley's head, and that the only person who wouldn't want that known was Janice. She must have broken into the trailer, snatched the camera, deleted the photos, and then returned it."

"Weirder and weirder."

I shrugged. "At least she brought the camera back." I finished repacking the box, using two pieces of paper to slip the hair in without touching it.

"Here, let me help you." He grabbed the shoebox from me and slid it back in its chronological spot. "As much as I'd like to further plumb Janice's psyche, we need to get what we came for."

"I'm with you. You open Lars's office?"

"Come see for yourself."

I gave Janice's a quick visual sweep to make sure it looked as it had when I'd arrived, locked the door behind me, and padded over to Lars's. The office was a mirror image of Janice's, down to the couch, desk, filing cabinets, and closet door on the opposite wall. Aeon was already inside, elbow-deep in the filing cabinets.

"Find anything yet?"

"Haven't had time. It looks like this place is mostly a storage room for past pageant materials, though. Check his desk."

All the drawers were unlocked. I opened them one by one, removing everything—pencils, erasers, paper clips, notepads—and giving it the once-over before returning it. "Nothing. Did you check his closet?"

"I'm on it. You look in the garbage and the couch cushions while I search the closet."

"OK, but it might help if the note told us exactly what sort of report we're looking for."

"It's about an inch thick, spiral bound."

My heart grew heavy and icy. "What's that?"

"A spiral-bound report. About an inch thick."

I was frozen. "Aeon, how do you know that?"

He looked up from the closet, where he was digging in the back. In the shielded glow of his flashlight, his expression was confused, and then calculating, and then, as if he hadn't ever had a thought before this moment, completely ingenuous. "That note. It said we were looking for a report that would incriminate Lars."

"But it didn't say how big the report was, or how it was bound." I tried swallowing, but my mouth was too dry.

"Oh, my bad. Must be my overactive imagination."

As he returned his focus to the rear of the closet, the enormity of my blunder fell swiftly and heavily from the sky, making it difficult to move my body toward the open door of Lars's office, even though escape was so close.

Here I was, a wily woman on the trail of a murderer, and I'd gotten into bed with the enemy. I was so caught up in Kate's embezzling and Lars's philandering and Janice's weirdness that I'd let Aeon lull me into complacency with his kindness.

If he had access to bomb-making materials in his past, he could certainly get his hands on cyanide now. And he clearly had the skills to access Ashley, or the people serving food and beverages to her. As to why? For the same reason he vandalized the college, or freed the cows, or bombed the lab: to bring attention to the cause of animal liberty.

What better target than a Milkfed Mary, Queen of the Dairy, representative of the entire Midwest dairy industry?

I squeezed my eyes shut and visualized moving. It worked, and my right leg shuffled a little, followed by my left. I was two inches closer to the door.

Aeon backed out of the closet. "You wanna come help me? I think I found something back here, but my hand is too big to squeeze in. Mira?"

He turned, and our eyes locked. I saw instant comprehension dawn. He straightened quickly, and his movement freed me from paralysis. I dashed to the door and was halfway across the dormitory when someone tripped me.

"You looking for this?"

I stared up into a new set of eyes that were in a face that was attached to a neck that was linked to an arm that was holding a one-inch thick, spiral-bound report.

Chapter 43

Delrita bent down to offer me a hand, but I brushed her away. When you don't know who your friends are, treat everyone like an enemy.

"I'm fine," I said, standing to rub the knee I'd skinned on my way down. "Where'd you get that report?"

She hugged it to her chest. "First, tell me who he is." She nodded at Aeon, who was shifting his weight anxiously from one foot to the other. He couldn't take his eyes off the report.

"Aeon Hopkins. He helped me break into Lars's office." I stood and flexed my knee. "You wrote us the note?"

"I wrote *you* the note," she corrected.

As much as I was on her team when it came to being suspicious of Aeon, there wasn't time. Something big was happening here, and I needed to know what it was. "Where'd you get that report?"

"Lars's office. I waited so long for you to show up and get it yourself, but I finally gave up. Figured I'd have to handle this all myself. That's when you two appeared."

"And how'd you get into Lars's office?" I backed up surreptitiously, enough so I could see Aeon on my right, still standing in Lars's doorway, and Delrita on my left, each about five feet away.

Delrita stared from me to Aeon and back again. She was struggling with a decision, and I let her. Finally, she sighed and plopped herself on the bed nearest her, crinkling the fabric of a blue crinoline dress tossed across the bedspread. "Lars gave me a key a while back. He said he loved me, that he'd leave his wife for me. It's the oldest line in the book, right? But my girls adored him, and I wanted to believe it, the whole package."

"You were dating Lars at the same time as Ashley?"

Delrita scoffed. "Ashley was nothing, a little blonde blip on his screen. I've known Lars for two years. I used to be a part-time receptionist at Bovine Productivity Management. It was Lars who convinced me to run for the pageant. Said no one would find out about my daughters, that my being in the pageant would give us more time together. We got plenty of that, here in his office, until Ashley squirmed her way in.

"That's why I went after Dirk, that big doofus. I wanted to get back at Ashley, but she could have cared less. She had her eyes on bigger prizes, so I had to get more imaginative."

"And you killed her?" I asked.

"Ha! You watch too much TV. No, I just hid in the closet in Lars's office and filmed their last boff session. I was going to post it online, but then someone killed Ashley, and I didn't have any reason to get back at her anymore."

Christ on a cracker. "But you still wanted revenge on Lars?"

"Exactly." She smiled, but there was no pleasure in it. "Hence this report, which he accidentally left in his office after that last time he screwed Ashley. And believe me, he wants it back. He's been frantic since it's gone missing."

Aeon's voice was low, growly. "What's the report say?"

Delrita tossed her hair over her shoulder. "Probably nothing you're interested in. Just a little info about ME, BPM's best-selling product and Lars's baby. This past summer, BPM commissioned a private study because of rumblings in the dairy community about ME's side effects. BPM hoped to set everyone's fears to rest, but they got bad news. The study found that using ME triples the white blood cell count in the milk, creating a salty product, and in rare cases, causes rapid and irreversible mammary growth when fed to rats."

A picture flashed through my mind: the Bovine Productivity Management representative at the Cattle Barn, the guy who had appeared oddly feminine, but I couldn't put my finger on why: he'd had actual breasts. I coughed.

"If ME goes down, Bovine Productivity goes down with it. They've invested all their capital in that product." Delrita shared this last point with all the satisfaction of a cat who'd caught its mouse. She had Lars just where she wanted him.

"Give me the report." Aeon held out his hand.

Delrita looked at me.

"I'll take it," I said. "I imagine BPM wasn't going to release it to the press?"

"This is the only copy there is. I don't think Lars was supposed to take it off company grounds."

A sudden explosion made all three of us jump as I accepted the report. The sky behind the wall of windows lit up in a spectacular spray of reds, blues, and greens. The fireworks had begun.

"I'm going to get this to the police and inform someone I know at the *Pioneer Press* about it. Thanks, Delrita."

"My pleasure," she said, her eyes sparkling.

Chapter 44

My brain was on overdrive. I had every reason to suspect that Aeon was Ashley's killer, and I needed to get him out of here so he couldn't hurt Delrita. Then I'd lose him in the crowds of the fair.

All my fairground exploration was about to pay off. There was a police station behind the Space Tower that I'd passed many times on the way to the campground. I'd give the on-duty officers the report and let them find Aeon on their own.

I addressed Delrita. "What're you going to do now?"

"My kids are waiting for me at the fireworks with my mom. After we watch them as a family, we're going to say goodbye to the fair for a long time."

"Perfect." I glanced at Aeon. "After you."

He nodded, locked Lars's door behind him, wiped the knob for prints, and led the way across the dormitory. Delrita followed close behind, and when I stopped, she almost bumped into me.

"What?" she asked.

I turned. On our first meeting, I hadn't been sure if she'd been missing eyebrows or if her hair was naturally so pale that they looked invisible. The knowledge I'd gained since then told me it was likely the former, but I wanted to be sure. I hated loose ends. "Can I ask you what happened to your eyebrows?"

She felt where they'd been, suddenly self-conscious. "They just fell out. I think it's the new Pill I'm taking. I need to ask my doctor to lower the dosage."

"I wouldn't bother. I think Janice Naired your face while you were asleep, a move she saves for the Milkfed Mary contestants who particularly piss her off. Everyone else, she just pinches a lock of hair or some jewelry from."

Delrita felt the back of her head and blew an exasperated breath of air. "I got out of that pageant just in time."

"With any luck," I said, following Aeon down the steps, hopefully the last time I'd have to traverse them. I continued behind Aeon and out a side door while Delrita walked toward the barn's main doors. He and I found ourselves on Underwood Street, which was less traveled than the main thoroughfares of the fair but still had foot traffic. I gripped the report tightly and kept Aeon a little forward and to my left as we marched toward Judson Avenue.

"I know a shortcut," he said, ducking into an alley. I took note of all the people around and decided to follow him a couple steps. He immediately stopped.

"Wait. I forgot my flashlight in Lars's office," he said.

A mental calculation told me Delrita would reasonably be out of the building by now. "I'll wait for you," I said.

Our eyes grappled. He knew I wouldn't be here when he returned, but he had no way to back down on retrieving his flashlight without exposing himself for the liar that he was. "Thanks, Mira."

My mouth was tight. "You bet."

As soon as he was out of sight, I oriented myself toward the Space Tower. This alleyway was disturbingly empty. I longed to be back in the safety of crowds. The darkness felt all the heavier because of the sporadic blasts of light from the fireworks.

An eerie wail sounded to my right, and my heart stopped. I'd been so totally focused on the clear and present danger that was Aeon that I hadn't noticed that the alleyway he'd led us into abutted the Haunted House.

All the liquids in my body turned to ice, and it felt like the ground was tipping. The horror of seeing Jenny Cot slip to the Haunted House floor, bleeding and unconscious, descended as I relived the moment.

From this less-public side, the building looked battered, with siding that didn't match the front, scrub grass all around. The unfinished appearance lent a particularly sinister element to the building, accented by the screams emanating from inside and the earsplitting explosion of fireworks overhead. I clenched my body and decided for the second time in a day that I wasn't too proud to run.

"What's the hurry?" a deep, breathy voice whispered into my ear at the same time a hand clamped on my forearm, the grip so strong it felt like I'd caught my wrist in a drawer. Something sharp pressed into my back, and fear shot through me like poison. "A girl shouldn't leave the State Fair without visiting the Haunted House, right? Don't worry. I'll come with you. No screams, though, or this ride is over."

My brain felt dipped in novocaine. I wasn't aware of walking, but my body was moving toward the Haunted House's deserted rear entrance.

Up close, I recognized it as the door Jenny Cot had been carried out of by the paramedics. I knew that when it opened, a wash of stale air and shrill screams would pour out. I instinctively struggled, but the person holding me tightened their grip on my shoulder and pressed the sharp object hard enough to pierce my skin. Warm blood trickled down my spine.

"You're doing great. Just keep walking. This could be fun."

The hand holding me reached forward to open the door. It was gloved, with a denim sleeve buttoned all the way to the wrist. To my left beyond the alley, walking in the brightly lit main street that seemed a mile away, people laughed and strolled, unaware of my terror.

I screamed, and one of them, a teenage boy, glanced my way. He appeared momentarily confused, then smiled and gave the thumbs-up when he saw I was entering the Haunted House.

I thought I saw a head of apricot fuzz peeking around behind the teenager, but his was the last face I saw before being plunged into the endless darkness.

Chapter 45

The essence of the haunted mansion crawled over my body like a million scurrying centipedes. Tears spilled down my cheeks at the visceral terror of returning to the place that had spawned nightmare after nightmare in my teen years.

My eyes adjusted to the dim glow of the Exit sign, and I saw scythes, glowing skeletons, and headless bodies stacked in one corner. In the other, gravestones and jugs of fake blood. A shadow scurried across the floor.

We stood in a storage room.

It smelled like dust and mouse pee. Dull percussive thumps reverberated through the walls, indicating the fireworks were still going on outside. Nearby, bloodcurdling screams suggested murder was taking place ten feet away. I heard a chain saw rev, and I moaned.

"Sort of a scaredy-cat, aren't you? I'll take that, by the way."

The report was yanked out of my hands. I'd forgotten I was even holding it.

"Why so quiet? You've been doing nothing but talking since you arrived at the fair, as near as I can tell. No point in stopping now."

"Who are you?"

"See for yourself."

I turned, slowly, expecting to look upon Aeon grinning like the Joker, a knife in one hand and the report and a bottle of cyanide in the other.

Instead, in the dim light of the room, I saw Lars Gunder, a horrible fire glowing in his face. I whimpered. I thought I spotted a hint of breasts under his jacket, but it may have been the dim lighting playing tricks on me.

My teeth were chattering. "You've got the report. That's what you wanted, right?"

"I also need the information that's inside of it. Since it's now in your brain, I'm afraid I'll need to take that as well." He tipped his head and lifted his shoulders, his body language telling me, *Sorry, that's the breaks, kid.*

All the blood drained from my head, and I grew dizzy. "I'm not the only one who knows what's in it."

"Delrita won't tell, and I can promise you that Aeon Hopkins is not long for this world. That gnat has been irritating the big boys for far too long. I'll be swatting him in about, oh, five minutes." He glanced around. "Killing you in a haunted house is a nice touch, don't you think? The butter-sculpting booth murder took some planning, but your death will be the scarier of the two, considering the setting. Your body'll lie here for days before an employee discovers your corpse isn't a prop. You'll be smelling by then. That's what you get for—"

Without any warning, my body made an executive decision. It leaped for the door that led deeper into the Haunted House. If it had consulted my brain, it would have been advised to remain in "play dead" mode, to be paralyzed by the knife and hypnotized by the voice of Lars describing how he would kill me.

By the time my brain caught up with my body's rebellion, though, I found myself in the Haunted House's murky bowels, pushing past an employee dressed in chains, wearing a joltingly childlike mask on his bloodied face, and holding a pair of severed ears.

I lunged ahead until I found myself in a small room. Blood poured down the walls, and in the outline of a door across the room, a dismembered skeleton dropped goopy intestines from one bony hand to another like a macabre Slinky.

It was the same room Jenny had hit the floor in.

I screamed, and it blended in with the many others, fake and real. A hand clamped onto my shoulder, and I whipped around to face a masked person, my heart beating like a million clocks. I scratched and kicked and ripped the mask off.

Underneath was a teenage boy.

"Dude, relax. It's just pretend." He held me off with one hand and reached for his felled mask with the other.

I breathed raggedly, peering behind him, expecting my captor to appear in the door at any moment. "How do I get out?"

He must have been trained to deal with panicked customers.

He pointed at the skeleton. "Just squeeze around Mr. Bones."

I jumped forward, ripped the skeleton out of the ceiling, and leaped toward the drape hiding a metal exit door. I moved the curtain aside and pushed frantically against the door, but it was jammed. Behind me, the kid who'd given me directions grunted loudly. I swiveled to see Lars leaning over him with his knife still out. He hesitated, unsure whether to carve the teenager or pursue me. In that moment of indecision, I gave up on the door and charged into Lars, catching him off guard.

He lost his balance momentarily but righted himself by grabbing at my hair. My head yanked to the side as he ripped out a chunk, but I didn't slow, desperate to put distance between him and me. I ran, careening off people, charging blindly from one room of the Haunted House to another. Behind me, I heard the steady thump of pursuit and people yelling at someone to watch out.

Breath ragged in my chest, I found myself back in the storage room Lars had first pulled me into. I made for the door just as it opened, and Mrs. Berns peeked her head inside.

She looked shocked. "Mira? What the hell is wrong with you? I saw you come into here with some guy, but I know how frickin' scared you are of this place. Don't lie to me. It was written on your face plain as mud when we walked past here." She pulled herself into the room and let the door close behind her.

"There's no time! We have to get out of here! It's Lars, he's . . ."

He caught me before I could finish the sentence, snaking one strong arm around my neck, pressing his knife into my jugular with his other. Mrs. Berns bolted forward, but he lashed out, striking her hard across the face with the butt of his knife.

She fell to the ground, bleeding copiously from her forehead. She landed on her stomach, her face pointed away. Blood pooled around her, but Lars's grip was too tight. I couldn't reach her.

I thought I smelled a hint of almonds, and then a wet rag was pressed against my nose and the world went black.

Chapter 46

The smell woke me.

It was an overwhelming stench, like pounds of festering hamburger rotting in a swamp. The feculent odor was so strong it thickened the air, making it difficult to breathe. My awareness shifted from my nose to my body. I was slumped on a lumpy pile, my arms and legs hanging lower than my torso, and the mass beneath me felt like fur over cold rocks.

I shifted, and my hand slid into an opening in the pile. I sensed wetness. I opened one eye and then the other. The room was dim. I couldn't make out dimensions. A light shifted in the far corner, and I heard the rumble of large equipment starting up, followed by a wash of fresh air.

An enormous door slid open, and the glow of the moon spilled into the space, illuminating the mound of dead cows that I'd been tossed onto, four times the size of the one I'd encountered inside the BPM main building. I recoiled, which upset my balance, sending me toppling to the base of the corpse mountain. I screamed, but it came out as a choked gurgle. I scraped at my arms and legs, trying to wipe the sensation of cold death off my skin.

A bulldozer lumbered through the opening. Lars, steering the machine, glanced over at the corpse pile, appearing suddenly alarmed. He switched off the hulking bulldozer, jumped to the ground, and sprinted forward, not relaxing until he caught sight of me shivering at the base of the dead animals. My arms and legs were covered in welts from my scratching, but I still felt infected with death. I couldn't shake the coldness.

Lars stood thirty feet away, staring at me as dispassionately as if I were a bug under glass. "Woke up a little early, eh? You probably want to be asleep for this. See, any animals that don't make it, we house them out here in the testing lab. Once the pile gets big enough, we load them up and bring them to the grinder, where they're turned into cow feed. Used to be we made dog food with this offal, too, but people are particular about what goes into their pets. What goes into their *own* food, that's a whole different story." His face twisted in an imitation of a smile.

I stared wildly around the testing lab. It was about three hundred square feet and built like a bunker. The garage door Lars had opened to drive the bulldozer through was the only visible exit. I'd have to get past him to escape, and then what? I was in an industrial park in the middle of nowhere.

"I saw the dead animals in the plant. You had a whole pile in there, too."

"I know you did. I watched the videotape. I have to tell you as a point of pride that we don't usually leave animal carcasses lying around our front offices. We run a very clean operation but needed to make an exception and ramp up the testing, using all available space. You see, the USDA is inspecting the plant next week. Seems people like your friend Aeon have been spreading vicious rumors about our products, enough so that the government felt they needed to get involved." He reached into his pocket for the same bottle of liquid he'd had at the Haunted House.

"I called them!" I yelled. "I called the USDA and told them about all the animals you'd hurt. They could show up any minute."

He chuckled. "You clearly haven't worked with the USDA before. They're chronically underfunded. They're not going to come out for an extra inspection just because some nobody called, especially since they're already coming next week." He tipped his chin. "But on to more pressing issues. You, and how you'll die."

He sized up the distance between us. He could reach me in ten strides. "I'm not a monster. I'll give you a choice. Either you go into the grinder awake and tied up, or you let me put you out again. That way, you won't feel a thing as you take your place in the circle of life." He started humming the Disney song.

I gagged. My chest felt ready to explode with fear, but I was trapped. The garage door stood to my left and behind Lars, the ten-foot-high pile of animal corpses lay in front of me, and the dark, uncharted expanse of the lab loomed to my right. The viscous stench of death made it difficult to concentrate.

Scooting back several inches, my back hit the wall, which I used to leverage myself into a standing position. My legs were shaky from the knockout agent, but my wits were returning. "You killed Mrs. Berns?"

"I'm afraid she hit her head pretty hard. A woman that age isn't likely to survive a fall like that."

A sob escaped my throat. "And Aeon?"

"Look to your right."

I peered around the side of the pile, keeping one eye on Lars. I saw in the shadows a bundle of clothes and skin that were Aeon. His body was twisted in an unnatural angle.

My voice was a husk. "He's dead."

"Not yet." Lars smiled the empty grin of a jack-o-lantern. "It was easy carrying you out of the fair and into my waiting van. Turns out people think it's funny when you tell them your girlfriend had too much to drink. I had to be a little trickier with Aeon, though. I lured him to the van by telling him that you needed him. When he got there and saw you out cold, he put up a little fight, but I zapped him with a stun gun before knocking him out. He'll be much easier to get in the grinder than you. That's what you get for trying too hard." He lifted his shoulders. "Now what'll it be? Awake and ground up, or unconscious and ground up?"

He snaked toward me, eating up the distance separating us in seconds. I stumbled backward and toward Aeon's body, trying to keep the pile of dead animals between me and Lars.

"If you don't stand still right now, I'll retract my offer. You'll go into the grinder awake." His voice was smooth and unhinged.

My heart beat like a machine gun, and I thought I'd collapse from fear. I had only one chance to escape, but it meant letting Lars put his murderous hands on me. "People will hear me scream."

"Not out here," he said with certainty.

I moved and Lars followed. When I was near Aeon, I let Lars close the gap a little, but he moved too quickly. I wasn't in the right spot. I needed three more inches, but there wasn't time.

Lars lunged.

I jumped back, twisting as I fell. I landed full force, face down on Aeon's body. He didn't make a sound, not even a whisper of air escaping. His body felt as cold as the animals'.

"That's better." Lars's hands coiled into my hair, caressing my neck and tugging at the sore spot he'd created when he'd yanked out my hair earlier. He leaned close to my ear, murmuring, "Such a shame so many beautiful girls have to die for progress, but ME is just too important. Think about how many more starving people we can feed if we can keep the Milk Enhancer on the market. You're sacrificing yourself for a good cause."

Lars jerked me up harshly. As he did, I turned and plunged the Swiss Army Knife I'd snatched from Aeon's pocket deep into his stomach and twisted it, using my last burst of strength. I retched at the gristly sound of the blade separating organs and intestines, but the knife had become an extension of my arm, and I couldn't let it go, couldn't stop it from slicing side to side.

Lars gurgled and shoved me away. He fell toward the wall, covering his leaking belly with both hands. "You bitch!"

I couldn't help Aeon, not right now. I sprinted past Lars, knocking him over as I ran out of the testing lab to the nearest security gate. I stared wildly around the courtyard, not sure if Lars was working alone. I plunged the bloodied knife into the gate's keypad, wiggling and jamming it until I triggered the security system.

Klieg lights immediately flashed all over the grounds, lighting the place up like the Fourth of July, and an alarm sounded inside the building and blared from bullhorns set along the top of the razor-wire fence.

I prayed that a sister alarm was going off at the Saint Paul police station.

Chapter 47

"So he killed Ashley because he didn't want the world to know that Milk Enhancer created man boobs?"

"More or less."

I was helping to dress Mrs. Berns's wound. She'd been given five stitches and some painkillers (*Finally! A legal prescription,* she'd said), and sent on her way.

The doctor had ordered her to keep the stitches covered for a few days, but Mrs. Berns wasn't on board. She said she wouldn't be able to get the attention she'd earned if people couldn't see the extent of her injuries. We compromised, with her allowing me to put gauze over the top as long as I didn't cover any of the bruising.

"He thought Ashley had stolen the report from his office after their last tryst. If the report's contents were leaked, his career and BPM were both dust. She'd been blackmailing him before that, saying she'd come out about the affair if he didn't leave his wife. He figured he'd kill two birds with one stone, so to speak."

"What an asshole." Mrs. Berns had always been the queen of understatement. "He *deserved* to get stabbed in the stomach."

I winced. The memory sickened me. The police had arrived within minutes of the alarm going off at BPM and called an ambulance when they saw me covered in blood. It was all Lars's. He was conscious when they took him away, but incoherent.

Aeon was still out, but the EMTs had assured me all his vital signs were fine. They wanted to send me home, but I refused to leave until animal control was called out. The sight of poor, terrified lab animals being led out of the testing building would haunt me long after the memory of stabbing Lars in the stomach faded.

After a promise that all the surviving animals would be taken care of, I was sent back to my trailer, but Chief Kramer had told me I better not go far. There would be a court date in my future, testifying against Lars.

"He's getting what's coming to him," I told Mrs. Berns. "Not only is he looking at life in prison, but he's also recently acquired breasts from drinking copious amounts of ME-laced milk. Apparently, he's been taping them down, but they're at least C cups. I saw them when he attacked me."

Mrs. Berns snorted with laughter, forgetting that sudden movements gave her a headache. At her wince of pain, I apologized for her injury for the ten-millionth time.

"For the love of Pete, would you just let it go?" she said. "There's nothing to forgive. We're all responsible for ourselves. You can't save another person from their fate, and you're not the one who noggin-bonked me."

I teared up as hundreds of tiny weights took off to greener pastures, thanks to Mrs. Berns's grace. "I love you," I said.

"You better," she grumbled, taking a deep pull off the hot fudge malt I'd bought her for breakfast. "I can't believe you were right about the cyanide in the ice cubes."

"That was just a lucky guess. No one thought anything of Lars being upstairs while the Milkfed Marys scurried around to get ready for Ashley's butter carving. After all, he had an office up there and was in and out all the time, and the place was highly trafficked that morning. When he slipped Ashley a glass of ice laced with cyanide, she didn't think twice, probably assuming it was one more of the secret little favors he'd been doing for her since they'd started sleeping together."

Mrs. Berns tsked. "How'd Carlotta take the news about her girl?"

"About like you'd figure. She was relieved to know who killed her daughter and why, but that doesn't bring her back."

"That poor woman. Just goes to show you can do your best with your kids, but you can't predict how they'll turn out."

I nodded agreeably.

"It's true that she and her husband are adopting all the cows you rescued from the testing lab?"

I smiled. That was some particularly happy news. "Yep. They'll live out their lives in green pastures until they die of old age."

Mrs. Berns and I sat in the warmth of that. I had a quarter-size chunk of scalp missing, a black eye that I must have acquired while unconscious, bruised wrists from Lars manhandling me in the Haunted House, a small puncture wound at the base of my spine, and a chloroform hangover, but it was way better than being dead.

"The best news is that Aeon is going to be OK. He has a broken arm and a concussion from scuffling with Lars, but he'll recover. I think seeing all those poor animals at BPM has reenergized him and his cause."

"So he and his group came to the State Fair expressly to blow the whistle on Bovine Productivity Management?"

"Yep." I gingerly rubbed at my black-and-blue wrists. "He planned on breaking into Lars's office all along, and if he didn't find anything there, he was going to hit BPM. It was just luck that Delrita practically handed the ME report to him. Now that the report is public, BPM is done for. By the way, I'm pretty sure Janice is going to continue on as chaperone of the pageant. I sent an email this morning tipping off the Midwest Dairy Organization about her little hair fetish, but I think 'eccentric' goes with the job description. Who else'll they find to take that gig?"

"Truth. And Kate? Who's going to do her job?"

I stole a sip of Mrs. Berns's malt under her disapproving gaze. "That's still up in the air. I called Chaz this morning to give him the scoop on Ashley's murder, and he told me Kate was turning herself in for embezzling, making a plea bargain with the attorney general. She was going to give up her gambling-addicted husband, who apparently did most of the actual book doctoring, in exchange for leniency."

"Good. I hope she loses that scab. And the bull? Did her husband set that loose, too?"

"Nope, unfortunately that was all Kate. I think she might be angling for an insanity plea if turning her husband in doesn't work out."

"Creative woman. Say, I've been thinking. Do you suppose the fair'd give me one of those little golf carts to ride around? I got hurt in the line of duty, after all." She made puppy-dog eyes at me.

"I'm not sure if they'd see it that way, but we could try," I said, smiling. "You want a piggyback ride in the meanwhile?"

"Pah," she said, finishing her malt and standing gingerly to strap on her épée. "A woman's got to keep her dignity. Speaking of, there's supposed to be a new gym opening up in Battle Lake. I've heard they've got a lady martial arts instructor who'll teach you how to kick some ass. I think her particular art is called Toe Can Do. Maybe you and me should join, learn how to defend ourselves. What with the way you're going, that'll come in handy."

I nodded. "I think it's called Tae Kwon Do, and that's not a bad idea."

"That's what I said. Toe Can Do."

"Of course." We stepped out of the trailer and into a beautiful late morning, sunny but with a hint of the crisp fall to come. "What do you think Kennie's up to?"

Mrs. Berns tossed her malt cup into a nearby garbage can. "I think we'll find out in just a few minutes. You look very nice, by the way."

"Thank you." I adjusted the headband I'd used to cover my missing hair.

We hobbled toward the Battle Lake booth. It was "I Love the Fair" day, and we were on our way to help Kennie, though she hadn't yet told us what the booth consisted of.

Today was also the day Johnny was supposed to show up, and I was embarrassed to admit how much I was looking forward to seeing him. I had emailed him early this morning to fill him in on Ashley's murder and Lars's capture, but I didn't know if he'd received the message before getting on the road. I was profoundly rattled from the previous night's events, taking care of Mrs. Berns so I didn't have to think about me, and I just wanted to lean on someone for a while. Mrs. Berns and Kennie were a good start, but they didn't offer the same benefits as Johnny.

"This might be the busiest day yet at the fair," I said amiably. We passed through the crowds, people generously making room for our bruised bodies, and came in sight of the International Bazaar.

"Oh. My. God." My jaw hung open when I caught sight of Kennie's stall.

She'd snagged space in the far west corner of the International Bazaar, though her theme was more Minnesotan Bizarre. She'd taken over a Moroccan booth for a day, and their colored scarves and hookah pipes had been moved to the side to make room for cardboard hearts and plywood lips. The top of the booth was emblazoned with a sign in all shades of red: SAVE OUR LIQUOR, GET A PUCKER: ONE KISS FOR $5.

"About time you two showed up," she called over. "I can't run this booth all by myself!"

Mrs. Berns and I looked at each other and then back at Kennie.

"A kissing booth?" I asked when we reached her.

"No one's exactly beating down your door to buy what you're selling," Mrs. Berns said, scanning the lack of customers. "Think maybe the Cupid costume was too much?"

Kennie glanced down at her white corset, black fishnet stockings, and fire-engine-red vinyl platforms. Fuzzy white wings were strapped to her back, and a camo bow and arrow hung over one shoulder. I had no doubt she could use it, if not to make someone fall in love with her, then at least to slow him down until she could close in.

"It's all in the spirit of the event," she said. "And the booth doesn't officially open until noon, so get your rears back here."

"I'm not kissing strangers," I said. "Think of all the diseases we could catch."

Kennie held up cardboard smiles taped to Popsicle sticks. "That's why I have these lip prophylactics. Hold them over your actual lips when you kiss." She dropped the lips and scowled, studying Mrs. Berns and me. "Too bad I didn't have time to get full face masks. You two are as ugly as butts with all those stitches and bruises."

"A few war wounds can't hide my natural charm." Mrs. Berns cackled and rubbed her hands together. "I think you've finally got something here, Mayor. I'm in." She propelled me into the booth ahead of her, up to the front counter, and shoved a set of lips-on-a-stick into my hand. "Let's save that liquor store!"

I turned away from the counter to face Kennie and Mrs. Berns, holding up the prophylactic lips to illustrate how stupid they looked. "You really expect me to do this all day just to raise money for liquor?"

Instead of answering me, they both stared over my shoulder, their eyes widening before matching smirks settled on their lips. "Maybe not *all* day," Kennie murmured.

I turned.

Johnny Leeson was standing there, the sun glowing behind him, outlining the beautiful curl of his hair, the strong slope of his shoulders, the gorgeous line of his tanned arms, naked below the short sleeves of his crisp white T-shirt. His Levi's were slung low on his hips, but I didn't have too much time to concentrate on that because he was looking at me with the most peculiar expression. It made me feel vulnerable and safe at the same time.

My heart pump-pumped a salsa beat.

Leaning forward, he lightly traced the outline of my cheek, a flash of anger crossing his face as his finger circled the bruise surrounding my eye. "I got your email."

He gently pulled down the hand I was using to hold the prophylactic lips to my face. With his other hand, he caressed my cheek as he leaned over the counter.

His lips met mine in a sweet heat that ignited fireworks all over my body.

Up close, he smelled like cinnamon and fresh air. His hand moved down my neck, touching the edges of the bandage there, and trailed down my back. He pulled away, too soon, and rested his forehead on mine, his hands still softly holding my face.

"How much do I owe you?" I sighed.

Acknowledgments

You know how when you were a kid, you'd collect rocks because they were so interesting? And then you'd put them in the polisher in your basement for a week, listening to the horrible racket of tumbling, grinding stone, and when they came out, they'd morphed from rocks to treasure? That's what Jessica Morrell does for my books. She's the polisher, my manuscripts are the stones, and the grinding sound is me complaining because it's irritating to get your rocks glossed. Yet I keep going back to her, hiring her to edit every one of my mysteries, some more than once. She's challenged me and taught me how to be a better writer every step of the way. Thanks, Jessica.

Special thanks to Greg Schraufnagel and Karen Hipple for letting me use their names and their artery-atrophying recipes. Who needs to make this stuff up? When you live in the Midwest, the weird food is real. Thank you also to Michael Jacobson for patiently answering my questions about the operation of small-town newspapers; all mistakes in that regard are my own. And, oh yeah—Lana Sorensen? Thanks for threatening to do me bodily harm if I didn't use your name in this book. Hope it turned out like you wanted.

Friends and family, thank you for going on this beautiful ride with me. Big love to you all!

Book Club Questions

1. Who was your favorite character and why?
2. What Minnesota State Fair food would you most like to eat? Least like to eat? What is the grossest thing you've ever eaten?
3. What is the importance of Johnny Leeson to this story? In other words, how does he relate to the central storyline?
4. Who were all the suspects in Ashley's murder, and what clues linked them to her? Who was the most likely suspect? The least likely?
5. In *September Mourn*, Lourey uses humor to analyze the serious issues of animal treatment and food production in the United States. How do you feel about the mix of environmental issues with mystery and humor?
6. Do you know where your last meal came from? In other words, who were the producers, shippers, cooks? What were all the ingredients? Is it important to know, or are we just too busy to worry?
7. How long should Mira stay in Battle Lake? Why?
8. If you were invited to attend a concert with Mrs. Berns or Kennie, who would you choose and why?

About the Author

Photo © 2023 Kelly Weaver Photography

Jess Lourey writes about secrets. She's the bestselling author of thrillers, comic caper mysteries, book club fiction, young adult fiction, and non-fiction. Winner of the Anthony, Thriller, and Minnesota Book Awards, Jess is also an Edgar, Agatha, and Lefty Award–nominated author; TEDx presenter; and recipient of The Loft's Excellence in Teaching fellowship. Check out her TEDx Talk for the true story behind her debut novel, *May Day*. She lives in Minneapolis with a rotating batch of foster kittens (and occasional foster puppies, but those goobers are a lot of work). For more information, visit www.jessicalourey.com.